CROW
Stone

OTHER BOOKS BY
GABRIELE GOLDSTONE

The Kulak's Daughter, 2010

Red Stone, 2015

Broken Stone, 2015

Tainted Amber, 2021

CROW
Stone

GABRIELE GOLDSTONE

RONSDALE PRESS

CROW STONE
Copyright © 2022 Gabriele Goldstone

RONSDALE PRESS
3350 West 21st Avenue, Vancouver, B.C. Canada V6S 1G7
www.ronsdalepress.com

Typesetting: Julie Cochrane, in Caslon 11.5 pt on 15
Cover Design: Julie Cochrane
Paper: Rolland Enviro Book White 55 lb.

Ronsdale Press wishes to thank the following for their support of its publishing
program: the Canada Council for the Arts, the Government of Canada, the
British Columbia Arts Council, and the Province of British Columbia through
the British Columbia Book Publishing Tax Credit program.

Library and Archives Canada Cataloguing in Publication

Title: Crow stone / Gabriele Goldstone.

Names: Goldstone, Gabriele, author.

Identifiers: Canadiana (print) 20220417482 | Canadiana (ebook) 20220417504
   | ISBN 9781553806653 (softcover) | ISBN 9781553806660 (EPUB)
   | ISBN 9781553806677 (PDF)

Classification: LCC PS8613.O447 C76 2022 | DDC C813/.6—dc23

At Ronsdale Press we are committed to protecting the environment. To this
end we are working with Canopy and printers to phase out our use of paper
produced from ancient forests. This book is one step towards that goal.

Printed in Canada.

For you,
Mom

Those, whose world became grey a long time ago when they realized what mountains of hate towered over Germany; those, who a long time ago imagined during sleepless nights how terrible would be the revenge on Germany for the inhuman deeds of the Nazis, cannot help but view with wretchedness all that is being done to Germans by the Russians, Poles or Czechs as nothing other than a mechanical and inevitable reaction to the crimes that the people have committed as a nation, in which unfortunately individual justice, or the guilt or innocence of the individual, can play no part.

THOMAS MANN, BBC radio broadcast, December 30, 1945

— PART 1 —

East Prussian
Refugee

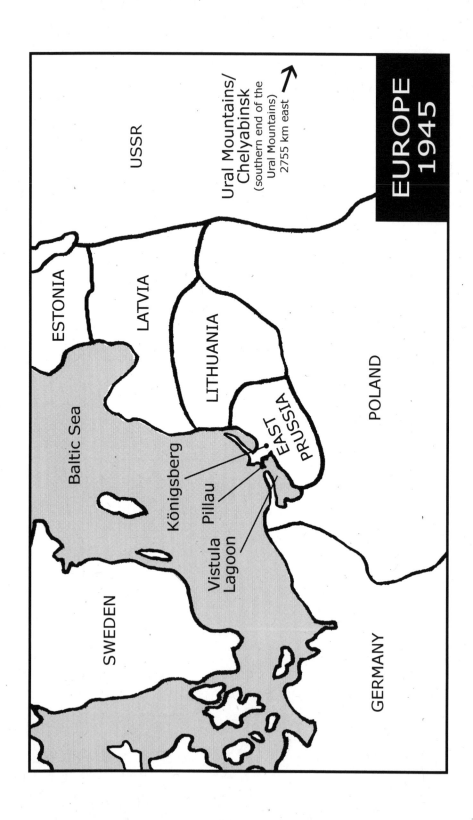

EUROPE 1945

ESTONIA

LATVIA

LITHUANIA

EAST PRUSSIA

Königsberg

Pillau

Vistula Lagoon

Baltic Sea

SWEDEN

GERMANY

POLAND

USSR

Ural Mountains/ Chelyabinsk
(southern end of the Ural Mountains)
2755 km east

CHAPTER 1

NOVEMBER 11. Today is Albert's twenty-fourth birthday, and he's coming home to celebrate. Well, not *home*, home, but what's become home — Königsberg — here, in East Prussia. I'm meeting him at the train station, the same station where we arrived when we were homeless children — kulak orphans. Will I even recognize Albert? The men all look the same in their grey field uniforms.

I glide over the polished marble like it's ice and I'm a child.

"*Achtung, achtung!*" The loudspeaker voice warns us to clear the tracks as the black locomotive roars in, squelching, snorting like a mad pig. It's on time. There might be a war raging, but German trains are always on time. Swastika flags wave a proud greeting in the swoosh of the train's arrival.

Around me is the regular jostling. Women, old and young, waiting for the return of their sons, husbands, fathers — or like me — their brother.

The soldiers all look old. They jump off the train to the platform,

not with a hop but with a thud. Heavy, dirty boots land on home territory with the weight of the war in their soles. Children run up to
papas, old women hug young men, lovers share kisses. Where's . . . ?

There he is! Dear Albert — my only brother.

"Over here!" I wave my arms.

Albert's tired face lights up, and he transforms into the impish boy
I know so well.

"Katya!" Albert strides closer, and we share a hug. He feels strong
and lean.

I pull away to study him. "Don't they feed you in the army? You've
gotten skinny, little brother."

He pinches my cheek. "You're no prize goose, yourself, dear sister."

I grab hold of his hand to lead him away. We have a friendship
that's grown better since childhood.

"Dearest Katya," he says. "You're like a little girl."

I turn to him. "I'm quite grown up, Albert." And to prove my point,
I ask, "Have you heard from David?"

"David?" He tilts his head sideways.

"I mean Klaus, of course." Many Aryans with Jewish-sounding
names changed them a few years back. But it's David who stole my
heart, not the Klaus he's morphed into. "I haven't received a letter from
him in weeks."

"It's a mess out there, Katya. Even a horse medic is in danger."

I stop swinging my brother's hand. The crowd becomes a blur, and
its noises swirl around me.

Albert releases my hand and steers me along by my elbow. "Let's get
out of here."

We pass long lines of knapsack-carrying soldiers queuing up to
board trains — their furloughs over.

"That'll be me in two days."

"Don't think about tomorrow . . . not now . . . today, we celebrate."

At the exit, SS men loiter with guns and dogs.

Albert mutters, "Even here."

"Even *what* here?"

"Deserters. They're making a big deal about anyone trying to leave the army. A big deal."

"Katya!" One of the SS guards steps towards us.

Albert stops. "Did they just call you? You have friends in the SS?"

"No, I don't. He must be calling someone else."

A black uniform stops in front of me. "Katya! Look at you! Don't even say hello? My, my."

The face is hard, the mouth cruel, the eyes familiar. It's David's brother — Helmut.

"And who's this? My brother would be jealous . . . if he weren't dead!"

"What did you say?" I stutter.

"Oh, you haven't heard? Sorry about that."

"Helmut . . . what did you just say?" I repeat, his words only beginning to become real.

"How thoughtless of me. I thought you knew."

"How . . . ?" I can't speak. A growing numbness distances me from the surrounding buzz of voices.

"Near Memel, on our east front. A bayonet wound. He was tending horses and wouldn't leave them behind. Him and his horses." Helmut bites his lip, as if . . . but no, Helmut has no emotion.

I blink my eyes, save my tears for later.

Helmut turns from me and faces Albert. "Well, you might have to introduce yourself. Katya seems to have lost her manners."

Albert tightens his grip around my hand. "I'm her brother."

Helmut now lights a cigarette and blows smoke into Albert's face. "Let me see your passbook, soldier-boy."

Albert becomes an instant soldier, saluting at attention, then grabbing for his soldier identification pass. I stand frozen, unfeeling.

Helmut holds the pass, but his eyes continue to assess me. "Everything in order. *Heil* Hitler, soldier."

Albert returns the salute while Helmut steps closer to me and plunks a quick kiss onto my lips. "Always wanted to try that."

I cover my mouth while he blends back into the faceless military presence that hovers like a swarm of hornets over the station.

"Katya?" Albert asks. "Are you okay?"

I blink my eyes and grab his hand. "Albert, you're here! It's all that matters."

"I'm terribly sorry about . . . what a cruel way to learn."

"I'll have time to cry for him later." I smile. "You're only here for two days. I'll not ruin it with my selfish grief. I want you to have a wonderful furlough. That's all that matters."

"But Katya . . . you can't just pretend nothing happened. You and Klaus . . . you cared for each other . . . you . . ."

"I've had lots of time to miss David, and this Klaus fellow in the army . . . I barely knew him. We've all been trying to fit in, just to survive. Cowards." I sigh. "And then we die anyway."

"What are you talking about?"

"Never mind."

"Katya, you are . . ."

"Incorrigible, they tell me." I force a smile, remembering Aunt Elfriede's view of me.

"Yes, you are incorrigible." But when Albert says it, I know it's a compliment.

"Let's go!" I pull Albert out of the suffocating building onto one of Königsberg's main streets as a tram swooshes past us — so close I can touch it.

"Nothing's changed here." Albert chuckles and holds tight to his cap. "This city is almost as dangerous as the front. How do you survive?"

"Albert, maybe you don't see it here on this corner, but Königsberg has changed. We'll avoid the ruined areas." British bombings back in August devastated huge blocks of the city.

Deking in and out among the traffic, we make it across the busy street. A half-block of tall buildings later, and we stand before Aunt Hannelore's own narrow red brick place.

CHAPTER 2

BY THE TIME I PUSH open the heavy door and invite Albert in, I've got David pushed away, too. "Let's get you something to eat. Aunt Hannelore is probably still out hunting with Susi."

"Hunting?"

"For food." I laugh. "It's become a daily battle. But don't worry. Since no one's here to tattle, I'll spoil you with extra butter on your bread and even some jam. We've managed to hoard some butter, but sausage to go with the bread . . . well, that's another story."

"Katya? I'm sorry about Klaus. I'm sorry we had to meet Helmut."

"Shush, Albert. No more." I shrug. "Klaus and I . . . we were just friends. Nothing more."

As a couple, David — or Klaus, as he later preferred — and I were doomed. I'll think about all this later. Soldiers die every day in this stupid war. Right now, I have my dearest brother here with me, and I need to be strong and happy for him. His furlough is so brief.

"Katya —"

I cover Albert's mouth, then turn and hum while I prepare his snack. Albert shakes his head and joins in with the tune. Everyone knows the popular song, "*Ich weiss es wird einmal ein Wunder geschehen.*" I know someday there'll be a miracle — Zarah Leander's hit from the movie *Die große Liebe.* We all want to believe that some kind of miracle — some kind of victory weapon — will end this never-ending war.

After a few bars, there's an awkward silence until Albert says, "It's horrible out there."

"You said that already."

"Katya, the Germans are losing. There's no way we can fix things now. No miracle."

Still holding the butter knife, I raise my hand. "So why doesn't the fighting stop? Why not end it now before more have to die?"

"Admit defeat? The Germans have much pride. Pride." He spits the word out like it's mouldy bread. "The Führer would never allow such a thing."

"Here." I push the rye bread into his hand and laugh. "Eat. So you don't go missing by getting too thin."

"Not unless you're eating with me," Albert insists.

And so we share the jam sandwich. I've never had so much butter on one piece of bread. It's good. I can do this. I can keep David far away.

"Remember those Bolshevik candies?" Albert asks between bites.

"The ones you hunted for during that May Day parade back in the Soviet Union?" This is the Albert I know so well. "You better not have any of those left in your pockets, dear brother. You'll end up in a concentration camp." I laugh at my bad joke.

Albert doesn't laugh. "You've heard of those places?" His eyes darken.

I nod. "Not really camps. More like jails." Run by hard-faced SS guards like Helmut. "Do you think that's where they sent the Jews?" I'd like to believe that all the missing people work in factories like mine — only further out east somewhere.

"Many are worked to death, others get shot, Katya." He turns away.

"Some say they're being gassed — by the thousands. Then they burn the — "

My throat hurts. "Explain what you mean. Gas? What burns?"

"I don't know, Katya."

I'm afraid to ask, to know. "What about women and children? Where are they being kept?"

Exasperation colours Albert's voice. "Let's not talk about this. Not today."

I can't finish the sandwich, not with the memory of Minna's bright eyes flashing before me — my fun-loving friend from the Richter estate, where we both used to work. Could Minna be in one of those camps — those prisons?

Maybe she's safe in Switzerland. That's where she told me she was going. It's been years now, and I've had no mail from her. Our golden days before the war, hunting for amber along the Baltic, seem like a mirage.

"Do you think the Jews are different from us?" I look at my brother, defiance in my stare.

Albert shrugs. "Jews, cripples, gypsies . . . ordinary people like you and me, Katya. The Nazis hate anyone who's different."

"Remember? We were once different, too."

"We're German, Katya. Full-blooded Aryans. The superior race."

"Surely you don't believe that?" I ask.

"I'm a soldier, Katya. My belief doesn't matter."

"Back home, in the Soviet Union, they labelled us kulaks." I motion Albert to sit down. "It's not just Nazis who hate."

Albert plops onto a chair. "We all need someone to blame. It's your fault, Katya."

"What is?"

"Never mind. Bad joke." His eyes twinkle. "I'm surprised you and David never married. You might have created new soldiers for the Führer. We're going to need them."

My face heats up and I drop my last piece of bread. Albert doesn't know that David had to be sterilized because he had epilepsy.

"You wouldn't understand." I shake my head, still too embarrassed to explain.

Albert picks up the bread, pretends to dust it off and stuffs it into his mouth. "Sorry, Katya," he mumbles while chewing. "None of my business."

The uncomfortable silence breaks when Aunt Hannelore's mantel clock chimes the quarter hour.

Albert smiles. "Time keeps ticking. My furlough will be over soon."

"I'll stop it! No more clock winding." We both grin at my stupid solution.

"Why is our world so crazy, Katya?"

"It's fear," I tell him. "We have to be brave."

"We are brave, Katya. You and me. We're brave. Always." He reaches over the crumb-covered table and squeezes my hand. "It's better than being proud."

I change the topic. "What will you do when this war is over, Albert? What will make you happy? A girlfriend?" I smile. Albert's shy with girls. "Or maybe a new automobile?" He's been obsessed with motors since he was little.

Albert shakes his head. "No, nothing that easy." He stares into the distance. "All I want, Katya, is a home . . . some place to belong."

This is why Albert and I get along so well. We share the same hole in our hearts. "Me, too, little brother. A real home."

I blink back useless tears as the kitchen's back door squeaks open and Aunt Hannelore appears, bringing with her a welcome rush of cold air.

CHAPTER 3

"ALBERT, YOU'RE HOME!"

It's been only a few months since our aunt's son, Wolfgang, was taken as a prisoner of war by the Americans. Seeing Albert in front of her must be painful, but a smile lights up her lined face.

"I am, yes . . . " Albert glances at me, "uh . . . sort of at home! Thank you for letting me visit."

Aunt Hannelore, strands of grey slipping from her bun, gives him a long hug. "You're always welcome here. You know that."

Born in the Soviet Union, now Germany's enemy, Albert and I have lived confused lives. These are uncertain times for everyone, in spite of the Führer's promises.

The thoughtful moment is broken when nine-year-old Susanna, Wolfgang's daughter, barges in. Seven-year-old Marianna tags close behind.

"Uncle Albert!" they scream in unison and scramble all over him. "You're here!"

"It's his birthday," I remind them. "Be gentle."

"Oh boy! Birthday cake!" Marianna pulls away and rubs her tummy, while Susanna keeps holding him tight.

Aunt Hannelore beams. "Yes, there will be cake, of course. I just got the eggs. Not an easy thing, you know. But I was able to trade. A guest left his cigarettes behind — Sulima brand. Any good, Albert?"

"Better than money," Albert acknowledges.

Aunt Hannelore's home, close to the rail station, is a guest house. It gives her much needed money — or cigarettes — and bustles with guests.

Just then, a kitten comes mewing into the kitchen.

"Fritzi!" Susanna calls out. "Uncle Albert, have you met *Meister* Fritz? He was my birthday present."

"I want a dog," Marianna pouts, skinny blonde braids falling forward.

"You'll have to wait a while longer," Aunt Hannelore tells her youngest granddaughter. "Dogs have to be fed and right now, we have trouble feeding ourselves."

"Turning nine was my best birthday ever," Susanna announces.

I nod. "Yes, Susi, it was quite the occasion. A squeaking kitten and lights bright like Christmas trees in August!"

"What lights?" Albert asks.

"When the British bombed Königsberg. You must have heard — "

"Enough talk," interrupts Aunt Hannelore. "Out of the kitchen, please. I have a cake to bake, and I'm sure Albert would enjoy a long soak in the tub. Katya, find him some towels. Albert, room five is empty. Last door on the left, second floor."

Aunt Hannelore likes to pretend that the war is far away. Any war talk in this house is quickly shut up.

"Nice to see you, Albert. Really and truly." But Aunt Hannelore's smile doesn't hide the sadness in her eyes. She gives Albert another hug and turns away to tie on her apron.

I lead my brother away. "I'll let you go for now," I tell him. "But I want to hear everything. Okay?"

"Yes, yes, skinny Katya." He lifts my chin with an outstretched finger. "But you must share, too. It's not good to keep things inside."

"I'm fine."

He drops his finger. "I want to hear about your life at the munitions factory."

"Later." I push him towards his room and wander back to Aunt Hannelore. I don't mind helping her out; she's not at all like grouchy Aunt Elfriede.

Susanna and Marianna have disappeared along with the cat. They lead a carefree childhood . . . in spite of the war.

Years ago — when I first came to East Prussia as a raggedy, hair-shorn twelve-year-old — it was Aunt Elfriede who took us in. Three gruelling years of slavery followed. Even now, when I remember those years, I get angry — angry at the sad little girl I was, and angry at the charity that pretended to be kind.

I wrap a tea towel around my waist and join Aunt Hannelore at the kitchen table. "What kind of *Kuchen* are we making?" I ask.

"Ach, Katya!" She shrugs. "We'll make up our own recipe with the ingredients we have. Eggs, butter, some sour milk and flour."

"We need sugar," I tell her.

"We do, but from where?"

We stare at each other with knotted faces.

"I know," she says. "Talk to Otto at the newspaper kiosk. He fought in that first war with my husband. Tell him I sent you." She dumps open a jar and hands me some coin.

I take off my makeshift apron and slap on my shoes. "I'll be right back."

It's good to keep busy. Stuffing the *Reichsmarks* into my pocket as I run, I head back to the train station and the newspaper kiosk. That must be Otto — the one-legged old man sitting on a three-legged stool.

"Otto?" I call. A craggy face looks up at me. "I'm Katya. Frau Hannelore sent me."

"Ah, my Hannelore, my *Liebling*. She owes me a kiss."

"We need sugar," I tell him. "Where can I get some? My brother's in town, and we're making a birthday cake."

"Go see Mariechen at the bicycle shop."

Maybe Otto does know everything about everything. "Thank you, Otto!"

"I'll take a kiss from you instead!" He offers up his lined, scarred cheek.

I blow a kiss and run.

The bicycle shop on the other side of the station rents bikes by the hour. A tandem one sits invitingly. After the war, maybe Albert and I can go exploring. A big woman hovers, hands on her hips, surveying the busy street.

"Are you Mariechen?"

"*Ja.*"

I stretch my neck around her and spy a big cloth sack of sweet treasure that looks like snow crystals but tastes like . . .

"*Finger weg!*" she complains and slaps my hand.

I lick the granules off my finger. We negotiate a price, and she pours the sugar into my clean kerchief. I tie it shut and then I'm off again, the half-pound of sugar secure in my grasp.

Running past Otto, he calls out, "Still no kiss? I'll take a piece of cake then!"

"Of course. But we have to bake it first."

"Lucky brother! All my love to Hannelore."

As I wait for a break in the traffic, I calculate how big the cake has to be. Albert, me, our two younger sisters, Marthe and Sofie, will be coming. Cousin Anni should be there. Doris — Susi and Marianna's mother — plus Aunt Hannelore and Aunt Elfriede. Ten people, for sure. Maybe Uncle Reinhold?

Back in the comfortably warm kitchen, I plop the sugar on the table.

"You were successful!" My aunt grins. "That Otto never disappoints."

"He seems lonely."

Aunt Hannelore blushes under her flour-smeared face. "Yes, we all need a little affection!"

David's smiling eyes flash before me.

"Katya?"

I blink David's face away. "Cake. Let's get it done."

Together we finish baking with those precious ingredients that no one takes for granted. Once the cake is in the oven, I go to the dining room to set the table. Aunt Hannelore has beat me to it, though. I count the settings. Ten.

Albert will be our only male — our guest of honour. Unless Sofie or Marthe bring guests. You never know with those two. My younger sisters have become strangers to me.

From behind me, Fritzi jumps on the table. "No, Fritz. Bad cat." I pick him up. He nuzzles against my chin, and I close my eyes and nuzzle back. Because it's November, there are no flowers to set on the middle of the table. But we'll have a *Kuchen* — that will be centrepiece enough.

"Come on, Fritzi. This is no place for a cat."

CHAPTER 4

CAT SECURE IN MY ARMS, I can't resist a final check, making sure the cutlery's lined up and the linen napkins sit perfect. Aunt Hannelore's voice behind me comes as a surprise. "Well, does it pass your inspection, dear Katya?"

"Of course," I stutter.

"You were trained by my sister, and I know she was a harsh taskmaster."

I shrug as the squirming feline jumps down and makes his escape.

"You've had a hard time of it, dear girl. I hope when this war finally ends, you find yourself a decent young man — if there are any left — and forget all this . . . all this . . ." Aunt Hannelore is about to cry.

It's been hard for her, too. The other war, the Great One, left her a widow. And now her only son is a prisoner of war. I'm grateful to focus on someone else's pain.

"Wolfgang will return," I promise her. "The Americans aren't cruel. He'll be safe with them." That's the consensus of the women I work with at the munitions factory.

Footsteps approach from the hallway, and Albert comes in. "What's all the sniffling about?"

Albert looks so strong, invincible and yet so vulnerable. How can that be? Maybe I still see my little brother the way he was, not what he has become — a seasoned infantry soldier for the German Wehrmacht.

Aunt Hannelore wipes tears from her face with the corner of her apron. "*Junge*, we're so glad to have you here." She gives him a quick hug. "Now that you smell clean." She smiles, sniffs and then sniffs again, this time with a frown. "I have to check on the cake. Wouldn't that be something if I burned it!"

As Aunt Hannelore runs into the kitchen, there's a commotion at the front door.

"I'll get it," Albert offers.

It's Sofie and Marthe. No male guests with them. Good. I don't like feeling like the odd one for not bringing a boyfriend along. They never knew about David, and there's no point in sharing now.

Sofie, Marthe and Albert hug and laugh as he helps them take off their coats. They pay no attention to me, and I scuttle away to help in the kitchen.

"Hey, Katya!" Sofie calls. "Aren't you even going to say hello?"

I retreat back down the foyer. This door greeting is backwards. I live in Stablach, sleep in the factory's dormitory. My sisters live at Aunt Hannelore's house — they should be letting me in.

"Dear sisters, of course I want to say hello. How are you?" I give Sofie a perfunctory hug. Do the same for Marthe. The girls are fashionably dressed, both with short bobs and heels. You'd barely know that there was a war going on, the way they look. Bright red lipstick painted on their lips. Aren't they daring? Lipstick is frowned upon by the Nazis.

"Doesn't Albert look wonderful!" The red lips swoon as one over their favourite brother, their only brother.

Then there's an awkward silence. We're all sizing each other up.

On the outside, Albert looks like every other Wehrmacht soldier, with his swarthy complexion from living outdoors like a farmer.

Marthe's happy mouth contrasts with a tinge of sadness in her grey eyes that I've not noticed before. It must be from working at the hospital. Sofie works as a secretary for some postal bureaucrat. She looks the part — posh and sophisticated. Maybe Marthe got the lipstick from her.

"You all look good. Great!" Albert grins his approval. He's not looking my way though, and that's okay. I don't need my little brother complimenting my looks.

Sofie does it for him. "Katya, you look good. But you should smile more." She reaches over to touch my hair. "And you might try a perm."

I pull back.

"It looks perfect the way it is," Marthe assures me. "Maybe try some lipstick, though."

Albert chuckles. "You girls and your vanity. What a change from the front. Red is not a good colour out there."

Heat rises in my face, and a quick glance reveals my sisters are also blushing.

"Where have you been, Albert?" Marthe's tone is soft, empathetic. "The front must be horrible."

Albert glances in my direction and mumbles something that sounds like . . . like . . . Zhytomyr? Did I hear him correctly?

"You were in Zhytomyr?" I shout. Zhytomyr is close to our home, to Federofka. "Did you see Aunt Helena?" Aunt Helena is Mama's younger sister. She was forced to stay behind when we left the Soviet Union, back in 1931. So much has happened since then. Like this war, for one thing.

Albert shakes his head. "No, I didn't see her. Zhytomyr and its surroundings are scorched to the ground. Windmills gone. You wouldn't recognize anything. Besides, that was months ago. The front has moved much closer."

Aunt Hannelore joins us from the kitchen. "Sofie! Marthe! You're back!" She pulls my hand and also grabs for Marthe's. "Let's get comfortable in the sitting room before the others arrive."

"Who else are we waiting for?" asks Sofie.

"Why Doris, Elfriede and Anni." Aunt Hannelore looks around. "What's happened to Susi and Marianna?"

At the mention of her name, Susi explodes into the room. "Did you see Fritzi? I can't find him anywhere." Marianna tags behind. "He ran away."

Albert jokes, "You've lost your boyfriend?"

Just then Susanna's boyfriend shows up on the other side of the window, on the empty flower box, pawing to get in.

Giggles explode as Susanna rescues Fritzi from the November chill.

"Okay. One guest accounted for. Three more to go," I note.

"Doris went out to Kreuzburg, to accompany Elfriede on the train. That sister of mine doesn't like to travel alone."

"How does she manage out there on the farm without Uncle Reinhold?" I ask. He'd been recruited for the *Volkssturm* a few months ago. It's part of our total war effort. Every man under sixty must fight.

"She still has her Polish workers — a new young girl and the same boy she's had since the start of the war."

I shudder at the thought. *Poor nameless foreigners having Aunt Elfriede as their boss.*

"Elfriede's train arrives at 1700." We're all used to military time now. Just then the mantel clock strikes four times. Still an hour to wait.

"Enough time for board games!" Susanna claps her hands in glee.

Marianna shakes her head. "I'm not playing. Susi always wins." Instead, Marianna's off chasing the cat.

We get out *Mensch ärger Dich nicht*. Rolling the dice, we have a knock-out war trying to move our game pieces into their homes.

"I win!" Susi cheers as she rolls a two and slides her last piece home.

The rest of us share relieved grins because sometimes losing is better than winning.

CHAPTER 5

THE DOORBELL CHIMES Anni's arrival. Dressed in her navy blue and white BDM leader's uniform, she greets us with a curt, "*Heil* Hitler." At some point during these war years, Anni graduated from being a mere member of the League of German Girls to being one of its leaders. While my two sisters raved about the Nazi girls' group, I was relieved to be considered too old for BDM membership when it became compulsory back in 1936.

I mumble a greeting to Anni, focusing on putting the game pieces away. Only Albert gets up and returns her salute. Since the summer, after the assassination attempt on the Führer, it's been important to show loyalty to all things Nazi. Anni gives me and my sisters a cutting look but doesn't push for more.

"You're looking good, Albert."

"*Danke*. So are you, cousin Anni!"

"*Sieg Heil*." Anni parrots the Nazis — victory is near.

"Of course." Albert can't possibly believe what he says, but it satisfies

Anni. I hope we can avoid talking too much about politics during this short birthday visit.

"Hello! You've made it, Anni," says Aunt Hannelore. "Your mother should be here soon. Have you heard from your father?"

"Nothing. He must still be training. Every man and boy is needed for the final victory."

"But your father's a farmer." Aunt Hannelore shakes her head. "Poor Reinhold . . . he's almost sixty."

"Even the old and young can fight if they have a good cause." Anni's chin goes higher.

Albert interjects. "Anni, the Wehrmacht needs more than old men!" He turns to me. "Katya, you're our munitions expert. How's that miracle weapon coming along?"

All eyes turn to me. "Why would I know? They don't tell me what we're building. I just stand in a long line and do the same thing, day in and day out. We've assembled countless bullets and grenades. It's never-ending work."

"Don't get discouraged," Anni says. "That's what the enemy wants."

"My job's boring, Anni. That's all I was trying to say." Why do I ever try to have a conversation with Anni?

"Still writing?" Her eyes narrow, as if accusing me. "Weren't you interested in writing articles for the girls' magazine?"

My face flushes. "I've . . . I've no time." It's embarrassing having my innermost passion examined by others. My novel, inspired by Minna, Thomas Mann and amber, is a Baltic love story. But it'll never get published. And writing articles for the *German Girl*? I couldn't do it. It's all just Nazi propaganda. No, the only writing I've done lately is to David . . . and that's over now, too. I bite my lips, my throat aching with unshed tears.

"Katya?" Marthe looks concerned.

Anni waves dismissively. "She's always drifting. Hasn't changed a bit." With a smirk, she turns to my sisters. "And you two fine young models of German womanhood . . ." Anni studies both Marthe and Sofie. "I'd wipe that lipstick off, if I were you."

Neither sister wipes their lips, and their defiance makes me proud. Anni, pretending not to notice, asks, "How's life going for you two?"

"I've seen more blood than I ever want to see again," says Marthe. "Can we please change the subject?"

Anni persists. "Sofie? And you?"

"I type. Whatever they tell me to do, I do."

"Everything?" Marthe glances at her sister, eyebrows arched above her twinkling eyes. Sofie's been dating someone from her office, and now she turns bright red.

"Let's stop this line of questioning. Seems we all have secrets." Aunt Hannelore glances at her granddaughter Susi. "Who'd like another game while we wait for Doris and Elfriede?"

"No games for me." Anni straightens up like a soldier and adjusts her BDM tie.

"How about you, Anni?" I ask. "Anything new with you?"

"Well" — now it's Anni's turn to blush — "I have a new beau. He's in the SS. That's all I can say for now."

Of course Anni's beau is from the SS. She's such a snob. I wish she wasn't here. She's ruined the friendly atmosphere of Albert's birthday celebration.

The tension breaks with the arrival of the last two guests — Aunt Elfriede and Doris.

"Mami!" Susanna runs over and hugs her mother. "I missed you!"

Marianna comes up behind. "I missed you, too."

Doris, I note, has a decidedly thick waist. *When was Wolfgang last here?* I mentally calculate the months since the June visit.

Doris sees me staring. "Yes, Katya. I'm expecting. Doctor says late February."

Albert clears his throat, his voice low and earnest. "Let's keep the Russians away from here at least until that baby's born."

Aunt Elfriede overhears and shouts at all of us. "No such talk is allowed. There'll not be Russians on my doorstep. I forbid it!" She shudders for effect — a drama queen, just like Anni.

We stand around in uncomfortable silence.

Aunt Hannelore calls from the kitchen, "Elfriede, come show me what you brought."

Aunt Elfriede beams with pride. "What would you do without me?" She lists off her treasures as she heads to the kitchen. "I've got bread, butter, cream, smoked ham, even some bacon."

My heart might be aching, but my stomach growls like a dog. *When was the last time I had any meat? We'll have a real feast.* Tail up, Fritzi scampers purposefully behind Aunt Elfriede into the kitchen. Even the cat is eager for a feast.

Today we will celebrate.

We chomp down on open-face rye bread sandwiches slathered with butter and topped with thin slices of Hungarian salami and thick slabs of smoked ham. We crunch gherkins and spiced pickled pumpkin.

"Delicious!" Albert announces after he swallows a mouthful. "What a treat! Our field kitchens serve only lukewarm pea or cabbage soup and *Zwieback* — if we're lucky. Those dry crackers taste more like cardboard than bread."

Aunt Hannelore brings out the cake, and we sing Albert the birthday song. A special treat is the real coffee that Sofie's brought along. Just the smell is enough! Ersatz coffee does not compare.

"Time for presents!" Susi hands Albert a picture she drew. It's of Fritzi playing with a ball of wool.

"This picture . . ." Albert reaches over and hugs the child. "This picture reminds me of why I'm fighting. I'm going to take it with me."

Albert also gets four pairs of newly knitted socks. Women throughout the Reich are knitting for the war. Except me. I've not been able to master the art of knitting. Instead, my gift to Albert is a stolen bullet casing. I've wrapped it up, and in the card I call it the miracle weapon.

Albert laughs, and I know he appreciates the joke. "With this bullet and four pairs of socks, I'll be the envy of my troop. You've no idea how wonderful it is to have extra socks. Winter's coming."

I nod agreement. "Russia will be cold. Remember Siberia?"

"Katya, I do remember Siberia. Why do you think I haven't been captured yet? Now, if I could get captured by the Amis, like Wolfgang, I'd go in a moment."

Anni stands up, hands on her hips. "Are you suggesting that my cousin deliberately — "

"Hush!" says Aunt Hannelore. "Calm down. He's just joking."

There we go again. Arguing about the war. It's impossible to avoid.

"Will you get time off for Christmas?" I ask Albert.

"Hard to say. I somehow doubt it." He laughs. "Having a birthday so close to the holiday doesn't help. I have to make this my Christmas."

"Oh, but we don't have a tree!" Susanna exclaims. "I know! Maybe we can find one and have a pretend Christmas."

I look at Albert. "Remember that Christmas when we decorated a little tree and celebrated in secret?"

"Ooh. A secret Christmas?" Susanna's all ears. Marianna stops her colouring — a late gift offering — and leans closer.

Albert and I take turns telling about how we celebrated back in 1929, in spite of the Soviet's ban of Christmas.

CHAPTER 6

ALBERT BEGINS. "It started with the new sled."

"Painted red." Papa's love, detached but strong, warms me up even now as I remember his gift to us children. "He told us that it was a *winter* gift, not a *Christmas* gift because — "

"Because Christmas was illegal," Albert finishes for me.

"Why?" asks Susanna. "Why was Christmas illegal?"

"Because religion became illegal," I tell her. "The USSR is an atheist country. Churches were all closed. Let Albert continue."

"Right. So our parents went off to some communist community meeting right on Christmas Eve and we — "

I complete his sentence. "We went sledding with our new winter toy."

Albert and I grin at each other.

"We could have gotten arrested," Albert says.

"Really?" asks Susanna. "For getting a Christmas present?"

"Yes, really," Albert confirms. "That's not the whole story, though."

I continue. "At the bottom of the hill, we crashed our sled right into a little evergreen tree and ended up dragging it back to the house."

Albert laughs. "Zenta, our sheepdog, got covered in snow. Remember, Katya? He looked like a silver wolf."

"And remember how upset Gerda was about the tree?"

Marianna pipes in. "Who was Gerda?"

"Our housekeeper," I tell her. "She helped our mama with everything. Cooking, cleaning, laundry . . ."

"You had a housekeeper?" Aunt Elfriede raises her eyebrows.

"Hush, Elfriede." Aunt Hannelore pats her sister's arm. "Let them tell the story."

"Yes, Gerda was afraid we'd all get arrested and end up in jail if we put up our little Christmas tree," I tell them. "The secret police were always watching for rule breakers. Any excuse to scare us kulaks."

"Kulaks?" Now it's Aunt Hannelore who interrupts.

"That's what they called the private landowners. We were all labelled," I remind her. We've tried to forget about what happened under Stalin and his Five-Year Plan for collectivization. Here in Nazi Germany, anything to do with communism is considered pure evil.

"Of course," Aunt Elfriede mutters. "That's how they all ended up at my doorstep. Kulak orphans. If it wasn't for my charity — "

"It was a good tree," Albert remembers, guiding us back to our Christmas story. "I put my toy cars under it and pretended that Nikolaus brought them."

Marianna's eyes grow big. "You mean *he* didn't come either?"

Susanna motions with her finger for her younger sister to keep quiet.

I laugh. "And I tied my doll to the tree's tip and pretended she was an angel."

Albert adds, "And then we sang a Christmas song."

"We did." I let out a deep sigh. It feels strange to share our secret Christmas celebration here. Now it seems trivial, and yet it was such a big deal back then. But that was ages ago and in another world. Never could I go back to that place.

"In the end, Papa did get arrested and we lost our home along with our windmill and our dog. And now here we are." Albert's voice no longer sounds like that excited little boy.

"Your dog?" Susanna grabs Fritzi, nearby on the floor. "I'm never going to lose Fritzi." He snuggles into her lap and starts to purr. "Can you hear him?"

"And we lost our mama," I add into the silence enveloping Fritzi's purrs.

Aunt Hannelore reaches over and puts an arm around my shoulder. "Such a sad place. Don't you agree, Elfriede?"

Aunt Elfriede shrugs. "It's Russia. Anything's possible over there, I suppose. We can't let those heathens into our Third Reich. It would be the end of the world."

"Christmas in East Prussia will never be like that," Susanna declares, and with a gesture of sisterly compassion hands Fritzi over to Marianna. "We'll never have only pretend presents. That's just stupid."

Night falls early in November, and Aunt Hannelore heads to the windows to pull down the blinds.

"Leave them open," Albert tells her. "I don't like feeling shut in." He laughs, like it's a joke. "I've been in too many trenches."

We all reply at once. "We must. It's the law. Total darkness in case of bombing."

"Oh . . . of course."

Silence settles over the room as Aunt Hannelore finishes pulling down the blinds, one after another. Someone lights the candles on the table and now our faces, cast in moving shadows, look eerie.

"How romantic!" Sofie announces. "We need some music."

Marthe jumps up and heads to the gramophone in the corner. She flips through the limited record collection. "Ah. The perfect song to brighten up our dark mood."

She pulls out a Zarah Leander hit. "*Davon geht die Welt nicht unter . . .*"

Marthe and Sofie dance together, but Anni is too severe, too stiff, to enjoy the music. Aunt Hannelore dances with both her granddaughters, while Doris dabs at her eyes, and I dance with Albert. There's not much space for dancing, but we wiggle along the perimeter of the room.

"I'm sorry about David." Albert's voice is low. "I only met him the one time . . . if I remember, he seemed to prefer horses over autos. But still, he struck me as a good person."

"I'm glad you got to meet him." I lean against Albert's shoulder. "Otherwise I might think I imagined him . . . my dear David . . . he was too gentle. Not made for a war."

"None of us are, Katya." Albert leads me past the gramophone, and the music swells. "Helmut . . . his brother . . . was he always cruel like that?"

"Consistently cruel." David and Helmut were opposites when I worked at the Richter estate. David was usually in the stables, grooming the horses, while Helmut joined the SS early on. He loved to poke fun at David . . . and at me. Always.

"I'd like to punch him in the — "

"Hush, Albert." I sniffle away tears and with bleary vision, look up at my soldier brother. "Just you be careful. Please."

"Excuse me, Katya!" Marthe nudges between us. "Albert, when are you going to dance with me?"

"Okay, okay, you men-starved women! I'll dance with each of you."

"I ache all over," Aunt Elfriede complains. "You can count me out of this dance party." She heads to the kitchen. "Besides, someone has to wash the dishes."

Typical of that woman, I think. *But she'll not guilt me out of this evening's festive spirit. I'll focus on the music.*

Marthe notes, "It's too bad Aunt Hannelore's record selection is so limited. She doesn't even have a copy of Lale Anderson's 'Lili Marlene.'"

"Time for the radio," Sofie suggests. "Maybe they'll play 'Lili Marlene.' Have you heard Marlene Dietrich's version? Even the enemy likes our song. I could listen to it forever."

We switch to the radio and use that as our dance music. It's all good until the Führer's voice comes over the air, interrupting "Schön ist die Nacht" — everyone's favourite tango.

Aunt Hannelore shuts off the radio. "We're not listening to him. I can't stand his voice."

Anni gasps. "You mean the Führer's voice? Aunt Hannelore! How can you say that? I . . . I . . ."

"Come now, Anni. We're family here. Can't we be truthful with each other?"

"I have to go." Anni quickly gathers her things and slams the door shut as she exits.

"Good riddance," says Marthe, glancing towards the kitchen. That door's closed, so Aunt Elfriede hasn't heard the insult against her daughter.

"You think she'll report us?" asks Sofie.

"For what?" I ask. "For turning off the radio?"

Like a candle flame, the party mood has been extinguished. We all head to our beds and our night terrors. Finally, I have time for my own thoughts — but my tears have dried up.

CHAPTER 7

ALL TOO SOON, Albert heads back to the front and I to Stablach, back to my life at the munitions factory. Stepping off the crowded train with my small suitcase, I'm bombarded by yelling. "Katya! Over here!"

It's Lili, my closest friend here in Stablach. I wave and hurry over. "Lili! We were on the same train and didn't even know it?"

"I guess so." She gives me a tight hug. "It's so good to see you. I have a lot to share." Lili's face glows. She has been visiting her boyfriend, Hans, who's been injured.

"Well, start talking," I tell her, as we squirm past other girls who, like us, are returning to the barracks after a day off. "I want to know everything!" Maybe her joy will blot out my sorrow.

Lili blushes and looks around. "Katya!"

"Oh, Lili." I move closer and lower my voice. "I don't mean *everything*." It's my turn to blush.

Nobody pays us any attention. Other girls, in their little groups, are too busy chattering among themselves. We leave the rail platform behind and head towards our barrack home — one of dozens of wooden one-storey structures built for soldiers who once trained here.

We hurry past one of the gated areas reserved for the French and Belgian prisoners. Blinds darken all the windows, and even the jeeps that growl back and forth have their headlights turned off. As a military installation, Stablach is a high-security area. Military police parade back and forth along the gated entry. It's part of the normal routine around here.

Lili stops walking and takes a deep breath. "That train made me nauseated."

"It's all that perfume. Too many girls returning from visiting their boyfriends." I laugh — it's becoming easier. "I was beginning to get a headache."

"I was gagging." Lili looks pale and gulps air like it's water.

We join the queue at the other security gate, show our passes to the handsome, unsmiling new Gestapo guard and enter our compound. At Barrack Eight we stop, and I put my suitcase down near the door.

"How about we leave our bags here and go for a walk?" I suggest. "I could use some fresh air myself. We still have time." Daylight's fading into a muted purplish grey.

Lili and I lock arms and saunter past the other barracks, all bustling with returning workers. We're comfortable with each other's silence. I don't make friends easily, at least not people friends. Give me a dog or a horse and I'm instantly in love. But people — I keep my distance.

I've been here, in Stablach, since this crazy war began. The whole town is built around the military installations. Half of the barracks are dormitories for the munitions workers. The other half of the barracks are occupied by war prisoners.

Of course, we have nothing to do with the half-starved French and Belgian men. Sometimes I catch them leering with undisguised lust through the barbed wire fence that divides us, and I feel sorry for them. It's a feeling I squash down because seeing the enemy as human can get me in trouble. People disappear overnight for even the slightest fraternizing. Every morning, the skinny men are loaded onto trucks to work on neighbouring farms.

"The cold air feels refreshing." Lili shivers and tightens her arm around me. "Better than that overheated railcar."

I should tell her about David, but something stops me. I don't want another's pity. I also don't want to be known as one of those sad girls. There's always someone crying about bad news from the front.

Lili and I work on the same assembly line inspecting brass casings — a preferred position. It's better than the heavy lifting in some of the other jobs, like lugging sulphur in twenty-kilo bags. While the assembly line with the conveyor belt of brass shells is noisy, every job in the factory has its drawbacks. Working beside a friend is a definite plus. Even without talking — on account of the constant grind of machines and the staccato of hammering — Lili and I connected and became friends gradually, without knowing it.

Once, when I first started working here, David came to visit. He'd brought me back to the barracks after a night at the cinema, and Lili was there, standing in the shadows with Hans. David and I had been arguing. He was going to war and didn't want me to wait for him. He wanted me to meet and date others. But I didn't, I couldn't. And now? Now I no longer have to wait for him.

I force back my tears, bite my lips and focus on Lili. "Tell me, how is Hans? Is the wound healing? How badly was he hurt?"

"It's a foot wound. He's in bed and taking total advantage of his bedridden position." She giggles.

"Is he in the hospital?"

"He was. Now he's convalescing at his mother's place. She rearranged the sitting room so that he can be a part of the household and not shut away in a bedroom." Lili sighs.

"What does that sigh mean, Lili?" I prod.

"Well, sometimes, you know, a little privacy is a good thing." She glances over at me.

"Definitely," I say. David and I shared that kind of privacy only once and I ruined it.

"Katya, I . . . I have a secret."

I shake away my regret and focus on Lili. "Out with it!"

"I'm going to have a baby!"

I gasp. Then, quickly recovering from my shock, I stumble on. "Are . . . are you okay with this?" Since Minna's abortion and David's sterilization, the topic of babies remains a difficult one for me.

Lili's eyes brim with tears. "I'm scared, Katya. I'm scared because I do want this baby, but — "

"Stupid war!" I finish for her. "When will the baby arrive?" I look at her tummy. Hard to see anything with her winter coat on.

"Beginning of March. We were together in June and had so little time to prove our love to each other. Then when that week was over and I missed one period, and then another . . . I felt so afraid . . . and he was back fighting. I tried to ignore what was happening. But I can't pretend any longer." She takes a deep breath. "So I finally saw a doctor."

"It's good that you saw a doctor, Lili. You can't keep something like this to yourself."

"I know. That's why I'm telling you, Katya. But when I went to visit my mother, I . . . I lost my courage." Lili looks over at me, wiping her eyes with the end of her scarf. "You're the only one I've been able to tell."

"You haven't told Hans?"

"No, I couldn't tell him either. He has enough to worry about. They're sending him back to fight . . . even before he can walk properly! The war's been so hard on Hans. These men . . . they're just like us, you know." She sniffs. "Not any braver."

"Lili, you have to tell *Chefin Hilde*. You can't hide it."

"I just want to wait until after Christmas."

We turn a corner and the wind gusts into our faces. "Let's get back," we say in unison and laugh.

Now for sure I can't tell her about David. She doesn't need to be upset. "Let me know how I can help, Lili."

"Thank you, Katya. I feel lighter already, not carrying this baby alone anymore." Lili reaches over and squeezes my gloved hand.

"This war won't last much longer," I say, trying to comfort her.

"That's what I'm afraid of, Katya. What happens when we lose the war? Then what?"

"Then the fighting will stop. Everything will be better. Hans will return, and you'll be a perfect little family. Make Hitler happy."

David and I would never have made Hitler happy.

"Lili, don't worry so much."

If only I could believe my own advice. But the November clouds above are heavy, and the feeling in my gut is like . . . like . . . like when the Soviet police forced us out of our home. That's the feeling I have — like we're heading to our doom.

I hurry my steps because fast walking energizes me, lifts me out of my doldrums. Soon though, I have to stop and wait for Lili, who's dragging her feet — like she's afraid of her future.

CHAPTER 8

EACH SUNDAY IN DECEMBER, there has been a little advent celebration in the Stablach dining hall for the girls who didn't go home on the weekends. It's now noon on Christmas Eve day. Four candles burning on the advent wreath seem out of place here, but then *we* must look out of place, too. I glance over at women gathered near the door, waiting for rides. Yes, even munition workers get off work early for Christmas.

What would we be doing if we weren't here? Some of us might be married and raising children. Not me, of course. Maybe I'd have read more Thomas Mann and become a real writer.

"Katya?" Lili calls out. "Let's go. Time to catch our train." Lili waits at the drafty dining hall entrance with her suitcase.

"Katya's always daydreaming," one of the women calls out.

"She'll end up spending Christmas here alone," another points out.

That wouldn't be so bad. Instead, I'm heading to Uncle Reinhold's and Aunt Elfriede's farm, in Kreuzburg, to celebrate the holiday with my sisters and extended family.

"I'm coming!" I tell Lili. You still can't tell she's expecting under her oversized coat, and she's still too afraid to tell anyone.

Kreuzburg is not far from Stablach — I can even bike there in the summer. But the train service is quick and reliable, and it's been cold and snowy for a couple of weeks now.

Fifteen minutes later, I'm jumping off the train. "*Frohe Weihnachten*," I call out to Lili. I hope things go well for her. Even if she can't share her condition with words, her family will see it for themselves.

"*Ja, frohe Weihnachten*, Katya!"

Uncle Reinhold waits for me at the tiny Kreuzburg station, and I'm surprised at the warm happy feeling that grows inside me. Uncle Reinhold has Papa's blue eyes that stare at me with Papa's same quiet twinkle. What's Papa doing now? It's been many years since he and I have shared a Christmas. I was only a little girl.

"*Frohe Weihnachten*, my dear Katya." Uncle Reinhold waves at me like he's ten years old, not almost sixty.

"Good to see you, Uncle!" I reach out to shake his hand.

Uncle Reinhold holds it tight and then forces a hug on me. "Dear Katya." He sighs with too much emotion. "How are you?"

"I'm good," I reply and push him away. "How's the ditch digging going?" Uncle has aged considerably. The Wehrmacht has ordered the *Volkssturm* to dig ditches to stop any Soviet tanks.

"*Mensch!* Hard work for an old man. Come on! Let's go for a sleigh ride, like in the old days." He leads me to a horse and buggy standing outside the station.

"Where'd you get the horse? I thought the Wehrmacht claimed all the horses."

"This old one's like me," he says. "Just good for around the house."

I love the sleigh ride. Uncle Reinhold has put bells on the harness, and the feeling of Christmas is strong and good — peaceful like the snow-covered surroundings.

I sniffle with nostalgic feelings. "How's Aunt Elfriede doing?" I ask. Saying her name dries my tears.

"Well, she's in her element. Has those poor Polish workers running from sunrise to sunset."

"Who else is coming for Christmas dinner?"

"The usual crowd — assuming they make the train. Anni and her young SS man, what's his name? Jürgen, I think. Then your sisters, each with a soldier, I presume. Aunt Hannelore, with her two grand-children and Doris. And you. How many is that?"

I shrug, suddenly feeling alone. What does it matter? "No word from Albert?"

"Nothing."

I'm more disappointed than surprised.

"Come on. Let's get some hot coffee into you. You'll feel better."

"Coffee or . . ." Ground up acorns or dandelion root do not make coffee.

Uncle Reinhold calls to the old horse and we're off. "Coffee. Real coffee." He sniffs the air. "Can't you smell it now?"

"No, Uncle Reinhold." I smile though, appreciating his attempt at a joke.

"Aunt Hannelore brought it along. Says it's left over from Albert's visit back in November. She came out this morning. Our nag, old Pauline here, has had her workout."

As I enter the familiar house, Marthe pokes her head around the kitchen corner. "Hello, dear sister." Aunt Elfriede's overweight dachs-hund, Max, toddles in behind her, tail wagging.

I'm surprised Marthe's here already. "*Frohe Weihnachten,*" I reply, bending down to give Max a good scratch behind the ear before straightening back up.

With flour up to her elbow, Marthe comes closer and gives me a hug. It's a good thing I've taken off my dark wool coat.

"Thank you," I mutter.

"You look like you needed one."

Why do my sisters always tell me I'm needy? It's most annoying.

"Is Anni here yet?" I ask, changing the subject.

"Not yet. She's still marching with some troop somewhere, handing out Christmas cheer. She's promised to be here by five."

We both look over at the big mantel clock. It's just past four.

"So we have an hour of peace without her propaganda," I say, glancing over at Uncle Reinhold, who's whistling as he goes through a pile of mail. I don't mean to offend him. Anni is his only daughter, but she's hard to take.

"I'm surprised you got off so early," I tell Marthe. "How are things over at the hospital?"

"Bad. The only reason I'm here early is because I have to leave early, too. I have a night shift starting at eleven."

"On Christmas Eve?" I sputter. "We don't even build grenades on Christmas Eve."

"Katya, soldiers die every day of the year."

Why does she have to be right?

Uncle Reinhold, along with Max, follows us into the kitchen. "Now all I need is a cup of that coffee to go with this newspaper, and I can pretend I haven't been digging ditches for Russian tanks to trip over for the last three months."

"Where's Aunt Elfriede?" I ask.

"Napping," says Marthe. "She was up early. Spent a busy morning in the kitchen."

"She needs her rest," says Uncle Reinhold. "You should both be familiar with that."

We give each other knowing glances. Aunt Elfriede's routine must not be disturbed.

"I'll make you a cup of coffee, Uncle." Marthe turns to the stove just as footsteps clatter down the stairs. "Oh, but that might be Sonja. She can make the coffee."

A girl, maybe fifteen, comes towards us. She's pale and pretty, with blonde strands escaping her bun. She must be the new Polish worker ordered to work for Aunt Elfriede and Uncle Reinhold. The other was sent away. Sonja stares at the floor, avoiding our own stares.

"Nice to meet you." I reach out to shake her hand, but Sonja doesn't take it, and I quickly let it fall again.

"Make coffee," Marthe tells her.

"*Ja, Fräulein.*" Sonja turns to the stove.

"You don't go home for Christmas?" I ask her narrow back.

Marthe answers for her. "She doesn't have a home, Katya." She rolls her eyes. "She's a prisoner, for heaven's sake."

How stupid. Of course, I should know that. We Germans have taken over all the Polish villages, kicked people out of their houses, divided families — just like what happened to the kulaks back in the Soviet Union. Waves of guilt pass through me.

"Our Polish girl will be back in her home soon enough," says Uncle Reinhold as he stuffs his pipe. "This war's almost over, and then the Poles will have their revenge." He lights a match and focuses on his pipe.

"Can we talk about something more cheerful?" I ask. "Just because it's Christmas."

Tobacco smoke rises, swirls in a lazy ring, releasing its musky smell. "Of course, my favourite Russian orphan. Of course."

"What about me, dear Uncle?" Marthe's smiling as she takes off her apron.

"You're all my favourite orphans."

We sit in quiet contemplation at the kitchen table, the radio playing soft Christmas music in the background, and I nod off in the warm room, Max cuddled on the floor near by feet.

CHAPTER 9

AS THE CLOCK CHIMES five, Sofie and Anni crash through the door, laughing and bringing a blast of cold air with them.

Max greets them with excited yelps.

"A fine bunch, you are!" Sofie exclaims. "Sleeping in the middle of the day. *Frohe Weihnachten*, everyone!"

I shake myself awake as Sofie's brandy breath comes close. She gives me a kiss on the cheek.

"Sofie!" I'm repulsed by her obvious intoxication and unusual show of affection.

Anni is more reserved, although she, too, has obviously had a few drinks. "Papi!" she cries out, and Uncle Reinhold quickly shifts from half-asleep to welcoming his only daughter home.

"Ännchen!" he mumbles. "My Ännchen von Tharau!"

"*Ja, ja*. But not from Tharau — not today. Today I'm Ännchen from Nemmersdorf."

"Nemmersdorf!" I exclaim.

"Thought that would get your attention. It's all quite calm there — now. A ghost town, really. We staged some more photographs — for film and propaganda purposes, you understand."

"But why?" I mutter. "To scare us?"

"Exactly. So we can summon up the courage to fight and prevent more massacres and ghost towns." She turns her head and I follow her gaze.

Aunt Elfriede has entered the room, and Marthe, Sofie and I all watch. How many times have we seen this family connect, with us on the outside? It reminds me of what we lost back in the Soviet Union. Our home village of Federofka is *not* a ghost town; It's all one big happy collective now ... with our milkmaid, Natasha, no doubt, as a brigade leader. But what did Albert report? Maybe Federofka burned to the ground with the Nazi retreat.

Sofie's the first to break the uncomfortable scene. "Let's pour ourselves a drink. For our — "

Anni finishes the toast for her. "For our victory, of course!"

"Of course," Uncle Reinhold mumbles in agreement.

Sofie brings out a bottle of Jägermeister Schnapps. "A Christmas gift from my boss," she titters.

Marthe gets the shot glasses and Sofie pours.

"To our Führer!" Anni toasts.

The herb-based liquor burns my throat.

"Clears the head, it does!" Uncle Reinhold says, wiping his mouth. "How about another one?"

"Now, now. Let's not all get drunk. It's Christmas Eve." Aunt Elfriede looks flushed after downing her schnapps. "We still have to go to church, you know."

Sofie raises her eyebrows. "Church? You go without me."

Anni agrees. "I'll keep the house warm."

There's a commotion at the door, and then Susanna explodes into the room. "Hello!"

"You made it, after all." Uncle Reinhold sounds relieved. We must all appreciate the energy of the children.

Doris comes in last, her round stomach protruding from her open coat. "The girls insisted that it's not Christmas if we don't come see you — just for the evening. I have to visit my parents, too."

"Of course," says Uncle Reinhold. "That's quite acceptable. You're always welcome here."

Aunt Hannelore adds, "We were just discussing our own church plans. Seems no one wants to go."

Young Susanna looks surprised. "But the Weihnachtsmann won't come unless we're in church." Marianna tagging behind, a squirming Max in her arms, nods agreement.

Sofie grins. "When the Weihnachtsmann comes by, we'll hide and he won't know we're here."

Marthe adds, "We'll pretend he's part of the Red Army."

"Not funny." Anni glares at Marthe.

Luckily, Susanna and Marianna are too excited by Christmas and the promise of gifts to worry about soldiers from the Red Army.

Uncle Reinhold, the two aunts, Doris and her two daughters and I head to the nearby church for a formal candlelit Christmas Eve service.

I can't say it feels normal, although it looks peaceful enough. There are barely any men. Just a few old ones and some injured young ones. Fear hangs like a garland connecting all our cheery Christmas wishes. Silent but menacing, just the same.

We hurry home in the falling snow to sit around the candlelit Christmas tree. The Weihnachtsmann has indeed delivered. Everyone likes the handkerchiefs I've embroidered with their initials, and I'm grateful for the Nivea cream, the nuts and the orange I receive. How did the Weihnachtsmann find an orange — especially this year?

We munch on chocolate-dipped *Schweine Ohren* and marzipan while the two Polish servants run in and out, providing us with our needs, and Max is on the lookout for crumbs.

Later, the Polish boy, Donat, heads to the barn to look after the animals. I'm tempted to follow, to check out my old room, but Susanna talks me into playing her new board game that Anni brought along.

Jagd auf Kohlenklau is a ridiculous game about catching coal thieves and stopping them from wasting energy. Even board games are now teaching tools to support the war effort.

We're all running low on energy. The rich foods and too many glasses of wine and schnapps have drained my energy. I notice Sofie's eyelids drooping, and soft snores coming from Aunt Elfriede have me exchanging grins with Uncle Reinhold. Marthe's long gone for her night shift.

Uncle Reinhold clears his throat. "We're all tired. Let's close the evening with a couple of songs."

We start with a grumpy rendition of "O du fröhliche" and end with the "Stille Nacht" lullaby.

I sleep over at the neighbour's, a *Frau* Schultz. When I first came to Germany, she once criticized me around a coffee table. Now, with her husband and both of her sons dead, *Frau* Schultz has lost her edge. Thus, our Christmas Eve ends with peace and quiet.

CHAPTER 10

NEXT MORNING, we indulge in a big breakfast of eggs, sausages, bread, butter and fruit preserves, including Aunt Elfriede's favourite — plum. Again, we drink real coffee. Sonja looks tired and serves us automatically, without expression.

I follow her into the kitchen to ask for more coffee. When she passes me the pot, I grab a clean cup. "For you," I tell her. "You need some real coffee, too."

She glances to the door, where a harsh Aunt Elfriede could come charging through at any moment.

"I'll keep her busy. You enjoy your coffee and have some bacon and eggs, too. I insist." With a smile, I add. "It's an order."

I re-enter the dining room, sit down across from my aunt and say, "You've had it hard, Aunt Elfriede, and I appreciate your efforts." Usually, the two of us don't have much to say to each other, and she jerks her head back as if I've slapped her. Everyone's silent and we're suddenly the centre of the room.

"How's your back?" I continue, pushing my nervousness aside.

That's always an intense topic for her. But to my surprise, she doesn't want to talk about her aching back.

"Ach, Katya," she says. "What's to become of us when this war is over?"

"Peace," I tell her. "You'll have Uncle Reinhold back to stay. No more fighting."

"Humph!" she sniffs, regaining her arrogant composure. "You young ones. For you the war's been one big party. You don't remember the last war."

"You mean the Great War?"

"*Ja*, that one. After it ended, the Germans were punished and the whole country suffered, even out here. This time it'll be worse."

"Maybe not," I offer.

She glares at me with impatience. "*Ja*. They'll take away my Polish workers. Prices will go up. So much to repair and rebuild. Nothing's going to be the way it was." She lets out a long sigh and then stuffs more sausage into her mouth. "Maybe the Russians will move in." Her words squish out around the mouthful of meat.

"Oh, Mami, don't talk like that," Anni warns.

Defeatist talk can put a person into one of those dreaded camps that everyone knows about, but no one mentions.

Anni glares at me like it's my fault her mother's upset. She then gets up and puts an arm around Aunt Elfriede. "Don't worry so much, Mami. Our Führer will figure it out. He's working on a secret weapon and — "

Uncle Reinhold laughs, chokes on his food and laughs some more. Even Max seems to join in.

"Papi! Why are . . . what . . ." Anni frowns at her father.

"Private joke," he says, clearing his throat. "Of course we will win this war, dear daughter."

"I wish Albert was here," I tell them. His birthday visit seems so long ago.

Sofie, next to me, adds, "And Wilhelm." She blinks her eyelids quickly to hide tears.

"Wilhelm?" I turn and ask her.

"Didn't you meet him?"

"I met ... umm ..." Someone in a uniform. "An *Unteroffizier*, maybe?" Military rankings still confuse me.

"You might have met Rolf." She pauses. "He fell, back in the fall." Nobody uses the dead word. Soldiers don't die, they fall.

"I'm sorry." Somehow I don't think of my younger sisters as ever knowing pain. To me they are forever little kittens playing their way through life.

"It doesn't matter. I didn't know him long." She pulls out her new Christmas handkerchief, sighs and adds, "Who knows if I'll get to know this Wilhelm any better."

Aunt Hannelore pipes in. "What about our dear Wolfgang?"

"What about him?" Uncle Reinhold moves over and puts an arm around her. "He's in American hands, Hannelore. The war's over for him. Your grandchildren will see their father again."

Aunt Hannelore nods and holds back tears, even though her eyes brighten with them. Doris, visiting her own parents, isn't here to contribute to the worry about her missing husband.

"When do you have to return to the *Volkssturm*, Uncle Reinhold?" I ask.

"Me?" He drops his arm from Aunt Hannelore's shoulders. "Yes, well, tomorrow night. Back to the ditch digging." He looks tired already.

And that's it. Christmas, 1944, done. We succeeded in pretending everything is as it should be. Maybe it is. Maybe this sense of doom is only in my head. Or maybe, with David now gone, none of it really matters.

CHAPTER 11

CHRISTMAS DAY, nine at night, and I'm taking the last train back to Stablach. My breath clouds the crisp, night air. It's been a cold winter so far and with the coal shortage, we'll all be freezing. Factories get priority to burn coal — that game Susanna and I played about the coal thieves is all too true.

Over the station's loudspeaker, Marlene Dietrich's sultry voice sings "Lili Marlene." Its melancholy tone matches my mood. Has my own Lili, my friend, had the courage to tell her family about her condition? It's not a good time to have a baby.

Listen to me. You'd think we'd already lost the war.

After clambering up the train's metal ladder, I find an upholstered seat near the exit, surprised to note that the car is almost empty. Am I one of the few required to work at six tomorrow morning? Or maybe my co-workers took an earlier train. There are serious consequences for being late to start a shift. Imagine our soldiers dying because they didn't have enough ammunition. That's guilt none of us could live with.

The only other passenger, a soldier, catches my eye and winks. I bite my lower lip and then give him a smile. He needs encouragement, and encouraged he is because he saunters over.

"*Mein Fräulein*, may I join you?"

"Of course," I stutter and inch closer to the window as the smell of alcohol wafts in my direction. Determined to be brave and kind, I add, "*Frohe Weihnachten*."

"So it is. I'm Siegfried." He plops down beside me. Our thighs touch. "Formerly Jakob. Take your pick."

Like my David. He changed his Jewish-sounding name to avoid unnecessary attention. I relax, feeling an immediate connection with this renamed stranger. "Nice to meet you." I smile at his honesty and forgive him his tainted breath. "You like being Siegfried?"

He shrugs. "I prefer Jakob. What does it matter now? There are no Jews left."

His statement sounds so nonchalant, but it terrifies me. "Where did they all go, Jakob? And what are they doing wherever they are? Working in munitions factories?"

I imagine a million Jews in long assembly lines, like in our munitions factory, all working feverishly on a big, secret project. Even the children. I see Helmut barking out orders at them with his cruel mouth.

I imagine my old friend Minna flirting with all the good-looking, young Jewish men — dazzling even the Nazis with her teasing eyes. Minna would manage. She wouldn't let some Nazi like Helmut destroy her.

Jakob's voice breaks into my thoughts like a snapping whip. "Dead."

"Who's dead?" I turn and look at this stranger.

"The Jews. They're all dead. Even the children."

I get this feeling in my stomach, like I've been kicked. "I don't believe you," I whisper.

"Yes, you do." Siegfried-once-Jakob stares hard at me. "We have camps for them to die in. You've heard of '*Arbeit macht frei*'?"

I nod. My old employer, Herr Richter, liked to joke about it. "Some die slowly from too much work, and others die . . ."

I edge away from this soldier, but he nudges himself closer, and I'm grateful when the train squeals to a stop. But it's not my stop, and I feel trapped by this soldier and his words.

When the train starts up again after a session of hissing and sputtering, I change the topic. "Did you see that newsreel about Nemmersdorf? Did you see what the Russians did to those poor villagers?"

"I saw what we Germans did in Ukraine. A little village ... close to Zhytomyr. Women and children stuffed into a barn and burned alive."

I hold my breath. My heart beats faster. Where was Albert? Wasn't he in Ukraine? Didn't he go to the Zhytomyr area?

"I was there," Siegfried-once-Jakob continues. "I heard the screams for mercy. I heard the shots that replied. I saw the blackened — "

"Stop!" I hold my hand up against his mouth. When he kisses it, I quickly drop my hand and look out the window, but there's only my reflection to be seen.

Of course, I know that the Germans are killing people, but do I need to hear it spoken aloud like this ... on Christmas Day?

Siegfried-once-Jakob now forces my hand up against my own mouth. "Did you feel my kiss? Is your hand still warm? Return it to me. I need a kiss, too."

I'm frozen, but my heart hammers madly, like ice pellets against a window. "Can you feel anything?" Siegfried-once-Jakob asks, dropping my hand and moving away.

I don't want to think about death. I lean closer to the cold window, trying to see past my reflection.

"We're killing everyone," he says. "Russians, Poles, Ukrainians and every single Jew — old, young and in-between. You and me."

I turn from the window and stare hard at him — at hazel eyes that look sadder than a lonely dog's. "Why are you telling me this? There is nothing I can do about it."

"There's nothing I can do about it either," Siegfried-once-Jakob agrees and stares past me out the window.

"So we just wait for our fate? We just wait for the Russians to come and nail our tongues to the table?" I shudder with the Nemmersdorf image.

"Of course not." He looks at me again. "We run. We run for our lives. Because once they catch us, we will each get what we deserve."

"It's Christmas," I protest, staring down at my bullet-making hands folded in my lap. "I want to feel cozy and happy for this one day of the year."

"Go ahead," he says. "I don't blame you. Your cozy, happy time is ending. The Russians will soon be here." Jakob gets up.

Involuntarily, my hand reaches towards him. "Don't go. I'm scared."

Siegfried-Jakob sits back down and gives me a long, lingering kiss. On my lips, this time. I don't fight it. I give in, make it last longer. Maybe this is all there is. A few minutes of connection with a stranger on a train.

Siegfried-Jakob pulls away. "Mine's the next stop. Thank you for the kiss. I'll remember it."

I nod, my lips bruised. I don't even know the name of the place he gets off at. He's an unknown. But then, he never asked me for my name. I stare again at my reflection and touch my lips. *For you, David . . . that kiss was for you.*

When I get to my stop and hurry towards the security gate, I start to laugh. If I tell Lili about this, she'll tell me I imagined the whole thing.

CHAPTER 12

THERE'S A BULLETIN posted on the barrack door.

Rumours about a major enemy offensive are BOLSHEVIK LIES!
Anyone attempting to flee will be severely PUNISHED!
NEVER SURRENDER!
EACH of you has a JOB to do.

I push open the door, escaping from the ominous words. I'd rather think of my train kiss as I drift to sleep on my narrow cot, and I don't hear any of the other girls come in.

The next morning, while splashing cold water on my face in the dormitory washroom, I grin into the mirror, unable to wash away the memory of Jakob's lips.

Lili comes up behind me. "I'm late, I'm late!"

"What else is new?" I reply.

"Your smile, that's new. Katya, stop smiling at yourself and move over. Let me at the mirror."

I duck out of the way as she combs her hair and examines her skin. "Ugh. I keep getting these zits!" Then she looks over at me. "Katya, you are positively glowing. Must have been a good Christmas."

Christmas? I've forgotten about it. "I suppose. And you?"

She backs away from the mirror, looks quickly around for others, then pats her growing stomach. "Still a secret," she says. "Wasn't a right time."

"Soon it'll be impossible to hide," I warn her. The bump seems quite obvious.

"I know. I'm such a coward."

"Come on, Lili. We can't be late. They're all super-sensitive right now. Did you read that sign on the door?"

"Yes, I read it. Fleeing? How would we even go? The trains are always overloaded with soldiers."

We walk as we queue for breakfast — foul ersatz coffee and stale bread without butter. There's a lot of whispering, a lot of pale faces. We're all tired and scared.

Later, at the munitions assembly line, the machine clatter makes conversation impossible. Is it memories of the kiss that make my day fly by? Perhaps Jakob was really David. Maybe Helmut was just teasing about his brother's death. Maybe . . . I rub my lips, not wanting to lose the way that soldier made me feel.

Chefin Hilde, the shift manager, marches towards us with a purposeful stride, and I focus on bullets, not kisses.

"More work here, less daydreaming." Chefin Hilde stares, hands on her hips, at our practiced hands, which expertly seal grenades passing by us on the conveyor belt.

Then the Chefin's gaze shifts to Lili's stomach, and contempt fills her eyes as she acknowledges the bump that grows despite all of Lili's attempts to ignore it. Chefin Hilde shakes her head.

"*Komm, Mädchen*," she demands, with a crook of her index finger.

I reach a rubber-gloved hand out to my friend as she's led out of the work space.

Later, at *abendbrot*, the spot I save beside me on the wooden bench for Lili stays empty.

Girls across the table from me whisper, and I can't avoid their conversation.

"Did you hear about Lili?"

"Who's the father?" whispers another, glancing over at me. "You must know, Katya. Tell us."

"Where is she?" I ask, speaking louder. "Does anyone know where Lili is?"

"Humph. Obviously, she went to pack her bags. She'll be off to that place for unmarried girls."

That place! "Where? Which one?" Homes for unwed mothers have sprung up everywhere.

They shrug and return to their vegetable soup.

At bedtime, when I pull back my sheets to sleep, earlier than usual since I have no one to chat with, I find a note.

Dear Katya,

I have to write this fast. Yes, I've been discovered and they're sending me to a home in Königsberg. Please come visit. You've been such a good friend. I'll miss you. You're always brave and I'm such a coward. I put the address on the back page of this note.

Yours,

Lili

Lili! You're not a coward. You have every right to be scared. So much talk about the Russian front. Not a good time for babies. But before the war even started — that wasn't a good time either. Minna was part Jew and having Helmut's baby. That was trouble enough. Is there ever a good time to have a baby?

With the coal rationing, these early weeks of January are colder than ever. The frigid temperatures seep in through doors, windows and cracks in the barrack walls.

The wind blows from the east, where the Red Army waits. Maybe they won't attack. Maybe they'll change their minds. Maybe our soldiers, our Albert and that Jakob, will stop them. Maybe Uncle Reinhold's ditch will swallow them up.

I want to travel to Königsberg and visit Lili, but train travel is now restricted. There's a big movement of troops to the eastern front and all the railcars give priority to soldiers. Civilians must stay put and believe that things will work out.

The order to stay at our work stations, given by Gauleiter Koch, our Führer's right-hand man here in East Prussia, is repeated everywhere. It's posted in newspapers, on the radio, at the rail station, as well as on new posters in the factory and our barracks.

Everyone needed for the final victory! Fleeing is treason!

Hospitals, schools, munitions factories throughout East Prussia have all been warned. Why so strict? Does Gauleiter Koch know something we don't know? Is he afraid?

CHAPTER 13

A FEW WEEKS LATER, on a Sunday afternoon, when the flood of troops has finally slowed down to a steady dribble, I bundle up against the January cold and board a train for Königsberg. Although it's not far, it's a stop-and-go kind of trip because the tracks need to be constantly cleared of snowdrifts. Underfed and underdressed forced labourers dig us out while SS guards loom nearby, also shivering, their guns poised to speed up the shovelling of any shirkers.

Lili's not staying at a Lebensborn home because it's not been possible to confirm Hans's genetic background. Instead, she boards at a rooming house in the suburbs also catering to unwed mothers. Once in the city, I ride the familiar Königsberg tram past the bombed-out buildings from last August and arrive in an undisturbed, peaceful residential area called Metgethen, where the streets are lined with huge stately homes.

I find the house after a mailman points me in the right direction. He reminds me of Georg, our postal courier in Wehlau ... so eager to join the Wehrmacht back in '37.

"Katya! You made it." Lili embraces me down in the front foyer.

"You look . . ." Can I say "big" and not be insulting?

"I look pregnant?" Lili laughs. "I can't hide it now."

"Will Hans have a chance to visit before the birth? He should see you like this!"

"I'm not sure." Lili shakes her head, her mirth fading. "I haven't heard from him since before Christmas. Katya, it must be awful out there on the front. He hates it . . . hates the cold . . . the constant noise." She covers her ears, as if she hears it, too.

I nod in agreement. "I have a brother somewhere out there, too. But let's not talk about the men. How are you doing?"

"I'm good, Katya. There're two other girls here like me with similar due dates." She pats her bulging stomach. "We knit fat socks for the skinny soldiers and wee little socks for our babies." She stops to show me how little, before she goes on. "Plus, we do light housework . . . no lifting . . . and cook. I can't complain about the food." She smiles. "Better than at the munitions factory, that's for sure."

"You're not missing anything there," I tell her. "It's all the same. Chefin Hilde still barks orders like a dog."

"Well, her I don't miss at all," Lili says. "Come, Katya, join me for a walk."

"Are you sure? It's cold out there."

"Listen, Katya." Lili lifts up her chin and takes on a supervisory voice. "It's important that mothers-to-be get fresh air and exercise."

I laugh. "They're looking out for you."

"Yes, they are. My baby might be needed in the Wehrmacht someday."

She struggles to pull on her high leather boots. We have matching pairs — cast-offs from the Wehrmacht. "My feet are swelling. I can barely fit into these boots."

Once we're outside, we walk on in silence for a bit, with just the crunch of the snow beneath our feet.

Having a baby changes more than just bodies. I remember Minna stopped talking to me when she came into the family way. She had too much Jewish blood in her to be considered a suitable mother. Not like that Gretchen. Gretchen qualified for a Lebensborn home — with Helmut as the father — and her baby was adopted by a proper set of Nazi parents. Whatever happened to Gretchen? But why would I care — we had nothing in common. But Minna . . . I need to see her again. Soon . . . after this war's over.

"Seems so peaceful, so quiet out here," I note. "Doesn't feel like a city." There's no traffic on the tree-lined street. No autos, no people — only horse tracks, tall trees, wrought-iron fenced yards. "It must be beautiful in the summer."

Lili laughs. "It is peaceful, isn't it? After that noisy factory, I appreciate the silence."

"Me, too," I agree. "It's strange that there can be a war happening on days like this."

"Do you think we're safe here in East Prussia?" Lili turns to look directly at my face.

"That's what they say on the radio and in the newspapers, Lili. Safe and sound."

She turns away. "And you believe what you hear?"

Lili has enough to worry about, so I reply, "Dear Lili, you must trust the war effort." I sound like Anni.

It's one of those rare winter days. No wind. Brilliant sun. Sparkling snow. Biting cold but not bitter. I breathe in this silent beauty, breathe it in like it's peace and happiness and exhale frosty clouds of fear, doubt and worry. They fade into nothingness, but when I breathe again, new fear grows right back.

Lili's baby is now expected at the end of February and that will come soon enough.

"Maybe you can hold it back," I joke. "For my birthday, on March seventh." From somewhere ahead comes a low moaning. "Did you hear that?" I ask.

"Sounds like labour pains." Lili's lightness turns dark. "I just wish I'd hear from Hans." She sighs and the sigh blends in with a repeated moan coming from somewhere nearby.

"You have to believe, Lili. You have to think positive . . . for the little one's sake."

"Of course." She giggles. "If I wasn't wearing this heavy coat, I'd let you put your hand here so you could feel the little guy squirm. He's a good kicker, he is."

"Will make our Führer proud, will he?"

"That's not funny, Katya. Let's not talk about the Führer and this horrible mess we're in. I want my baby to be healthy and happy and never see a war."

Again, there's moaning. It's rolling towards us over the sparkling snow like a low wind. "What is that?" I can't decide if it's an animal or a human.

Lili moves closer to me, holds onto my sleeve. We're approaching a slope, coming to a dip in the park we've been strolling through. Horse tracks mess up the perfect snow.

"Someone must have fallen down the ravine up ahead." Lili lets go and quickens her step. I follow. "All this snow, they must have lost their footing."

Queasiness grows in the pit of my stomach. We come to the edge of the ravine and there beneath and in front of us are maybe a dozen horses — bleeding and dying. Beautiful horses. Are they Trakehners?

I cover my mouth to control my retching.

"Who did this?" Lili wails. "Who would do this?"

One of the horses attempts to stand but falls on top of another. For the first time in my life, I wish I had a gun.

Red blood on white snow. Groans of pain on silence. Horse flesh in agony. Who would do this? Is this senseless act a war tactic? Is self-destruction the only way to stop the enemy's victory? A crow settles down onto the branch of a nearby tree and adds its derisive caw to the chaotic scene.

"Let's get out of here," Lili urges, hands on her stomach.

Frozen to the spot, I stare at the blood staining the snow in the dip below us while a non-human sound sputters out of me, not unlike the crow's caw.

Lili tugs at my sleeve. "Katya, let's go."

I cover my mouth, close my eyes and find my human voice. "We can't just leave them to their agony. We need to find someone with a gun." When I reopen my eyes, Lili's shaking her head at me.

"No, we can't get involved, Katya." She pulls me and I follow in slow motion. Ahead of us, an SS soldier leans against a tree, cigarette dangling between his lips.

Anger emboldens me, and I approach him while Lili hangs back. "The horses . . ."

"Leave," he orders. "Get back home. What are you doing out here?"

"But the horses . . ." I step closer to him. "You must do something!"

"Go! The Russians are coming. Get out of here!"

A Wehrmacht truck rumbles close and squeals to a stop. The SS soldier climbs on, waving at us with his rifle. "*Sieg Heil!*" The truck drives on.

"I'm cold, Katya. Let's go back. We tried. My baby needs to get warm."

And we leave the dying horses to their fate.

Later, I catch the evening train back to Stablach. For now, Lili is safe — we are all still safe. But the blood of those dying horses stains my hope for the future.

CHAPTER 14

I WAKE UP LATE on the cold, dark morning of January 24. Rubbing sleep from my eyes, I manoeuvre down the narrow corridor to our spacious, sparkling clean, green-tiled washroom. Twenty sinks line one wall. Empty. No girls fighting for a spot at the mirrors. No one banging to get into a cubicle. I pull the cord to flush and the toilet's gurgle seems too loud.

I want to indulge in the novelty of all this privacy, but something must be wrong. Minutes later, I dash through the cold, across the windblown assembly field towards the dining hall for another breakfast of watery oats and ersatz coffee. Up ahead, just in front of the cafeteria, a noisy crowd gathers around the information board.

Girls shriek and stumble over each other.

"What's going on?" I stretch up on my toes to read the bulletin board.

"Look for yourself!" A woman pushes past me. "I have to pack!"

"I knew it!" someone else mumbles. "The bastards! Now we have to run for our lives. How dare they do this to us!"

I read the handwritten letter posted on the wall.

Attention!
The Red Army has broken through.
Soviet tanks are rapidly encircling Stablach.
Ships wait in the Pillau harbour to transport civilians to safety.
Leave immediately.

Chefin Hilde, usually so prim and neat, looks frazzled. "Just go, girls. East Prussia is cut off from the west. I had a phone call." She pulls both shaking hands through her hair. "This is it! Go, save yourselves!"

How will we flee? How do we get to the harbour, to the ships in Pillau? It must be a hundred kilometres. Maybe if we cross the frozen Vistula Lagoon it'll be shorter. But first, I better go back to Kreuzburg. Then I'll figure out the rest.

The constant hum of conveyor belts and machinery is no more — the munitions factory sits eerily silent. No smoke billows from its stacks. Army jeeps, overloaded with military personnel, scurry out of the compound in a steady stream. What happened to the prisoners of war? Their barracks seem deserted. Soon it'll be only us women left behind.

I collect my thoughts. *Immediate flight? Then I need to eat something.* "Any breakfast left?" I call out.

Nobody answers.

"Come along, Paula," I say to a quiet girl standing nearby, staring at the official evacuation notice. "Let's go eat."

She shrugs and just stares at me with fear-filled eyes.

I accept her indecision as a yes and yank her with me towards the cafeteria doors.

Other women run back and forth. Some scream, some whisper and natter in disbelief. I hear Nemmersdorf over and over. Images of the dead from the newsreel flash through my mind even though I swallow them away. Paula and I slurp the cold coffee and shovel in the soupy porridge in silent haste.

Back at the barracks, the mayhem is worse. We trip over each other.

Do I need my toothbrush, my Nivea, or should I pack light? Paula looks over at me. "Socks," she says. "Take all your socks."

"Good advice, Paula." Extra socks, of course.

I grab my small knapsack and stuff it with a few toiletries, a change of underwear and the extra socks. No room for a book. I pull on my coat and head back out, scarf trailing behind me.

Outside, the luckiest girls jam into vehicles queued up outside the factory grounds. How did they manage to secure petrol? The Wehrmacht has been confiscating civilian fuel for months now.

From beside one auto, an older woman waves Paula over, and Paula tugs at me. "That's my mother. Come with us, Katya."

"No, you go! I'll be fine."

Paula runs to the woman, who hugs her tight. I fight back tears, lonely for my own mother's hugs.

Others sit patiently on suitcases, legs crossed, waiting for rides — only their white faces give away their fear. No one will be picking me up. I'm on my own, and my heart pounds while my body demands action, demands flight.

With fingers shaking, I struggle to button up my overcoat and tighten the woolen coat's belt more than necessary, as if buckling tight will contain my fear. The scarf I wrap around my neck and half way up my face is not just for the cold. It's my cocoon, my nest, my inner sanctum where I mumble ... God, help me. Then I adjust the knapsack over my shoulders and distribute its weight over my strained shoulders.

At the storage shed, I grab my bicycle and walk it along tire tracks through the dirty snow. Heading past the empty patrol station, the realization hits me like a snowball: *our Wehrmacht won't protect us anymore and, like those dying horses, for us there is no mercy shot.*

I deke past a congestion of vehicles — honking horns, grinding gears, spinning tires — as they jostle for position on the snowy road. The recent cold snap has turned the snow hard and when I follow on the tire tracks, it's like riding on concrete. Still, with this heavy traffic I'm constantly forced off the road and into the deeper snow. I struggle to stay balanced, my gloved knuckles tight around the handlebars.

After a bit, I'm pedalling along the snow-packed rut of a walking trail parallel to the road and the rail tracks. When a train approaches from the southeast, it doesn't even slow down at the Stablach station. As it passes, people cling precariously to the frosted sides, their luggage and boxes tied on top. The railcars look like Nickolaus sacks, overflowing with too many toys.

It must be minus twenty or more, but my vigorous pedalling keeps me warm; only my hands — my fingers — sting with cold pain. I wipe at my eyes, vision blurry with frost crusted on my lashes. Waves of nausea pass over me as the frost bites.

CHAPTER 15

IT'S FIFTEEN KILOMETRES to Kreuzburg. In the summer, I can do this in less than an hour. But today, the hour drags into two ... then three hours. Autos pass, back and forth. Horses pull wagons loaded precariously with wooden boxes and furniture. All head westward towards the ships waiting on the Baltic.

By the time the road sign announcing the fringes of Kreuzburg comes into view, my fingers are frozen into a crunched position. My face is numb, and my lashes are so thick with frost that I can barely see.

Uncle Reinhold and Aunt Elfriede's farmhouse lies on the western outskirts of Kreuzburg, close to the school I once attended when I first arrived in East Prussia. Now it's not students but Wehrmacht soldiers trudging into the classrooms with weapons and supplies. I cycle past and let the bike, like a horse, finds its way, finally dropping it in the snow with careless exhaustion before I enter the once-despised house.

"Hallo! Anybody here?" Maybe they've left already, on their own — without me.

No. I follow the smell of baking into the kitchen. Aunt Elfriede stands near the stove, wrapping baked potatoes in towels. She looks over at me with fearful eyes

"The Russians are coming," she says. "I heard it on the radio."

Max, roused from his nap over by the warm stove, gives me a short hello bark then snuggles back to sleep.

"We have to leave," I reply. "Now!" Eyelash frost melts and dribbles like tears down my face. I stare at the pile of potatoes and drool like a dog. "Could I have one?" I beg, rubbing my hands together over the heat radiating from the wood stove. My numb fingers thaw with needles of excruciating pain.

Aunt Elfriede's glare is cold. "You want my potatoes? You think I have extra?" Her voice screeches with indignation. "I barely have enough for us. I can't feed you, too." She shakes her head. "I'm taking only a few and hiding the rest for when we return. We'll need food later. You'll thank me then ... when we sit around the table and have dinner ... you'll all thank me then. I plan ahead."

Max, picking up on the tension, folds his ears back.

This woman, once spurned by my father, has tormented me for so long. What else would I expect from her? I turn to leave.

"You're going alone? So foolish," she says. Max, standing as tall as his short legs allow, barks in agreement.

I stop. She's right. It is foolish. This is something I can't do alone. I need Sofie and Marthe. "I'll find my sisters first." I know where they're working in Königsberg. It should be easy to get to the hospital and the post office. Those are important places, after all. "Then we'll head to the ships in Pillau together."

At the door, a pair of Uncle Reinhold's thick socks sit stuffed into some old boots. I cram them into my knapsack and leave Aunt Elfriede behind with her precious baked potatoes.

Aunt Elfriede comes to the door. "That's Anni's bike. Is that how you came? And now you just throw it into the snow? You ungrateful Russian orphan, you are — "

"Incorrigible," I fill in for her.

"You better leave the bike here. Anni will need it in the spring. Pick it up!" Max takes her side and barks his agreement.

I leave the bike resting against the giant linden tree. Biking is too cold and difficult anyway. "She's welcome to it," I tell my aunt. "I was just returning it. Tell her, thanks."

Aunt Elfriede stomps back inside, slams the door, and I begin the twenty-kilometre hike to the big city. The bumble train, the one that stops at all the small towns along the way, rumbles past me, through Kreuzburg, at a snail's pace. Like the other train, it's overflowing with people and their belongings. Curiously, this train isn't heading to the big city, but away from it.

Shrugging off the sense of foreboding and ignoring the gnawing hunger in my stomach, I pull up my coat collar and join others following the train track towards Königsberg. The wind, now blowing in from the Baltic, wants to push us away. And it's snowing again. This January must be one of the coldest and snowiest ever, and my high boots fill with snow. The walking, though, warms me up.

At least I'm not alone. Alongside the track, the road is packed with decrepit horses pulling overloaded wagons. Families carry each other, old and young. After another two hours of trudging, we near the town of Tharau. I'm looking forward to a rest but notice people coming towards us.

"Go back!" someone yells. "Don't go to Königsberg. It's not safe! Russian troops are coming that way."

And so the jumble of people turns around. Hours later, my thoughts weighed down with worry about my two sisters, it's dark and I'm back at Aunt Elfriede's door. *Where else could I go?*

"Why are you here again? I thought you were going to Königsberg?" At least Max, in between Aunt Elfriede's legs, wags me a welcome.

The smell of soup wafts to my nostrils, and my mouth waters with hunger. "Königsberg is surrounded. We have to get to the ships another way. Over the frozen Vistula Lagoon. It's the only path to the Baltic left open." I swallow my pride. "Can I sleep here tonight? I promise to leave in the morning."

Aunt Elfriede shrugs. "I suppose it's necessary. Where else would you go? I'm waiting here for Reinhold. He'll know what to do. And Anni."

My crusty aunt doesn't like being alone. She's afraid, like the rest of us.

"Have some soup," she offers. "I made it for Reinhold, so don't take too much."

The soup is hot and goes down in easy sips. She watches me eat. "Where are the others? If things are so bad, why aren't they here? Hannelore, Doris and her little girls? Where are they? We should travel together."

"If the Red Army has encircled Königsberg, they might be trapped in the city," I tell her between spoonfuls of soup. "Or they might be on route. It's difficult to travel in the snow." Fear that I might not find my sisters, that they might also be trapped by the Soviets, settles into the pit of my stomach, leaving no room for more soup, and I drop my spoon.

"I have to wait here. They will find a way to me," Aunt Elfriede insists. "I'm not leaving without Reinhold and Anni." She looks over at my unfinished soup and shakes her head. "I thought you were hungry?"

Just then a noisy motor rumbles to a stop in front of the house. I rush to the door in time to see Uncle Reinhold jump off a Wehrmacht truck and stagger to regain his balance. He's stooping like an old man. Too much ditch-digging. He pulls himself up the stairs and announces, "Elfie, we have to go. Now!"

Then he sees me as I close the door behind him. "Katya, what are you doing here? You should be on the road. Elfriede, we have to hurry. No time to waste."

"Ach, Reinhold! I prepared some food ... but must we really go? Can't we just sit quietly and let the war happen? We won't bother anyone. What would they want with an old woman?"

"Revenge, my Elfie. They want revenge. I'm getting the cart out of the stable, loading up a spare wheel, and you load the food. Don't forget blankets and warm clothes. No time to waste," he repeats. "Hui!" he yells, like he's urging his horse on.

"What about the others?" I point out. "We'll never find them in the crowds. Maybe we should wait a bit longer." For once, Aunt Elfriede and I can agree about something.

Uncle Reinhold stares at me hard with Papa's blue eyes. Finally, he blinks and nods. "Good. We'll stay until tomorrow morning. Hannelore and her granddaughters ... well, they will have to find their own way. Königsberg is kaput. We can't enter that firestorm searching for them. They say the chestnut trees are blooming from the heat of burning buildings."

Aunt Elfriede howls like an animal, and Uncle Reinhold takes her by the shoulders and shakes hard. "Stop it, Elfie!" Max barks agreement.

It works. She pushes him away and claps a hand over her quivering mouth, gazing around the room like she's looking for an escape. Then she glares over at me. "What are you staring at? Get the preserves from the cellar."

I head to the cellar to collect Aunt Elfriede's plum and cherry preserves lined neatly along the shelves. Helping my aunt and uncle prepare brings back memories of another evacuation. I was eleven when the secret police came and told us to leave our Federofka home. Can this be happening all over again?

Of course not. This time it's different. We'll be able to return once the front passes. The soldiers will move on, and the farmers will retreat back into their homes.

"Just take a jar or two of each," Aunt Elfriede calls down. "We have to save the rest for when we come back. We still have a long winter ahead of us."

I wrap the jars in towels taken from the linen closet and notice tablecloths soaking in a laundry tub. That used to be my job ... now it's the Polish girl's. Where is she?

"Where are the Polish workers?" I ask as I re-enter the kitchen, arms stacked with more towels.

"They've vanished," Aunt Elfriede says. "This morning the cows were milked, and so I paid no attention. And then at lunch, there was nobody here. Heated up my own soup, I did. Stoked the fire myself."

"Why would they stay?" Uncle Reinhold asks. "They have their own families to worry about."

CHAPTER 16

SOMETIME DURING that dark afternoon, I spot a piece of mail over by the pile of old newspapers used to start cooking fires. It's a postcard with all too familiar handwriting, a postcard from Albert, dated January 17, 1945.

My dear ones,

A quick note to let you know that I've been taken captive by the Russians. All is well. I hope we will see each other again soon.

Albert.

The door flies open and a gust of wind brings in my two sisters. Marthe and Sofie made it! Marthe accepts my tight hug, but Sofie backs away.

"We have to go!" she yells, stomping snow off her boots. "The Russians are here!"

"Stop screaming!" I yell back. Max, agitated along with the rest of us, joins me with some sharp yelps.

Marthe covers her ears, and Sofie grabs the old, overweight canine while I take a deep breath, trying compose my emotions.

In the silent pause, a mantel clock chimes the quarter hour. "We need to calm down," I suggest.

Sofie argues back. "No time for calm. We've got to get out of here!" She drops the fat dog and he scampers away.

For the moment, I'm just so relieved to have my sisters back and that we'll be going through this turmoil together. "I heard from Albert," I tell them, trying to take the focus off our own desperate situation.

"And?" Marthe asks. "Tell us!"

"He's not injured, is he?" asks Sofie. "Or . . . ?"

"He's in custody. Soviet custody." I pass her the postcard. "Says he's doing fine."

Sofie and Marthe put their heads together to read the card and then Sofie looks up first. "That's probably all he's allowed to write. The Russians are the worst. He's doomed."

Marthe collapses into a nearby chair, the card fluttering to the floor. "Poor Albert. It's not fair."

"Yes, and it'll be us soon, if we don't hurry." Sofie shakes her head. "Did you see that newsreel? Did you see what they did at Nemmersdorf?"

I rescue the postcard and nod. Everybody's seen what happened last October at Nemmersdorf. Our Nazis made sure of that. Tongues nailed to table tops. Raped women and children lying in the fields, dark stains between their legs.

"We can escape," I tell her. "Those people in Nemmersdorf weren't prepared. We have time." I sound more confident than I feel.

Uncle Reinhold comes back from the barn, where he milked the upset cows, not milked since morning. "Two more, eh? Good to see you. We'll take turns. Keep the wagon for those most tired and for our food and clothes. Our old horses will have a hard time. The Wehrmacht borrowed the good ones."

Stolen is what he means. All those beautiful horses . . . dying in that snowy ravine. Or the Trakehner horses at the Richter estate . . . forced to be soldiers on the Eastern Front. What did David, as a vet, have to see before he died? David . . . no time to think about him now.

"Uncle Reinhold," Marthe sobs. "We shouldn't wait. Let's go to-night." Max paws at her legs, as if wanting to be included.

"What about our Anni?" he asks. "We must wait for her." Her photo grins at us from a nearby shelf. Anni is his only child.

"She'll be with her BDM," Sofie reasons. "They probably have army trucks to travel in. The party looks after its own."

"Elfie wants to wait," he argues back. "Just in case."

"For how long? We have no time," Marthe wails. She can't hide her desperation. I've never seen her like this.

"Let's turn on the radio," I suggest.

Uncle Reinhold shrugs. "That will be useless. Hitler, Goebbels and Gauleiter Koch are not going to give us directions on how to save ourselves, if that's what you expect. The radio might play some enter-taining music. An operetta like *Die Fledermaus* or something by Wag-ner."

I giggle at the idea. Both Marthe and Sofie glare at me like I'm crazy. Maybe I am.

"You're right, Uncle Reinhold." Sofie's voice is sharp, but she's re-gained her composure. "Koch is gone, and I'm sure Hitler's sitting pretty in his teahouse over in Berchtesgaden, admiring the winter scenery or looking at some useless map. We have to save ourselves."

"You sound cynical, Sofie," I tell her. "You weren't like this before."

"All the party officials at my office just disappeared, Katya. Suppos-edly there's a ship in the Pillau harbour reserved just for them." She laughs, but it's a hard laugh with no joy. "No one left to help us ordi-nary people."

"That's where we need to head . . . to Pillau . . . to the Baltic Sea." Uncle Reinhold's voice is grim. "A two-day journey, if we're lucky, in this weather. Straight over the Vistula."

We wait out the evening and a long restless night. Every sound has the potential of being a Russian tank. I sleep very little. Even Max seems restless, and his whimpers permeate the dark house.

The next morning, with still no sign of Anni, Aunt Elfriede weeps as we load up to head onto the road and join the thousands of others.

But first, the cows, pigs and goats are set free to roam. I can only imagine the state they'll be in by nightfall. The chickens don't have that problem — they've been slaughtered and roasted.

Max barks nonstop and because everyone is too busy, I'm the one who picks up the needy dachshund.

"We can't leave him behind, can we?" I ask.

Uncle Reinhold shrugs while Aunt Elfriede pretends not to hear me.

"Katya, remember Zenta? Remember when he ran after us?" Sofie asks.

"Of course, I remember." Zenta, my beautiful black and white sheep dog I left behind, back in Ukraine. He didn't understand why he couldn't join our exile to Siberia. I'm not doing that again.

Max stops his frenzied barking, but his long, stuffed sausage body still quivers. The two of us have never gotten along all that well. We'll see how long we last.

CHAPTER 17

WE TURN OUR BACKS on Kreuzburg, face the wind and head northwest, to the Baltic, to Pillau, to where the ships wait that will bring us to safety — away from East Prussia, from the Red Army. We must cross the Vistula Lagoon. This cold has been good for something, after all — it's frozen the lagoon and given us an escape route.

We don't get very far before we're forced to stop. A Wehrmacht truck blocks the road, and soldiers direct the wagon traffic off the well-travelled route.

"The army gets the good roads and we get the back roads," Uncle Reinhold mutters. "Of course!" He pulls at the reins. "Hui," he calls and the horses careen off into the woods.

We join a caravan of wagons bumping along a rutted side road traversing the countryside. It's more sheltered here in the woods with the beech trees, but the snow's deeper, the walking more difficult for us and the horses. We pass snow-drifted fields where the occasional stubble of grain peeks through.

We walk and we walk, following footprints of others ahead of us.

It doesn't take long before fatigue sets in, and so we trade off, alternating between bouts of exhaustion and the chill of sitting still on the wagon. The long caravan of complaining wagons squeal loud in the brittle cold — like pigs about to be butchered.

A grim hush settles over our group. Every step I take, I'm moving towards an unknown, leaving behind a troubled, but secure, past. Here we are, in beautiful East Prussia, once my promised land, where Papa said everything would be better. Now it's the middle of winter, and we're again fleeing from the Russians. I'm so tired, even my narrow cot at the factory barracks seems inviting.

Sofie says, "I've had enough of this. Where will we sleep?" She's at the reins, giving Uncle Reinhold a chance to walk and warm up.

He has visited with the wagon ahead of us. "I've talked to others," he replies. "They've been on the road three days now. If there's a farmhouse along the way, we'll invite ourselves in. It'll probably be empty. Otherwise, we'll use a barn. If there's nothing, we'll have to sleep on our wagon."

"Outside?" Sofie shrieks. "We'll die in our sleep." Frost tinges her lashes and her hair is white — like an old woman.

Uncle Reinhold doesn't answer as he takes over the reins.

I jump down and join people from another wagon. They've been on the road a week now . . . coming from a village further east, closer to Wehlau. The woman, Else, insists on telling me what happens when you freeze to death.

"My bedridden mother, eighty-eight years old next month — and dead on the road. What could I do? I couldn't bury her. I couldn't even shed a tear for her."

I shudder. This is like our childhood trip to Siberia all over again. Back at our wagon, I don't share what I've heard.

"Where's Max?" I ask, realizing that I haven't seen the dog for a while.

"I thought he was with you." Aunt Elfriede's muffled voice emerges from under a feather duvet. Only her nose is visible.

"No, I left him on the wagon."

We look and call out for him. "Max! Here, Maxie!" Nobody finds him.

"Someone else has him," Aunt Elfriede decides. "At least he's wearing his sweater."

I'm surprised at my aunt's attitude. And that's it. No more Max.

Before nightfall, Aunt Elfriede sits up and reaches for the basket of food. "We've got to make this last." She doles out baked potatoes and chunks of roast chicken like she's serving on a white linen tablecloth instead of a straw-covered wagon on a snowy road. She makes sure no one gets more than the other.

Uncle Reinhold shakes his head. "Elfie, the girls have been walking — give them some extra meat."

"You worry about the horses. I'll worry about this!" She licks chicken grease off her fingers like a toddler. We all eat with our fingers, each of us with the manners of a child and the hunger of a dog.

"I could eat more," Marthe whispers to me. "Should we ask?"

Sofie, shaking her head at Marthe's timidity, asks for us. "Aunt Elfriede, that was delicious. How about a second helping? I'd hate to see the Russians ending up with this food."

Terror flits across Aunt Elfriede's face. "That will never happen." She passes out chicken bones and we suck on them for the next hour like they're candy. It's obviously hard for Aunt Elfriede to share her limited food supply.

The first night, we sleep in an empty barn. The second night, it's a cold church with uncomfortable pews. Our detour off the main roads is making this trip longer than necessary and the snow doesn't help.

For long hours we trudge. Sometimes Soviet bombers fly above us, so low that I think they'll crash into the trees. I cover my ears and pray, expecting death over and over. For meals, Aunt Elfriede becomes more and more stingy. The only thing she generously shares is her misery.

After the third day, I've had enough. "Sofie, Marthe . . ." I tell my sisters, as we drag ourselves alongside the wagon.

"What?" Sofie asks. "You're ready to give up? We all are, Katya." Condescension drips from her voice.

"No," I answer. "I've had enough of Aunt Elfriede. I don't want to spend the last days of my life under her power."

Marthe listens in. "She's just scared, Katya. Like us."

"Sure," I agree. "But she's making a bad situation worse. Besides, I want to find my friend, Lili. She was supposed to be having a baby soon, and maybe she's in this caravan. She might need my help."

Sofie argues back. "Katya, don't be ridiculous. Look at all these people." Behind and ahead of us, an endless stream of wagons, horses and families. "It'll be impossible to find her."

She's probably right, but I know that Lili's mother lived in this area. Maybe Lili finally had the courage to share with her. "I have to try."

"If you wander off, we'll never find you again." Marthe sounds plaintive.

"We'll all meet again in Pillau, when we board the ships. I'll watch for you." The need to see my friend tugs at me with an unreasonable insistence. "You stay with Aunt Elfriede. That might be the best. I'll find you, I promise."

"Katya, don't be stupid." Sofie shakes her head. "It'll be even worse in Pillau. There'll be more people."

Marthe dares to speak the truth. "I want to get away from Aunt Elfriede, too. She's a miserable woman to be around. Can't the three of us stay together? Sofie, don't you agree?"

She shrugs. "I suppose."

Marthe understands me too well. I smile. "All right then. We'll face this together ... without Aunt Elfriede." Relief to actually be rid of the horrid woman renews my energy and, when Marthe puts a reassuring arm around Sofie, I'm relieved to see Sofie lean in closer.

Minutes later, we explain to Uncle Reinhold that we want to rest and watch for a friend.

Aunt Elfriede pops her head out from under her multiple duvets. "Well, we're not waiting for you. Reinhold, we must hurry. The Russians are coming ... the Russians are coming." She ducks under the covers again and shuts us out.

"Yes, Elfie." He turns to us, with resignation and sadness on his face. "Your choice, girls, but don't wait too long. Each person has to look out for themselves. God be with you." And then he reaches behind our aunt and passes me one of the food baskets.

"Are you sure?" I ask him, clutching the container filled with potatoes, preserved fruit and chicken.

"I'll tell her it fell off the wagon," he replies. "You need to eat."

"Reinhold!" Aunt Elfriede calls from her blanket tent. "Let's go!"

"Yes, Elfie. Let's go."

Poor Uncle Reinhold, alone with Aunt Elfriede. He'll have to manage. The two of them, wagon loaded with their precious belongings — china, linens and silver — continue on towards the harbour. Marthe, Sofie and I dawdle along the edge and watch the wagons roll by, watch families without horses, dragging their sleds by hand.

"You think we did the right thing?" Sofie questions. "Now we're truly on our own."

"Absolutely," Marthe replies. "I completely agree with Katya. Aunt Elfriede has never looked out for anyone but herself." Then she turns to me. "Who's Lili?"

"She worked at the munitions factory with me. Got sent to a maternity home on the edge of Königsberg a few weeks ago. She's having a baby soon."

"And she's out here?" Marthe asks.

"Probably. She wanted to see her mother."

"And cousin Doris. Remember? She's expecting, too," Sofie points out.

"I hope she stays put," Marthe says. "Better to stay in Königsberg with her two girls than to be out here in this crazy cold."

"Maybe, but my friend Lili wanted to go home to her mother."

Darkness creeps upon us without the winter sun making an appearance. We need to find a place for the night. Maybe leaving the wagon was a bad idea — every choice is a bad choice. Soon a message gets passed along the caravan of tired people.

Sofie repeats the message. "There's a barn up ahead."

We hurry our steps, eager for shelter and some rest. With dozens of other families, we crowd into a barn to sleep on straw.

CHAPTER 18

I NEVER USED TO BE excited about seeing a barn. Sleeping on itchy, dirty straw was never a treat before. Now, just to stop walking will be wonderful. My sisters and I jostle other road-weary travellers as we choose a spot to build our nest.

"We should move towards the centre," Sofie suggests. "It's going to be cold here by the door."

"What do you think, Katya?" Marthe asks. "Any spot suits me — I'm exhausted."

It's unusual for either sister to ask for my opinion. "I say we stay near the entrance. This way we can leave in a hurry, if we have to." *We might get ambushed by the Russians and need an easy exit*, I think. "Let the women with children get the warmer middle area."

"Agreed!" Marthe lays down her coat and splays herself upon it. "It's less smelly out here, too."

Sofie surveys the situation and then reluctantly drops beside her. "This will have to do! Makes me feel like I'm a pig, sleeping out here."

"Come, Sofie," Marthe chides, with a tired smile. "Let's pretend we're storks."

"Marthe, how can you make this seem like a game of pretend?" I flop down beside them and look out into the greying day. Will we be safe here?

From the direction of the farmhouse comes a wobbling light. It's a woman carrying something heavy. As she comes closer, I see she's carrying a pot. Beside her is a child with a flashlight, lighting her way. Then another child comes out of the house with a stack of dishes.

The spicy turnip soup is the best soup I've ever tasted, even though I'd considered turnip to be pig food. After the meal, in spite of the conditions, I fall into a heavy sleep, surrounded by the heat of other dirty bodies.

Moaning sounds wake me. Looking around, I spot my two sisters, entwined like kittens, nearby. I sit up, pull straw out of my hair and hear the moan again. It sounds like an animal in pain.

Of course, we're in a barn. I remember the horses back in the ravine and snuggle back down to sleep . . . just for a few more minutes. But the moan becomes a shriek, a human cry of pain. In the semi-darkness, I strain my eyes for the source. Around me people stir. We're all becoming aware of this sound. We're all trying to ignore it.

"No . . . o . . . o . . ."

I struggle, first to my knees and then, still not seeing, I stand up straight. There — in the far corner — a figure huddled against itself.

"Katya, stay here." Marthe tugs at the hem of my coat. "Don't get involved."

I shake my head, whispering, "I'll be back. I just have to check."

I tiptoe closer, careful not to step on anybody, drawn to the sound like a moth to a flame. I'm not the only one.

Others are gathered around the moaning woman, and I'm stunned to see . . . "Lili!"

"Lili!" I repeat. "It's you!"

A sweat- and tear-stained face looks up at me. "Katya! You must help me. The baby's coming."

She doubles over as a spasm rocks her.

"Someone's gone to the farmhouse for help," a voice beside me says. "We need clean cotton, hot water and scissors. Just hold on, dear woman, it won't be long."

Lili reaches out to me and I push through the circle and hold her thin, shaking hand. I squeeze it, unable to speak. I've never attended a birth — kittens and puppies don't count — and I feel helpless.

Her moans crescendo into screams of agony. Is this supposed to happen? Do babies tear their mothers apart? I squeeze her hand again, not sure what to do.

Luckily, someone with more experience moves past me and takes charge.

"Get me some snow!" the old woman orders. "Just a bucketful."

I'm grateful to be useful. The snow gets rolled into a rag and stuffed into Lili's mouth. "Clamp down on this." Lili continues to moan, but now with muffled intensity.

Two women help Lili, her face glistening with sweat and tears, into a squat position. Someone else soothes her forehead with a snow-dipped cloth. My heart lurches every time Lili grunts like an animal. The sounds of her agony, amplified in the cavernous barn, force me and those around me to cover our ears. Her groans decrescendo into a whimper and then rise up again like some discordant symphony. I hold my breath in the quiet moments . . . listening . . . waiting . . . then, before the hot water and clean towels arrive, a baby's cries punctuate the air with the insistence of life. A tiny red and purple human, complete with a shock of dark, wet hair, gasps for air. Born greedy. Born angry.

Lili pants, out of breath, weak but demanding. "Let me see him," she whispers. Her eyes are closed, but she repeats, "Let me see my boy."

I laugh with relief and joy. "Lili, you're wrong. He's a girl."

"A girl?" Lili's eyelids twitch but stay closed.

"You have to open your eyes, my friend." I laugh as one of women, done cutting the cord, wraps the newborn in a blanket. "She'll be beautiful, just like you," I tell my friend, her face streaked with dirt, sweat and straw.

Lili opens her eyes as the naked, new life is laid against her. "A girl," she mumbles against the baby's head. "You are my little girl."

"Get more towels," a woman acting as midwife demands. "She's still bleeding. Hurry."

Women around me scatter, while I keep holding Lili's hand, squeezing it with a reassurance that I don't feel.

"What day is it?" Lili's voice is barely a whisper.

"It's February fifth," I tell her.

"My little girl's birthday. February fifth," Lili repeats the date and kisses the baby's wet head. Someone passes me a hot, damp towel, and I gently clean Lili's worn-out body while a last convulsion of pain shudders through her body . . . and the afterbirth leaves her empty and exhausted.

"More towels," orders the woman who's taken charge. "Someone get more towels. She's losing too much blood." She shakes her head. "This woman needs absolute rest or she won't make it."

I squeeze Lili's hand tight. Of course, she'll make it.

Someone else cleans the blustering newborn and passes her back to her mother. Everyone in the barn is awake now, and with the sound of approaching planes, the reality of our situation hits us again like a sharp gust of wind. We have to keep moving. We can't stay here.

"What's her name, Lili?"

Lili fingers the newborn's toes. "She was supposed to be called Hans, like her father." She looks up, eyes swimming with tears. "Now he is a she." She smiles. "So she'll be Hanna." And Lili falls asleep with tiny Hanna breathing close by.

The other women and children stream out of the barn with the first hint of daylight.

"What now?" asks Sofie.

I look over at Lili and the baby, not sure what to do. The friendly farm woman solves the dilemma for me. "You can't stay here," she says. "It's not safe. You heard what happened in Nemmersdorf?" Her eye shine dark with fear. "I'm leaving, too. We'll make room for your friend on my wagon. Until she's stronger."

More droning fills the air like distant thunder. Not even Papa's windmill would protect us from this storm. Time to get moving. Planes, like migrating birds, swoop overheard. It's impossible to tell if they're friend or enemy. For now, it doesn't matter.

We guide mother and newborn onto a wagon loaded with an array of baskets and boxes. An old woman sits at the reins. "We can manage her for a bit. She needs to recover . . . poor woman. My grandchildren, they can walk for a while."

"Thank you," Lili murmurs. "Hanna thanks you. I'll repay you some day." She closes her eyes and we cocoon the two in blankets. They'll have to warm each other.

CHAPTER 19

OUR WESTWARD TREK towards the Baltic continues in spite of the bad weather. Above us, planes swoosh back and forth. Maybe the Luftwaffe has finally come to help us. When bombs fall not far from our caravan, it's obvious that it's enemy planes above us. Smoke greys both the sky and the snow — filling our nostrils and lungs and irritating our eyes. But we can't walk faster, can't take a detour; we can only trudge forward, against the wind, step by cold step.

We must get to Pillau, to the harbour, to the boats waiting for us. I've never been on a big ship. Perhaps it will be like a train, with upholstered seats and window views. Perhaps there'll be a dining room. I check my pocket and finger my wallet. Everything I have is in there . . . my savings bank book, two hundred marks in cash and my identity card.

"Katya? Are you still here?" Lili's awake. I move closer to the wagon.

"Rest, Lili. You're not missing anything." I pull the blanket higher around her, tuck in the sleeping, ruddy-faced baby. "When your daughter sleeps, you must copy her. You need to regain your strength. Things will get better." I'm offering encouragement — courage I don't have — it's all any of us can do as we shiver through another day.

Walking keeps us warm, but Lili must keep herself warm. "So cold," she mutters, eyes wide open but strangely unseeing.

"Keep breathing, Lili," I beg.

Lili closes her eyes, and I stroke sleeping Hanna's cheek before pulling the blankets back over them. Once again, I focus on the snowy trail, on putting one boot ahead of the other. The planes are gone, but a silent sky seems as ominous as a busy one.

We trudge through forests, through empty villages, down winding roads, past forlorn farmhouses. The snow makes everything look the same. I daydream . . . not about the future . . . that seems too blurry. I daydream about the past, about Mama and Papa, about my baby brother Emil . . . about trees.

Hanna's screams bring me back to the present.

"Lili?" Dread clutches my stomach.

Maybe it's the minus twenty temperature, or the bumpy ride, or maybe it's just hopelessness. Maybe it's the blood that won't stop flowing. Lili's skin, grey like the dirty snow around us, feels colder than life. Her eyes stay shut.

I reach over Lili's dead body and pick up the pink-skinned newborn, fingers clenched with life, face distorted with the rage of hunger.

I call to my sister. "Marthe, hold Hanna."

She looks at Lili, who's now fallen sideways, stiff and lifeless. Marthe gasps, tears streaming down her face, and takes the infant.

The grandmother at the reins stops the wagon. We unload my dead friend. Heads shake in sympathy as her grandchildren clamber on to take Lili's spot. Hanna wails, protesting her hunger . . . or maybe she knows . . . maybe she's mourning her mother. I'd like to howl with her, but that would waste energy and do no good.

My sisters and I move to the side of the trail, trip over a ditch . . . did Uncle Reinhold dig this? With a borrowed shovel, we quickly dig a shallow grave. I bow my head and say a silent prayer for Lili. Then, with Marthe clasping the tiny child against her, we continue walking alongside the wagon.

"Should have waited and buried the baby with its mother," the grandmother observes.

"Don't say that," Marthe sputters. "This baby wants to live." She holds the screaming newborn tight, as if smothering it will keep it alive.

"You have to find another nursing mother," the grandmother tells us. "And fast."

Sofie and I leave Hanna with Marthe and run from overflowing cart to overflowing cart trying to find a woman who will take the baby.

At the end of the day, when we're tired and discouraged, cold and hungry, and Hanna's silence now feels more threatening than her screams, the grandmother points, "Over there!"

I head in the direction she points. Another burial is taking place. This time it's a doll they're burying. A perfectly formed face, lashes long like on my old rubber doll, framed by a white lace bonnet.

The infant lies on the ground and is being covered with snow. Her mother is easy to spot. She stands longest by the makeshift plot.

"*Komm, Mutti!*" An older child tugs at his mother's shawl.

Sofie brushes past me and approaches the woman. "We need you. We have a newborn with no mother. Will you nurse her?"

And so tiny Hanna gets a new mother. We find paper and pen and exchange names. Later, later, we'll work the details out.

My sisters and I shuffle off in silence. I tag slowly behind, sniffling away my tears for little Hanna and the family that never was — for Hans, who never held his daughter, for Lili, who lies frozen in the snow. Somewhere above, planes rumble, but they come no closer.

Our new wagon friends have moved on without us, and darkness falls with no shelter in sight. The three of us need to keep each other warm, like we did back when we were children sharing a bed in Feder-ofka. We can't make a fire . . . can't risk being seen. Without the comforts of a feather duvet, we take turns being in the middle, sharing body heat, rubbing each other's toes when we're not keeping our hands under our armpits. No one sleeps.

"Did you hear that?" Marthe whispers into the dark.

"Shush," says Sofie. "Just stay still."

While the sky remains quiet, the night is full of sounds. All are amplified in my mind by fear and by the strain of listening. Maybe it's the cold that makes the slightest noise seem louder. Cracking twigs, snow sliding off branches with dull thumps, wild animals shuffling . . . all might be potential footsteps of enemy soldiers.

At the first sign of light we start walking again. The planes reappear closer, louder, slower — I spot the Soviet red star on their wings — and we're deking in and out of the woods for protection. Even this forest trail is now crowded with Wehrmacht vehicles — tanks, trucks and soldiers. Lines of tired, dirty men zigzag back and forth in unmilitary-like confusion. I pity these doomed soldiers. Like Albert, they have no choice but to fight for their country. No doubt they'd rather join us and try to fend for themselves.

Marthe, always the mind reader, says, "I hope Albert will be okay. He's better off as a POW."

"At least he's not dead," Sofie agrees.

"Not yet," I mutter. "The Soviets starve their prisoners or work them to death."

"Be negative, then," Sofie replies. "Like always."

We don't say another word about Albert, but I think about him as I trudge. Maybe he gets served regular bowls of soup and sleeps on a bunk made of birch logs. Cabbage soup and bug-infested barracks sound welcoming right now. Again, when the Soviet planes fade away, I renew my belief that we will indeed reach Pillau.

Our trek stalls as we wait by a narrow bridge for a convoy of military vehicles to stream by — the open backs of LKWs are crowded with soldiers. Their faces all look the same, haggard and grey.

From somewhere in the column of refugees a voice calls out, "Soup ahead!"

The words are passed down the line and we all hunger for the warm cabbage or turnip soup that will be passed out. The Wehrmacht is looking out for us after all.

Sofie, Marthe and I have only one container to fill among us and we take turns sipping the lukewarm liquid.

"At least little Hanna has milk to drink," Marthe remarks and passes the tin mug to me.

Poor Lili. I add salty tears to my soup.

CHAPTER 20

TIME BLURS INTO one long nightmare. Too risky for fires. Too risky for sleep. Too risky for walking on roads. My eyes sting from keeping them open in the dry, cold air. I trip over my own feet — appendages at the bottom of my legs that seem to belong to someone else. To conserve energy, we communicate without words and just trudge on.

But the trudging becomes panic when distant rumblings grow closer, when the planes aren't headed somewhere else, when the planes are right overhead.

Soviet planes drop Soviet-made bombs. As I cower under a snow-laden beech tree, debris falling around me, gloved hands stupidly over head as if they could shelter me from a lethal weapon, I wonder whether it was Russian and Ukrainian girls like me who built these bombs. I'm being repaid for the weapons I helped build the last five years.

"Katya!" Marthe calls from the shelter of her tree. "You okay?"

"I'm good. You?"

"I wish they'd just go."

"Shut up," Sofie reminds us. "Just shut up."

Marthe crawls through some snow towards me and I hold her as she trembles with fear. "It'll be fine. We're still together," I murmur.

I'm unable to tremble or to cry. As the planes hover and drone, I picture the enemy. There was a boy once, Sasha. We'd shared a barrack with him during our exile as children out in Siberia. He'd be wearing an enemy uniform now. He was once my friend, the boy who danced under the northern lights with Albert and me. How did we end up this way? Why are we killing each other? I squeeze Marthe tighter as another bomb whistles nearby.

Our trek passes countless bodies — old women and young children. At the first small grave, Marthe falls to her knees and I follow suit while Sofie, impatient, stomps her boots. But as we pass body after body, we also become impatient with the indecency of these deaths. The wind blows snow away from the shallow graves, exposing corpses of the unlucky East Prussian women and children

We plod on. Once on the ship, we'll be able rest. Then I'll worry about what comes next. Rumours are that British troops will be kinder than these Soviets. That is our goal — to stay away from the Red Army.

"Did you hear the news?" a woman asks, as I lean against a tree, catching my breath.

"What news?" Marthe asks her, slumped nearby.

"Another ship down."

"What are you talking about?"

"You heard about the *Wilhelm Gustloff*? Torpedoed. Thousands drowned. That was during the last week of January. Now it's another ship. *Von Steuben*. Same story." The woman moves on, telling others her grim news.

"That woman should shut up!" Sofie shouts.

"Come on, Katya," Marthe pulls at me. "We weren't on those ships. We still have a chance."

Perhaps joining the dead would be better, yet still I step forward, still I avoid the vacant stares that litter the sides of our trek.

Relief comes with the infrequent passing of the Wehrmacht. Sometimes they stop with soup, thin and colourless like the soldiers who serve it and walk on. Fighting exhaustion each step of the way.

"Hey, Katya!" It's Sofie.

"What?"

"Where were you? I've been calling your name over and over." Sofie's face — blotched with shadows and frost — reminds me of somebody.

"Marthe stopped to talk with someone behind us. I'm going to wait for her."

"I'll wait with you." Mama. That's who Sofie reminds me of, not Mama in the kitchen but Mama dying on her bed, in Yaya. "How are you doing, Sofie?" I reach a hand out to her — to touch her frosted face.

"Don't touch me!" Sofie backs off. "How do you think I am? We're all the same." She sobs. "You look like an old woman — an ugly old woman."

We let the stream of other old women and old little children plod past us, many on foot, some still lucky enough to have a live skeleton of a horse to pull them. Do horse bones make good soup?

It's sometime in the afternoon, according to the sun which has finally poked out from the grey clouds. Sunlight seems out of place, but I relish its presence and allow myself a moment to bask in its warmth. Then it's gone again. Taken away by a drifting cloud of smoke. Behind us, I spot Marthe holding a blanket. A man stands beside her. Around them is a constant flow of people, but the two figures stay put. Sofie and I move towards them.

"Sofie, Katya," Marthe says. "Thanks for waiting. This here is Hugo. He needs to find his wife and their other child. I said I'd hold onto little Erika for him. Such a sweet girl."

The blanket stirs and a little face with eyes blue like blooming flax pokes out. A bedraggled teddy bear hangs from one of her mittened hands.

"I'll be back, my dearest Erika." Hugo kisses his child. "Be good. I will find your *Mutti*." He backs up a step, turns toward Marthe. "This isn't easy, but I just can't . . ."

"Go. I'll look after her. She'll be no trouble. I'll see you at Pillau. At the boarding gate. We won't board the boat without you."

Marthe's assurance makes me uneasy. This is a not a time to promise anything.

And with a last lingering look at his daughter, Hugo steps against the current of people, back towards the east, while the three of us melt into the west-moving stream.

Marthe, with the youngster whose head leans on her shoulder, explains as we walk. "I met Hugo at the hospital. He served as a medic bringing in the wounded until he himself got hurt. Lower back injury. No more lifting for him. He's such a nice man. Totally devoted to his wife and children. Poor girl, she's only three and she's had to walk until it's almost killed her."

"How did he get separated from his wife?" I ask.

"Come now," Sofie sneers, skirting around a woman who's kneeling beside a crying child. "It's not hard. If we're not careful, we'll get separated, too. Look how easy it was to lose Aunt Elfriede."

"Well, that was no accident," I admit.

Sofie and Marthe both laugh, and I can't help but join in. It feels good.

Our laughter, however, is cut short by screams. And then I hear it, too . . . the grumbling sound of tanks.

"Where did they come from?" Sofie's eyes dart around and I follow her gaze. Around us, trekkers scatter like chicken into the surrounding woods.

Marthe doesn't waste words. With the young girl in her arms, she's running.

A monster of a tank cuts our stream of refugees in two, right where we stand. People scramble to avoid being run over. Ahead of us, desperate families keep heading west, looking back in terror.

My heart stops. I stare in disbelief. A soldier in dirty white camouflage jumps off the frost-covered tank. A Red Army soldier! Face distorted by a scowl, he points his rifle, its bayonet flashing in the sunlight, right at me.

CHAPTER 21

PINCER-LIKE HANDS grab me from behind. I twist and turn but can't get loose. Glancing towards the woods, I spot Marthe with the child, cowering behind a bush, and nearby there's Sofie, peeking out from behind an old linden tree. I kick, squirm and finally wiggle away from my unseen captor, only to have the sharp point of a bayonet against my throat.

I swallow the words I can no longer speak. *Wait for me!* The bayonet prods deeper and then retreats. I reach for my throat and my glove gets sticky with blood. I collapse in the snow, sobbing with terror. Am I going to bleed to death like the horses? I pull off my glove, finger my throat but feel no gash, just a surface scratch. Sobbing, I scramble back up, shake wet flakes off me and try to run.

I stumble over legs, arms, tree roots. Whimpering fills the air. Was that me? Someone screams. Did I? Snow blurs my vision. The cacophony of tanks and shrill drill of mortar confuses me. I need to keep running. I need to move faster . . . I need to hide with my sisters . . . I . . .

"You!" A bayonet pokes my stomach. "*Frau, komm!*"

"*Nyet!*" I scream back.

The soldier lowers his rifle. "You, Russian?"

I nod, swallowing down my fear. "Maybe." Should I tell him where I was born? Will it help? "Ukraine," I stutter.

"Me, too!" His eyes sparkle. "From where?"

"Federofka," I tell him, blinking snow from my eyes.

He shrugs, shakes his head but keeps the gun down.

"Near Zhytomyr," I add. My eyes dart around, looking for an escape route.

He shakes his head. "*Nyet.*" He laughs. "We're everywhere. You can't run. It's over. Hitler kaput!"

I can't stop shaking, and it's not from the cold.

"*Frau, komm,*" he says again. His tone now gentle, friendly almost, while images of the Nemmersdorf newsreel race through my mind.

"I found our translator!" The soldier shoves me towards another soldier. Maybe his superior? A captain wearing a *ushanka*-hat.

The captain raises bushy, frosted eyebrows. Then he lets out a torrent of Russian words.

"Translate!" the first soldier orders.

"Please repeat," I tell him in Russian. I need to keep calm, to focus. "Speak more slowly."

The Soviet officer offers a contemptuous smile — miniature icicles dangle from his thick moustache. Now he speaks slowly, and I understand. "You will be sent to Russia to work — to fix the bridges, factories, homes. All broken by you Nazis — fascists!" He spits at my feet. "Tell the others."

I look around me at the dozens of East Prussian trekkers, herded like sheep to this place in the woods, cowering under the bayonets of Red Army guns. Like me, they're all shaking with cold terror. Where are my sisters? What happened to them? I stare into the trees, trying to catch sight of them.

A soldier yells. "Find wood. Make fire! Tell them."

I translate, and we bend over and search the snow for dead branches among the dead bodies. The Russians watch carefully, guns pointing, making sure no one goes too far. One grey-haired woman darts away in a foolish, desperate attempt. A shot rings loud and she collapses . . . her blood pooling on the snow. Other shots ring out further away. Smoke hovers everywhere.

I finger my throat. The blood's dry, crusting over. I swallow and focus on picking up twigs or stripping bark off trees. Low murmurs mumble around me. The sounds of praying? Perhaps. I add my own. God, please don't let them get angry or drunk. God, please don't let them shoot us, don't let them touch us. God, save us. God? I straighten up and look at the guns, at the faces. There is no God. Not here.

The captain yanks me away from the others. "Stay close by me!" he demands.

I spend the rest of the day beside him, translating orders. In between, he asks me about my family.

"I have two sisters," I tell him.

"*Gdyeh?*"

Where are they? I shrug.

He gets jumpy. "We must find your sisters!"

Why? Doesn't he have enough prisoners? Have I been too honest?

"It's an order!" he demands. "Bring me your sisters." He pushes me away with his gun.

Terrified and confused, I back off. I head towards where I saw them last. The tank still blocks the road and bloodied bodies litter the area. No sign of my sisters.

Right behind me is the captain. "*Gdyeh?*"

I shake my head. I don't know where to look. My sisters are gone.

He shoves me forward and repeats. "Find them!"

I move away from the bonfire and the Russians and head aimlessly down the road, not sure what I'm supposed to do. When I glance behind me, the soldier waves me on. I continue down the narrow road, forest on either side, fading flames and voices behind me. Up ahead, on the right, a trail leads deeper into the woods — no doubt leading to a farm. Do I follow it?

"*Gdyeh!*" the Russian bellows. "Find your sisters."

I turn onto the trail and follow imprints in the snow. Who made these steps? Marthe? Sofie? Soldiers?

Up ahead, nestled in pine trees, stands a timber-framed farmhouse. Smoke dances out of its chimney. The scene belongs on a Christmas card.

Behind me, the Russian repeats, "Find your sisters!" He lifts his gun towards the house for emphasis. "You hug them, maybe you cry together. You eat. Get some sleep. In the morning, you introduce me. *Versteh?*"

And then he walks off — without touching me. My knees grow weak, and I collapse into the snow. The Russian soldier didn't even touch me!

On the road, a vehicle approaches, its headlights off, rumbling motor getting louder. I crawl for cover behind an old chestnut tree and watch as the Russian who left me here waves at the truck, rifle high in the air. The truck stops, he jumps into the cab, cold metal clanks on metal, and the truck rumbles away back towards the bonfire, back to the camp of Russian soldiers.

I turn to the farmhouse.

CHAPTER 22

I DON'T KNOW WHAT I'll find in this timber farmhouse — don't know what I want to find. I don't expect to see a family sitting down to dinner. All the families are streaming down the snow-packed roads towards the Baltic. They've left their homes behind . . . unless . . . I can't imagine the unless.

That Nemmersdorf film can't happen again. Maybe it was all made up. Or maybe, like Anni said, they just wanted to scare us.

Snow seeps in over my boots. The smell of smoke burns my nostrils, and I cover my mouth, my nose, breathing through my frosted scarf. Even here, in the shelter of trees, flecks of ash darken the snow. I edge closer to the Christmas card house.

Do I want to find Marthe and Sofie? What about that little girl, Hanna? No, that was Lili's child. Erika. That's it. Is Erika still with Marthe? The confusion of the last few hours plays tricks with my memory.

So close to the enemy and still whole. How can this be? Lili's gone, dead and buried in some snow-covered ditch, and here I am . . . un-touched . . . like I'm invisible.

Is this house a trap? Will there be drunk Russians waiting inside? I could try to escape, but it's dark, cold . . . where would I go?

A crack of warm, yellow light escapes between the shuttered win-dows. Sunken footprints lead to the door. Heart hammering, I knock and without waiting for an answer, I enter. Warm air envelops me.

I need to rub my eyes at the sight. Marthe sits reading a book to the little girl. They're squished together in a big comfy chair. A kerosene lamp shines from the table next to them.

"Marthe?" I squeak, closing the heavy door behind me.

She gestures me to be quiet, then grins with satisfaction. "Erika has finally fallen asleep." Marthe gently closes the book, puts it on the table and gets up, carrying the sleeping child, and moves towards a door.

"Bring the light," Marthe whispers. "Shine it just from the doorway, so I don't trip over anyone."

I unfreeze myself, pull off my gloves and leather boots and follow Marthe, lamp in hand.

In the next room, six or seven shapes huddle together on the floor. Is one of them Sofie? Marthe lays the sleeping child down at an empty spot, covers her with a feather comforter, and we tiptoe out. We're about to close the door when the little one calls out, "Mami!"

Marthe looks stricken. Then there's silence and Marthe smiles as she closes the door.

I bring the light back into the kitchen and set it on the table.

"Katya!" Her voice continues to be low. "You made it. We were sure the Russians had caught you. What happened?"

"Marthe, please let me just eat something and sleep. I'm exhausted." The warmth of the room makes my eyelids droop.

"First, explain what happened." She stares hard at me in the yellow light and her tone is harsh. "They raped you and then they let you go again?"

I shake my head — startled — at words I'd thought but that spoken out loud sound so much worse. She motions for me to sit down and puts her finger to her lips. In a soft tone, she asks, "Why did they let you go?"

I gulp as I realize the harsh truth. They let me go so that I could find my sisters. It's a trap. They aren't safe here. The Russian watched me enter this farmhouse. Do I tell Marthe this?

"They wanted me to get some rest."

"Really?"

"And they told me to find my sisters. . . . I saw the smoke . . ."

We sit in silence — hearing only the snores from the next room.

"I told them not to light that wood stove." She shakes her. "No matter. It's going out now."

She looks over at me. "Besides, they'll find us sooner or later, with or without you." Marthe's pretty face is grim in the kerosene's light. I turn from the fear in her eyes to the checkered tablecloth. Red and white. Red and white like the horse blood in the snow-filled ravine.

"We'll have to get the others up before sunrise," Marthe decides, looking at the closed door. "Everybody needs sleep, but one of us has to stay up and guard." She glances back at me.

"I'll stay guard," I tell her, taking the hint. My little sister amazes me. When did she become such an adult? I was always the one who made the decisions for everyone.

"Good. Thanks, Katya. Wake me — "

"Two hours, okay?" I reply. I need to try and have some semblance of authority with her.

"I was going to ask for one, but I'll take the two. Thank you. And Katya?"

"Yes?"

"I don't blame you. The Russians will find us sooner or later. They're everywhere."

Tears of fear and exhaustion stream down my face, and Marthe pats my wringing hands. "Dear Katya, you've always been like a mother to me. Now we must each look after ourselves."

She slips into the other room, and I sit alone in this stranger's kitchen. Using the edge of the tablecloth, I wipe away my useless tears, then stick a finger into an open honey jar. Who lived here? What's happened to them? I suck the honey and reach for more. Why didn't the Red Army stay here? Did they find another farmhouse to spend the night?

The kerosene lamp grows dim. I glance around and on the frozen windowsill, I find a candle to light. Its single flame offers just enough light so I don't bump into things. I go back to the entry door — open it to confirm no one's there. Through the trees, I notice flickering light and hear what sounds like singing. Of course! For the Soviets, this is a time of celebration. They're having a party out there. What a miracle I wasn't raped — yet.

Going through the pine cupboards one by one, I look for anything edible. Behind one emptied jar, I find a chocolate bar. Probably a gift, hidden and then forgotten. I bring the candle close and see its pretty wrapping of the Swiss Alps. That's where my *mischling* friend, Minna, wanted to go. It's where Thomas Mann went, too. I wonder if he still writes novels.

I break off a piece of chocolate and put it in my mouth. The chocolate's dry — tasteless. Albert once got chocolate from a Russian guard back in Siberia. When he shared it, I told the others to suck on it to make it last longer. Now I follow my old advice and suck on this chunk of dry chocolate. But it'll never last long enough.

From outside comes the sound of a gunshot and I freeze. Nothing else. Snoring from the next room. I sit, tense, shivering with terror, waiting.

Sound travels far in the winter, I remind myself. I keep shivering — cold and fear have taken control of my body. With shaking steps, I search for a blanket, but they must all be in the other room. I dare not disturb them. A jacket hangs in the broom closet. I pull the oversized wool housecoat over my shoulders. Its weight comforts me, and the long sleeves hang past my hands.

I sit back down, hugging myself, and watch the white candle drip wax onto the red squares of the gingham cloth. A clock on the shelf no longer ticks — stuck at three-thirty.

In the distance, there's laughter and singing, but here in this farm-house the silence grows thicker, heavier . . . I drop my head to the table and close my eyes.

CHAPTER 23

LIFTING MY HEAD from the table, I massage my sore neck and notice candle wax, dried and stuck to the gingham tablecloth. That won't be easy to clean. I'll need to scrape it and then use an iron to melt the rest. As I finger the cold, hard wax a rumbling motor grows louder. Like receiving a slap, I'm jolted awake, and now I remember everything.

The dark of night has changed to grey. Morning, even if the hands on the clock still say three-thirty. The vehicle comes closer . . . now it's just outside the door.

Muffled cries emerge from the other room. The others! I'm supposed to be warning them . . . giving them time to avoid the Russians. That's them! I jump up, my chair crashing to the floor in the process.

Too late! The door swings open and in swarms a blast of Russian soldiers. There's three of them. In the dim light, they flash their guns around into the darker corners of the room. I need to distract them, let the others have time to get away.

"Just me," I say in Russian, a language I haven't spoken since childhood. It's my only weapon. I repeat my words in Ukrainian. When I was growing up both languages came easily.

"You speak Ukrainian?"

"Yes. I was born there ... near Zhytomyr."

"Zhytomyr!" Is it homesickness breaking out across the face of this young Soviet? "Not far from Kiev."

For a moment, he hesitates. Will the two of us share a conversation ... he and I, both longing for our homes? But then another soldier calls out, as if he's just discovered the bedroom door.

They break the door open with their rifles. Why must they be so rough? It wasn't locked, they could have tried turning the knob.

I hold my breath. One soldier stays with me, the homesick one. The other two disappear into the room and soon storm back into the kitchen.

Within minutes, the house is in shambles. Duvets cut open, feathers everywhere. "*Wo?*" The Red Army soldier's German question about where they are cuts into any bond we might have had.

I shrug my ignorance. I don't know where they went.

Two of them run out the front door, and I get up to follow.

"*Bleib.*" My soldier pushes me back down onto the chair.

It doesn't take long before the two soldiers return with Marthe and the girl. Where are the others?

The child screams in terror, but Marthe's terror is silent, her face, white; her eyes, big and dark, remind me of Mama's.

"I'm sorry." I mouth the words. Please believe me, little sister.

She nods, and I feel strangely relieved — in spite of the Russians, my sister doesn't blame me.

"Tell her to shut the mouth of the child," my soldier tells me.

"Or else ..." another soldier adds, motioning a trigger with his fingers.

"Marthe, if she doesn't stop crying, they'll shoot her."

The child understands and stops crying. Her hands grip Marthe's neck more tightly.

"How many others?" a soldier asks.

I translate to Marthe, who never retained any of her Russian or Ukrainian language skills. She was only four when we left for Germany.

Marthe shakes her head. "I don't know. We had a window partially opened, ready for a quick escape. When we heard them enter, we all climbed through it. The others could run faster than me because I had . . . I had this little one."

What about Sofie, I want to ask. The soldiers look from me to Marthe.

"No more," I tell them. "Just Marthe and the child."

"You lie!" One of the soldiers shakes his fist in my face. "Footprints outside."

My soldier stares at me, and I turn away. The three Russians retreat to a corner and yell, shake heads and flap their arms with impatient gestures.

Then my soldier — the homesick one — comes up to me and says, "You come with us. She stays here with the child."

"No, no, no!" I scream. "*Nyet!*" I add and shake my head while the rest of me trembles.

"She mother. She not work. She stay."

The Red Army solider grins with smug victory while I bite and tear at the hands that grab me, dragging me away into Soviet custody while Marthe stays behind with the stranger's child who's saved her.

And Sofie? No time now to worry about her. Now each of us is on her own.

CHAPTER 24

I'M EXPOSED TO THE wind in the back of the army truck, but we
don't drive for long before the LKW stops. We're at another farm, this
time with a barn that's filled with at least two dozen trekkers.

There's no way those people will all fit on the back of this truck. Yet
somehow this mass of crying, terrified women — yes, they are all
women — is shoved aboard. I smell their fear, right in my face. I
breathe their unwashed clothes, their foul mouths.

I'm not very tall and there's no fresh air at my height. I want to
squirm to the edge of the crowded LKW, but it's impossible to move.
The truck starts up again. I can't see where we're headed, but it's so
bumpy it must be a rutted side road.

Maybe someone I know will be picked up — then I won't be so
alone. All these people around me and not one familiar face.

I wish Marthe could have come along. We could have shared the
care of that small child. Am I going to be sent back to Russia? It can't
be. *Nyet!* It's not fair. Why me? What about Sofie? Where did she go?

Wheels churn, grinding beneath the wheels of the truck. Muddy slush flies around us. Rocking, more churning back and forth. Then the engine stops and we jam up even closer to each other. Someone's metal zipper tears my cheek.

"*Vykhodit!*" comes the command. Nobody understands until one of the Soviet soldiers starts throwing people off. We get it now.

Once we stand — cower — on the muddy mess of a road, a soldier shouts out, "*Ot sebya!*"

He wants us to push. Ah, yes, the truck is stuck. We're ankle deep in thick muck. Mild temperatures have melted the snow. Too bad for these Ivans — they should have stayed on the main road. No, it's too bad for us. The Red Army soldier pushes and shoves women against the truck and demonstrates how to push.

"*Ot sebya!*" he repeats, grunting with effort. "Hard. Harder!"

We're all weak with hunger and fear. We have no strength to push. Even though there must be forty of us, we barely budge the army truck.

The three Red Army soldiers decide it's a good time to share a bottle of vodka with each other. But we're not allowed to rest. We must continue the futile pushing. We look like pigs who've rolled in the mud, groaning like women in labour.

After an hour, maybe two, help comes in the form of more soldiers from another Red Army truck. They attach heavy chains and pull our marooned vehicle out of the mire. By then our original captors are decidedly drunk. With the success brought about by their comrades, they're all ready for a celebration.

And what are we supposed to do?

Guns pointing, a drunk solder slurs an order at us. I translate. "Get back onto the truck. Sleep!" I mutter the words under my breath, then seeing a gun move closer, I call out the order again, louder. Other drunk soldiers now poke and prod at us women. "Now!" I add with unnecessary emphasis.

Just as I'm about to climb aboard, the driver of the rescue truck, wearing what might be a captain's uniform, calls me over. "*Frau, komm!*" Those dreaded words we all fear.

Images of Nemmersdorf explode in my mind, and I hesitate.

He calls again and, whispering a prayer, I let go of the truck's metal edge and shamble towards him.

He's drunk. But rather than wearing a sneer, his face shows curiosity. "You understand Russian? You speak Russian? *Warum?*"

Why do I speak Russian? If I tell him I was born there, maybe they'll send me back, and I'll never be allowed to leave.

He repeats the question. "Why you speak Russian?"

I shrug and wish I could join the others.

"Hey!" With a victorious, red-eyed leer, the Soviet soldier puts his face right up to mine. His breath stinks of liquor and smoke and rot. "You, Russian." He pokes me hard. "You, Russian-born German. You my prisoner." His leer changes to a smile, like he's just shared a joke. "You my translator. *Frau, komm!*"

And I'm pulled up into the cab of another truck, beside him, and now I'm more than afraid. Two other Russians join us. I sit squished between the dirty, drunk men and make myself as small as possible. The man on my right, not the driver, lets his hands rove over my thighs. I keep still like I'm a statue, or a body — a dead body.

The driver, who's just backed out of the rut and is trying not to get stuck again, slams on the brakes. He slaps the drunken, roving hands away from my thighs while letting out a torrent of Russian words. I've no idea what he's saying, but now I'm left alone, untouched, and for that I'm grateful. I start breathing again.

We drive maybe fifteen minutes, past scorched trees and smouldering buildings, until we come to a farmyard that's not burning, with an intact barn. A huge linden tree stands at the entrance with a carved wooden bench beneath. A farm family must have once lived here, perhaps for generations. The driver gets out and motions for me to follow.

It's almost evening now, and ice forms again on the spring puddles. When he pushes me to walk in front of him, towards the barn, I slip and fall. He turns and pulls me up, gentle, almost. "*Aufpassen*," he mutters. This Soviet solider wants me to be careful? His concern is almost funny.

Inside the barn, half in light and half in shade, must be close to a hundred women.

"Tell them," he tells me, "they must prepare themselves for work. They must repair what their men destroyed. Tell them!" He sounds gruff, as if he's remembering something painful.

We stand at the entrance, and the Russian captain shoots his gun for attention. Two other soldiers have dragged over the carved bench, and I'm yanked up to stand on it.

"Tell them what I told you!" he bellows. "Loud."

I tell them. Most of the women just stare at me, the mouthpiece of the enemy. Have they understood? Do they know who I am, a German, like them? But of course not. I was never a German just like them, was I?

"Essen!" a woman pleads. They're hungry. So am I. I repeat this request.

"Nothing. No food. Maybe tomorrow."

I repeat this.

A brave woman retorts. "We will die if we don't eat. Then you won't have any workers."

I repeat her words to the Russian. He rubs his hand over his days-old beard before speaking. "Tell them I will find food. Tomorrow."

I tell them and a murmur of hope rises in the crowded barn even as the sun sets.

CHAPTER 25

I BECOME THE Russians' voice. When a Red Army relief truck, operated by unsmiling, young Russian women, arrives later in the day with soup, I translate the shouted directions for lining up to my hungry co-captives.

As I move to join the line for my own bowl of watery turnip soup, the Russian commander calls out, "*Nyet!* You stay with me."

"But I must eat, too. I'm hungry." Famished. The smell of the soup makes my nostrils twitch and my stomach cramp.

"I feed you. Better food. *Frau, komm.*"

Again those movie reels of the Nemmersdorf massacre flood my mind. When will I be raped? And by how many?

With a longing glance over my shoulder, I'm pulled towards a group of Russian soldiers hunkered around a blazing fire. A vodka bottle gleams in the flames' light as the drink is passed around. Several men are already drunk. They undress me with lusting eyes.

In spite of my fear, saliva collects in my mouth, and I lick my lips. Is that roast chicken wafting through the smoke-filled air? What will I do for food? I don't want to find out.

"Sit," the commander commands.

I sit. It's a folding camp chair — a German one. I see the name Krupp engraved on the edge of the seat. The Russian captain calls out to someone but does not leave my side. Moments later, a gold-rimmed china plate heaped with chicken smothered in greasy juices, along with a thick slab of dark bread, is dropped on my lap.

"Eat." Silver utensils clatter down to the ground beside me. From whose dining room did they come?

My Russian captor smiles as I attack the food like a ravenous dog. I eat too fast, not chewing properly, too afraid to slow down and savour the crispy skin and moist white meat.

Snow's melting now . . . almost spring . . . must be March. My birthday is somewhere around now. I hesitate, then wipe the plate clean with my tongue. No one pays attention to my animal manners.

The men drink more. Get drunker, livelier — like the fire that's being fed with fence boards, carved chairs, a child's dollhouse. Cramps spasm my stomach; I've eaten too quickly — or maybe they're from fear.

Beside me, the Russian commander belches and wipes his mouth with his sleeve. Turning to me, he asks, "Full?"

I nod.

He reaches over and flings my made-in-Bavaria china plate against a tree, where it shatters to the ground. "I'll take you back to the others now. You must sleep, but in the morning you stay with me again."

He's letting me go? I take a deep breath. "I can manage on my own," I tell him. I don't want the others to notice this relationship between us — don't want them to make assumptions.

He accompanies me anyway, deking past drunk soldiers sprawled in haphazard, relaxed fashion against broken cribs, chesterfields, bookcases. More fuel for the fire. A couple of LKWs sit nearby loaded with more stolen furniture, even a forlorn-looking piano.

If only the Russian soldiers would stay away from the vodka, maybe then they could stay away from the women, too. This commander, however, has not touched me.

Throughout the night, women sob in feeble protest as they're pulled out of the barn. The chosen ones. I hear the men's grunts, their slaps, the women's weeping, and all I do is pull my coat collar up higher ... cover my ears ... try to sleep. Once there's a tug on my hair, but I talk back in Russian, and then I'm left alone. Maybe I'm too ugly, even for a Russian.

Or maybe, maybe I'm protected because I know their language. I have another purpose. Finally, being born a Russian-German might help me.

Night turns to lighter and lighter shades of grey, and the soldiers, recuperating from their night of sex, vodka and partying, are silent — except for their snores, which rumble like distant army tanks. Near me, women curl up with private shame against the cold, ugly reality of a new day.

There's a makeshift toilet at the back of the barn, and I step over and around the shivering heaps of bodies. So many women. Where are they all from? The air stinks worse than a manure pile. I try not to breath.

"Katya! Katya!" It's a weak voice, but it has a distinct whine that I'd recognize anywhere.

A thin arm rises above the huddled figures. Could it truly be Anni? I approach and see a wreck.

"Katya! You've no idea how happy I am to see you."

"Anni, what's happened to you?" She's obviously been raped, and yet the question slips out of me. Her blonde hair, usually severely braided, is a mess. Her face — a map of scratches. Her BDM shirt torn — exposing her brassiere.

"Oh, Katya. Please stay here with me."

I crouch down near her. "Anni, I'm so sorry."

Anni's shaking. She grabs my hand. "I'll never be able to look at a man again. No man will want me." Her whiny voice trembles.

"Shush, Anni. It'll get better."

"I lost count of how many. They're animals, Katya. Animals!" She hugs herself tight and sniffs with plaintive indignation. "I was saving myself for marriage and now I'm ruined. What will my mother say?"

Aunt Elfriede might be in the same situation. But I dare not say this to Anni.

A Russian voice hollers loudly. "*Aufstehen*, Katya. *Versetzen!*" He's calling me to translate. "Now!"

"I have to go, Anni. They need me to translate." I stand up and leave her, broken and weeping.

But she has a last word for me, my East Prussian cousin. "You never were a real German. You traitor . . . you Russian lover!"

I want to slap her. I want to slap her hard. But I don't. Instead I meekly follow the voice of the commander. I have to survive. Whatever it takes.

Snow melts and drips like a ticking clock. Days turn into weeks. Women get thinner while trees thicken with buds. We live in the barn like animals — filthy, bug-infested animals.

Every day, more women are dumped into our barn. Instead of harvesting hay, the Red Army soldiers harvest people. Collect them and then store them in this overcrowded barn.

We entered this barn as humans, but eventually we become the animals that once lived here.

CHAPTER 26

SNOW DISAPPEARS. One bright, warm day, we're finally called outside. The sun hurts my eyes and highlights our scabs, dirt and fear. After we line up, a Soviet officer, grinning broadly, makes an announcement.

"Hitler *tot*." And that's it. The Red Army soldiers cheer and clink bottles. "Hurrah! Hurrah!" Laughter and self-congratulations deteriorate into general mayhem.

But they leave us alone. They keep the celebration to themselves. It's a loud one, with singing and dancing. If Hitler's dead, does that mean the war is over? No one knows.

Next afternoon, the captain enters the barn and calls me. "*Versetzen! Katya, komm!*" His slurred words surprise me. He's always been sober and able to be in charge. His bloodshot eyes fail in their attempt to focus on me. I look around helplessly at the others.

His arm does what his eyes can't manage. He points at me, and Anni nudges me forward. I approach the drunk Russian with all the trepidation of a mouse encountering a cat.

"Name?" The captain blinks at me with his reddened eyes, dark irises looking lost.

"Katya," I remind him, in a low voice. I sense that everyone's alert now, staring at us.

"Katya." The Russian wobbles like a toddler learning to walk, leans against a barn beam to support himself, then smacks his lips, like he's tasting food. "Katya. Good name."

I want to disappear. What does he want from me?

He nods his head in the direction of the exit and I follow, wobbling now myself. Slamming the barn door shut behind me, the Captain spits out his need like vomit. "My commandant is coming, and I'm too drunk." The Soviet captain bows his head to the ground like a contrite child. "Katya, *pomogite* me."

"*Pomogite?* Help you?" I repeat. "How can I help you?" His request flabbergasts me.

He looks up, red eyes pleading. "Too much vodka. Clear my head." He puts both hands against each side of his head and rocks back and forth. "Oi. Oi. Oi."

He has a hangover and his boss is coming. I rouse myself out of my stupor and lead my Russian captor to a nearby stream. He struggles to remove his shirt, and I help him, exposing a strong, pale, hair-covered chest. The situation feels so intimate, and embarrassment heats up my neck and face.

"Oi," he mutters to remind me of my purpose.

I dunk his head in the water, over and over, and my own blush cools down as he sputters like a drowning cat. The cat I thought would play with me, like I was a mere rodent, is nothing but a sputtering, drowning feline.

I expect someone to come and shout at me, but we're left alone. The other Russian soldiers still sleep off the victory of Hitler's death. I'm curious about his death. Who finally managed to kill him? Or maybe it was a bomb. Maybe I can ask this drunk captain when he sobers up.

"*Spasibo. Danke.*" The captain sputters and grins at me. He looks better than he did — fresher, less grey — his eyes brighter. He grabs his shirt, dries his hair and face with it, and then puts the filthy khaki army top back on.

"*Spasibo*," he says again, looking once more like a Soviet captain and not a half-naked man.

I get the sudden urge to ask him about Sasha. He'd be in the Soviet army now. Maybe this soldier, who's being so vulnerable and trusting with me, has met him.

"Do you know Sasha?" I ask, as the soldier buttons up his shirt.

"Sasha? I know Sasha." He laughs. "Many Sashas. Which one?"

How can I describe greasy-haired, belligerent Sasha? "The one who always wants to break the rules," I tell him. Sasha convinced Albert and me to sneak out of the transition camp where our kulak family was sent during collectivization. Sasha took us rabbit hunting. "Good hunter," I add, feeling stupid even as I speak.

The Soviet soldier laughs loudly, so loudly he hurts his head again and holds it between his hands, like before. "All Soviets are good hunters. All Germans are rabbits. Ping. Ping." He mimics a sharpshooter.

"My brother is a German soldier," I tell him, needing to somehow find some self-respect.

"Your brother is finished." The Red Army captain clears his throat and grabs onto me for support as he pushes himself up off the ground. "My commander will be here soon. *Spasibo*." He pushes me away. "Now go! Back to the others. Soon there will be new orders. Things will change."

I hurry away, tripping over my own feet, back to the barn. What will these new orders be? Will we be released or will we be sent to some desolate gulag in Siberia? A shudder passes through me. My co-prisoners have no idea what might await them. Siberia with its cold and the bugs . . . Anni has no idea. But maybe that's better.

What about Marthe? Is she in the same situation as me? Perhaps that little girl will protect her. And Sofie . . . she hasn't any Russian language skills to help her out; she'll have to rely on her charm. By now her pretty dress will be torn . . . her permed hair messed up. What about the old ones . . . Aunt Elfriede and Aunt Hannelore . . . where are they? Doris, Susi and Marianna . . . are they safe, or are we all now caught in this net of Soviet revenge?

So many questions . . . and I forgot to ask who killed Hitler.

Before I make it back to the barn, a big black automobile flying the hammer and sickle flag drives into the farmyard, our prison compound. A gun is fired, and an important-looking Russian commandant steps out of the vehicle.

The hungover soldiers shake themselves up. Chaos ensues as they bark at each other, my captain barking the loudest.

The visiting commandant watches, a bemused smile on his face, while the guards poke, shove and drag us like sacks of potatoes into a semblance of order.

When we're all standing, staring at this visitor, my captain and the newcomer salute each other and exchange words.

Then this visitor shouts at us. "Hitler *kaput*!" He smiles, revealing stained teeth, and looks us over, shaking his head. He turns and retreats into the farmhouse with the captain. We continue to stand, staring at the armed guards, whose drunken eyes squint into the brilliant spring sunlight.

Half an hour or so later, the high official gets back into the black Mercedes with its waving Soviet flag and, horn blaring, exits the farmyard. My captain comes looking for me. "Katya!" he calls.

The others nudge me forward. They know that I am his mouthpiece. What would they think if they knew I helped this man . . . that I saw him half-naked? I grin and shrug my shoulders. Who cares what they think?

"Tell the others they must march. Fifteen minutes before we go. Tell them to take what they can carry. No more."

As if we have anything to carry. "Where are we going?" I ask.

"Long march. Until we get to unbroken rail track. East, towards my country."

"But . . ."

"Weeks. Yes." He grins. "No more vodka."

"Will we get food?"

"Food?" He looks confused. Maybe that general, or whoever he was, didn't tell him about feeding us.

"We need to eat. We can't walk all day and not eat." My voice rises uncontrollably.

He nods, rubbing his freshly shaved chin, then his face lights up. "Spring is here. Food grows. We all eat."

We leave our weeks' long barn prison and start walking east — towards the Soviet Union. A long chain of German women.

— PART 2 —

Soviet Starosta

CHAPTER 27

WE STUMBLE ALONG past the polluted streams, as pussy willows lose their kitten plush, morph into pollen-dusty worms, then leaf into green leaves. Spring insists on life in spite of burned-out houses, charred trees, blackened fields. I don't wipe away the tears trickling down my face when we encounter a pair of storks — industriously mending their nest on a broken chimney. We're all crying and no one asks another why. A warm breeze tickles my face as we trudge along, five in a row — a wide river of crying women — from dawn until dusk.

We don't talk . . . we have nothing to say.

At night, it's still cold. We huddle like cows on the thawing ground, drinking water from puddles like orphaned dogs. Rivers, contaminated with death, littered with empty prams, broken furniture and bloated bodies, continue to flow. Death contaminates us all.

At least I can sleep. Sheer exhaustion promises me that dreamless escape. As the grass sprouts, I eat it.

Weak, old or sick women collapse. Gunshots mark their final escape. Is death dreamless, too? My legs keep up a rhythm all their own ... keep moving me forward. Or are they moving me back-ward ... back to my home? I always wanted to go back, holding tight to David on a proud Trakehner horse. Not defeated like this. I'm grateful to be wearing boots, but how long will they last with this mad march?

The weather changes after the full moon. For three days, it pours. Cold rain that makes me shiver; it quenches my thirst and cleans me, too. Still, I'm not clean for long, and soon I'm muddier than ever. We get stuck walking in each other's footsteps, but I'm determined not to lose my leather boots. I'm determined to re-enter the Soviet Union with proper German footwear. Until one day, some squelching mud rut swallows up my left boot, and there's no time for me to fight for it. I take off the other boot and cradle it like a child as I continue walking barefoot.

For my complaining stomach, grass isn't enough. As a side dish, I eat sand and small stones. Pretend food. It gives my stomach some-thing to do — so it doesn't forget why it's there. Crushed rock with grass is better than nothing.

One warm day, when the sun is high in the sky, we're told to stop. A commandant comes and announces soup ahead. Red Cross relief workers spoon it out.

"Katya!"

Who's calling my name? Shielding my eyes from the sun, I look around.

"Katya! Is that you?"

I keep looking. And then I spot ... I see ... Natasha ... one of the relief workers in the makeshift field kitchen.... Can my squinting eyes be deceiving me?

I open my mouth and close it again — speechless. Natasha, our family's servant girl from another time — when Papa was a kulak, before he became an enemy of the people. Later, after our Siberian exile, I'd seen Natasha as a *kolkhoz* worker. She'd given me food, straw-berries from my mother's garden — rather, from our former garden. It had all become part of the *kolkhoz* — the collective.

Back then, Natasha had stolen my clothes, including my favourite green velvet dress that Mama had made me. Today, Natasha wears a filthy Red Cross apron over her tattered-looking outfit, as tattered as mine. Cleaner, maybe — nobody's clothes could be dirtier than mine.

"Natasha?" In spite of myself, my eyes brim over with tears. She's not a girl anymore, yet I still recognize her, because of her dramatically beautiful eyes.

Natasha gives me a studied stare. "You haven't changed that much, you know." Then she hugs me, and I squeeze back with a desperate gratefulness. When did we become such friends?

"How can this be?" she murmurs into my shoulder. "We've both grown up."

I shake my head, unable to control my weeping.

She pushes me back. "Look at us, us two! I'm so happy to see you. The war's almost over. Your Hitler is dead." Natasha stops smiling; her dark eyes cloud over. "I guess the war's not over for you. Where are they taking you?"

"I don't know. Siberia, I suppose."

"Your favourite place!" Natasha looks around the makeshift relief kitchen. Everyone's busy doing their little job — peeling turnips, stirring pots, passing out colourless soup that looks more like dirty water. The long, straggly line of hungry POWs seems endless.

Natasha runs into a nearby tent and re-emerges with something round wrapped in a towel. "This will help you."

It's bread, a whole loaf of dark bread. I inhale its yeastiness. Food has a lot of power — for eating, trading, for living.

"Thank you. Thank you." Then, to take the attention off my hopeless situation, I ask, "What have you been doing during these war years? You haven't been working for the Red Cross, have you?"

"No. I just traded my *Ostarbeiter* badge for this Red Cross badge last week."

"*Ostarbeiter*?" What does she mean by 'East Worker'?

"Surely, you heard? Your Nazis rounded up wagonloads of us young women and children throughout Ukraine. They sent us to work in your factories. I worked in Breslau. It was not fun. Nazis hate Slavs almost as much as they hate Gypsies." She stares at me, opens her mouth, then closes it again.

"Like the Jews," I add.

"Yes, like the Jews. And like Stalin hates you Germans. I don't envy you, Katya. There are many reasons for me and my country's people to spit in your face."

"You hate me?"

"I could hate you, Katya — except, I know you. I knew your mother. I know you aren't a Nazi. You're like me. Just a person who was in the wrong place at the wrong time."

I hug her again, the loaf of bread between us, and notice that, like me, she has no earrings in her ears — only empty holes. I still owe her some earrings.

Now Natasha and I are both hoop-less.

CHAPTER 28

WITH THE LOAF tucked into my sweater, giving me voluptuous breasts I've never had, I rejoin my fellow prisoners. The unexpected reunion with Natasha makes this endless trudging easier. Or maybe it's just the smell of the yeasty bread wafting from my breasts.

I look back, but Natasha's waving her hands in an animated discussion with a couple of relief workers. Her loud laughter fading as I move away.

The two of us were so different as children. She, the dark-haired servant girl, whom Papa called a lazy Gypsy, and me, the pale, reserved landowner's daughter. Back then, I envied her free-spirited approach towards life. Now here we are connecting again, both crushed by the circumstances of this ugly war.

"Goodbye, Katya!" she shouts above the commotion. "Someday we'll meet again!"

"Do you know that Red Cross worker?" a fellow prisoner near me asks.

"Long ago," I mumble.

"Slavs. They're dirty," she tells me.

I move away, wanting to keep my memories, and Natasha's bread, to myself.

We continue our march. March? This is more like a dirge. An ever-eastward funeral procession. Did Minna march like this? While she pretended to be an actress, was she on a death march, too? How naive I was — naive and stupid. We all were. Can ignorance be a crime? Shame over my ignorance mixes with self-pity for my filth, my exhaustion, my fate. Walking is good for thinking; I'm not sure what thinking is good for.

More soup kitchens serve us along the way. More relief workers. No more signs of Natasha.

Scorched remains of war dot the landscape. Some days we're forced to stand still and listen to long announcements bellowed over our heads about our sins — our fascist crimes. Sometimes we hear about workers' rights, about the paradise that Comrade Stalin has built. But it's lost on us. Prisoners of war are not workers. We're slaves. We have no rights.

Whispered rumours, like fluff from dandelions, float around . . . into my ears, my nose, my mouth. Rumours about gas chambers and starving Jews. Can they be true? Are they exaggerations? Did Minna stay safe in Switzerland? Or was she also sent to one of these death camps? Maybe that's where I'm headed. And what about Albert? Is he working in a gulag somewhere, or is he still marching like me?

At least Marthe isn't marching. That little girl saved her life. Why couldn't I have stayed in East Prussia with her? Tears of self-pity blur my vision, and when I stumble, a gun prods me forward.

In front of me, there's a kerfuffle, like a hen fight but without feathers. Guards rush over and the squawking turns into muffled cries. A shot, then silence. We trudge past a body, blood trickling into the thirsty ground. I keep walking, choosing life over death. Every step is life.

Late one morning, electricity fills the heavy air and it's not from a thunderstorm. The sun shines bright as Red Army vehicles passing us by blare their horns, the hammer and sickle waving in the wind. Guns fire at random, soldiers laugh and dance.

We keep marching while they celebrate. From somewhere comes the message, passed along from woman to woman. Nazi Germany has capitulated. The war is over.

"*Urah! Urah!*" They shout their battle cry — drunk with victory. They sing, sometimes they even skip. Their vigour scares me. We trudge past another burned-out village. Did Siegfried-Jakob do it or maybe Helmut? Or was it Albert? Did he spread the kerosene or light the fire?

We pass a neglected orchard where apple trees blossom, delicate white and pink petals against a blue sky. I want to put my nose against them and breathe in their scent. I want to be a bee meandering from blossom to blossom. I want to suck up the nectar.

"*Dawai!*" A guard prods me with his bayonet — like a hornet's stinger. Yes, Papa, we truly are caught in a hornet's nest now.

All the rail tracks are broken and there's no freight train to give respite from this endless trudge. My blistered, bleeding bare feet shuffle me forward. I feel exposed, vulnerable and ugly.

Women and children, looking as bedraggled and hungry as us, line up in the decimated villages. As we pass them, like a slow parade, they throw rocks at us. Some spit. They call us names. Nazis. Fascists. Murderers. I've never been in a parade before. I'm usually the spectator.

One constant, as we drag our bodies along, are the crows. Like shadows, they follow wherever we go. They hover, jeering at us with belligerent caws, hoping for some food, for some meat — for a cadaver to peck at. They've become bolder. I feel the wind from their wings as they swoop close, sharply eyeing the pickings.

And then, in the middle of the day, when the sun blazes hot and even the restless crows are resting, we're screamed at. "*Stoy!*"

We stop. My knees buckle, threaten to give out completely. Ahead of us, blurry in the shimmering heat, sit a dozen or so cattle cars on unbroken tracks. Finally! I crane my neck, but see no engine attached.

The boxcars — doors wide open — now no longer seem so welcoming. Close up, they appear like dark pits and without even entering them, their stench enters me. I want to stay outside, where's there's scattered grass to nibble and a breeze and clouds that might offer rain. Even a cold rain is better than the insides of a freight car. Last time I was on one of those . . . claustrophobia swells in me as I'm shoved into the dark, smelly cavern and swallowed up by childhood memories.

CHAPTER 29

THE SOVIET GUARDS count us aboard. "*Adeen, dva, tree . . .*" One, two, three. I'm number forty-one.

Sixty tired, starving German women are stuffed into one railcar, and soon it stinks, not of animals, but of sweat, bodies, defeat. I can't breathe this air, but I do.

The hot day turns into a muggy night. No water. Women pound and scratch the wooden walls, but I don't think anyone hears us. Or maybe they hear us, but they don't listen. I say nothing — save my energy. In the privacy of darkness, I nibble on Natasha's bread, but without water the crumbs sit in my throat like pebbles.

Night moves on, light returns. I try to sleep this nightmare away. It rains on the second night, and the leaky railcar fills with water. We lap it up. I measure the passing of time with the size of Natasha's bread. It shrinks, dries up, grows mouldy in the moist conditions. My sweaty breasts itch.

We step on each other for a chance to plaster our faces against the cracks of our freight box, our tongues stretching out for drops of clean water. This rain saves our lives.

One night, towards dawn, I nibble at the stale bread and this time someone does notice. Like a snarling cat, the woman pounces and the intensity of her attack squeezes a scream out of my throat.

"Bread!" The shout goes around, and Natasha's dry loaf breaks apart like bird crumbs onto the filth of our floor.

The good thing with all this commotion is that our jail keepers finally open the sliding doors. They command us out and we fall forward — only, we don't all fall forward. Of the sixty women counted into the freight car, only forty-four fall out onto the damp grass.

Soviets are meticulous counters. That's one thing I remember from childhood. They count us again. Then two of them pull themselves up into our makeshift prison, holding their noses shut. They don't last long in the putrid air and jump back down.

The soldiers argue among themselves, then they point at us. "You and you!" They motion with their rifles. Two women are chosen to carry out the dead or almost dead. I don't blame the guards for delegating and mutter a prayer of gratitude that it wasn't me.

We're lined up, in proper counting order, maybe twenty metres away from the railcar, as the bodies of my co-travellers get thrown out. Countless hours and sixteen bodies — except, they're not all dead. Gunshots finish off the almost-dead. These hardened soldiers have mercy, after all.

Now every new dawn, a bucket shows up inside our wagon. The sixteen dead are replaced with more women. I ask one where she's from, but she turns away. No one wants to talk about the homes we've left behind. After the new passengers are loaded up, squeezed in, the train jerks forward.

"Hallelujah!" someone mutters.

Every few hours, the train squeals to a stop, rousing me from my trance-like state. I uncrumple myself and on shaky feet join the others trying to peer outside. We fight to be one of the lucky ones near the slatted walls — to gasp for fresh air. We don't like to share; even air is grabbed onto for dear life.

At one stop there's banging, pounding against our freight car. Angry shouting.

The Soviet guards shout back. "*Ukhodi!*"

But the angry voices don't go away. They must be Polish, because I don't understand anything except the word Nazi.

Someone in the freight car translates. "The Poles want to kill us."

I shrivel up some more. What kind of future is there for a German? The whole world hates us. Once I was hated for being a German in Russia. Then I was hated for being a Russian in Germany. Now the Poles hate me, too. I can't escape the hate.

Gunfire erupts, and through a crack, I spy Soviet soldiers threatening an old man carrying a pitchfork.

"The Soviets are protecting us?" I question with wonderment.

"They need us more alive than dead," someone replies.

"You heard what we did to the Jews . . . we killed Gypsies, too." The voice comes from a dark corner. "We deserve this . . . and more. We are all guilty."

Then there's silence.

We? Why is everything always my fault? My father was a kulak, and I was punished for being his daughter. Then I was an orphan and derided for being too Russian. And now, now they call me German, and I must take the blame for Hitler's crimes.

I try to sleep, to shut out the taunts, but the sweaty, squirming bodies of other women invade my thoughts and my space.

I glare at a woman who insists on howling out the miseries that we all feel. "Shut up!" I tell her, but she just howls louder.

I sit up with a bolt of insight. I'm being sent back into the Soviet Union to find Papa.

Yes! This is my chance! What has he been through during the famine and these war years? Here I am, thinking only of myself. Dearest Papa . . . you sacrificed everything for us. When we cross the border, I'll find you, and we'll find our windmill.

And Albert, my little brother, maybe you'll be in the same camp as me, and we'll be together. And we'll figure things out, like before. You and me.

We'll be a family again.

That thought nourishes me as the Poles continue to bombard the freight car with rocks and pitchforks, as the heat rises in our cramped quarters, as the stench becomes unbreathable.

It's night and we're moving again ... eastward ... always further east. The train groans and hiccups beneath me. The air gets cooler, less stagnant. Crouched over, my head on my knees, I sleep. In dreams, I see the windmill, its arms blowing in the wind. Mama holds Emil as he chortles, his pudgy fingers reaching out, while linden blossoms float gently around us like snow. I laugh.

"Hey, you! What's your name?"

An elbow pokes my shoulder. I open my eyes into the darkness.

"Katya," I tell the night.

"Stop the laughing. You're upsetting the others."

"Laughing?" I repeat. "I was laughing?"

"Yes, laughing. Others are crying and then you start laughing. It's insulting. It's maddening."

While our moving jail cell chugs on, the lice crawl over our skin, suck our blood and multiply. They grow fat while we grow skinny. Scratching and breathing — it's all I have energy for as days and nights turn into weeks.

I don't know when the train drags us across the border into the Soviet Union. Or maybe there is no border. This freight car is my world, and it's clearly under Soviet control. Nobody stops a freight load of women sent like livestock to their doom.

CHAPTER 30

"*VNE! TRAPEEDCA!*" Out and hurry.

Like limp flowers, we tumble out of the reeking freight car into the heat of a spring day. I pinch my eyes shut against the blinding sun.

"*Zakaz!*" They demand order, attention.

We sway in sweltering heat, overwhelmed by thirst. Some women faint and fall to the hard, dry ground. They stay there, unattended, while flies buzz around, tickling and irritating. Crows swoop down onto nearby leafless, scorched trees to watch the show — waiting. I hate them more than I hate the guards.

Five in a row we stand, waiting.

"*Osmotr!*" a guard shouts.

Inspection? Of what? Us?

Then he counts, "*Adeen, dva, tree . . .*," up to five. We're led to some black-painted barrels with rubber hoses poking out.

"Strip!" comes an order.

A woman near me mumbles. "Shower? We'll disappear without our dirt."

134 / Gabriele Goldstone

"Shut up and scrub!" another woman tells her. "Look, there's even soap!"

The water's pleasantly warm and showers life back into me. The few minutes it patters down onto my skin feel precious. Lice, legions of fat, blood-infested parasites, pour off me and drown. I step on them, on my stolen blood.

Another five women are called to the outdoor showers, while we, dripping wet, still naked, are led to a low building. Inside, electric lights glare with cruel brilliance — more direct than the sun. A man in a white coat sits at a desk. He wears a stethoscope around his neck. Next to him sits a young woman with a medic armband and a Red Army cap. Her eyes are slits of hate.

"*Frau, komm!*" Such familiar words. It's my turn, and a remnant of shame takes hold as I shyly step forward in my louse-less nakedness under the glaring light. Like the others before me, I criss-cross my arms, trying to cover my ugliness from the light, but the female medic slaps my hands apart and my shame turns to anger that I can only hold in with clenched fists.

She shoves me towards a scale onto which I obediently step, and the doctor adjusts the weights for a moment. He mumbles a number and his assistant scratches something onto paper. Then without warning, his huge hands pinch me — grab for the fat on my buttocks. It's at this moment I know that this is not a doctor — he's a vet, and I am merely a piece of livestock. The stethoscope placed between my shrunken breasts shocks with cold as the man's blue eyes leer into my face.

"*Gut. Gut,*" he soothes with mock kindness. He gives the nurse sitting at the same table another number. "Grade two," he tells her.

To me, he says in German, his Russian accent thick like his hands, "*Arbeit macht frei. Ja?*"

They're familiar words, too. Nazis used them and now they mock us. Now I must work for my own freedom.

"*Wie lange?*" I ask in German, not ready to give away my Russian language advantage. How long? What is my prison sentence?

The doctor shrugs. "*Ich weis nicht.*"

Maybe he really doesn't know. He's just doing his job.

"*Warum?*" I quickly add, grateful that he's actually answered a question. "Warum?" Why? Why me? But I'm pushed away without an answer.

"Next!" he hollers.

I go to the back of the line, where clothes are thrown at me. Clean, louse-free, but not new. Shabby rejects from some dead woman. I am in Russia — a different Russia than the one I left. This Russia is now the country of heroes. And German Russians like me continue to walk that no-man's land of not belonging to either country.

What's happening in East Prussia now? How are my sisters and the others doing while I'm being degraded into livestock status? Tears of self-pity run down my face. I no longer know tears of shame.

We're divided according to our health. The strongest ones are to be sent to Siberia for tree felling. The middle ones — like me — will go to the coal mines. The weakest ones will stay here, wherever here is.

Maybe they'll just wait here until they die. No work . . . no food.

CHAPTER 31

MY DESTINATION — coal mines in the Ural Mountains.

"East of Chelyabinsk, in the Kurgan Oblast." A talkative guard shares the information with me between puffs on his *makhorka*. We're standing outside the trains, waiting as prisoners get reshuffled.

"Not as far as Siberia." He grins like he's responsible for my good fortune. "Not so cold in the coal mines. Lots of coal needed for electricity," he explains. "For building tractors. No more tank factories. Soldiers can be farm workers again."

I can't work in a coal mine. That's men's work. I'll never survive. Never.

We re-board the stinking freight car and wind our way up and down the mountains. There's more room, now that we've been divided according to the meat on our bones. We spread ourselves out. Though our bodies get skinnier every day, we spread our wretchedness out, like carpets that need airing. Earlier, we'd been forced to wash out the freight car, but some lice linger — hungry and eager to propagate.

Heat oppresses us worse than ever, and the guards double our water ration. Instead of one bucket a day for thirty people, we now get two buckets. My tin cup disappears — lost or stolen — and I have nothing to hold the water. Most of it slips through my hands before I'm able to sip. There's no chance for refills. Too many others who need their mouthful. We're all each other's worst enemies.

Except Renate. Renate and I lock eyes one morning at the water bucket. Thirst and envy prompt me to beg. "Would you lend me your cup?" I ask. It's a rusted tin can, with no handle.

She nods, passes it to me, and I'm able to drink the water in leisurely small sips. I savour the tepid liquid like it's a fine wine.

"Don't take all day with it now," she says. But her eyes are smiling.

"Sorry. Here you go. Thank you." I hand back the misshapen can.

"You were in one of my classes." Renate keeps studying me. "You were the new girl."

I'm stunned. "In Kreuzburg?"

"Yes, Herr Meisner's class. He was so boring." Renate grins and shakes her head.

"You were there?" I was only at the school for a short while. Aunt Elfriede wouldn't let me go — said she needed me for housework.

"Yes, you're Katya, right? You were freshly imported from Russia."

"Yes," I mumble, my teenage awkwardness returning. Awkwardness comes naturally to me. "Sorry, I don't remember your name."

"I'm Renate. Don't worry. We all looked the same back then in those uniforms." She rolls her eyes. "So, how do you feel about being back here . . . like this?" she adds.

We've managed to squeeze past the women queued up for water, and we find ourselves a private corner. Not like real privacy, but the kind available in a crowded freight car — a corner where we can hear and see each other in the half light.

"I'm terrified that I'll never leave," I tell her.

"But isn't Russia your home?" Renate prods, not unkindly, just curiously.

"East Prussia is my home now," I tell her.

"There won't be anything left of Kreuzburg, even if we do go back." Renate's eyes spill over with tears.

"I left Kreuzburg when I was fifteen," I tell her, watching her cry with a cool detachment. "I moved to Wehlau. Then Stablach. I can live anywhere."

Renate blinks away her tears. "I lived in Königsberg, but that's a wreck, too." She grins. "You're Anni's cousin, right?"

"Yes. The perfect Anni. She got left — "

Renate interrupts. "The perfect Anni! That's a good description. She was always full of herself — even before she became this la-dee-da leader in the BDM. Lorded it over everyone. Well, not over me. I was never into that Hitler Jugend stuff. You?"

"Me? No. I've never trusted politics . . . or uniforms." I remember how Uncle Leo pranced in his OGPU uniform when I was a child in the Soviet Union.

"This Stalin is not a good leader," says Renate. "He should follow our Führer's example and shoot himself."

I gasp. "Is that how Hitler died?"

"You didn't know? Yup. Him and Eva Braun. Cowards. The whole lot of them, and here we are paying for their — "

"Hey, you two. Out of my corner!" It's Dagmar, a big-boned, tall woman who radiates hostility to everyone around her.

A defiant look settles on Renate's face as she crosses her arms, but I tug at my new friend's sweater. "Let's go." I pull Renate along, out of the corner. We must choose our battles. We don't need more enemies.

Exhausted from our exchange, I scrunch myself up near some sleeping women and nod off. It's the best way to pass time and conserve energy. The mayhem of a freight car is not the kind of place to have thoughtful conversations. Too much noise. There's the clattering of the rickety train, and someone's always moaning with either pain or self-pity, or maybe they're actually dying.

A few hours later, a young girl — no more than fifteen, I guess — goes through a messy miscarriage. She probably didn't even know about her condition. Probably didn't even know how to get pregnant. Raped — and now bleeding much too much.

Luckily, someone in the boxcar knows what to do. We make room so that the girl can lie down. I help collect rags, remembering Lili, and we try our best to stop the bleeding. She dies anyway. Probably for the best. Maybe dying would be the best for all of us.

With cat vision — used to seeing in the putrid light — I glance from face to face. Are the others like me, scared young women thinking that death would be better than life?

No. The shriveled-up woman next to me is old enough to be an *oma*. She should have been left behind at the classifying station. Her good health will kill her. She hasn't said a word in the last few hours, doesn't look at anyone. Maybe that's the way to do it, just sit alone and keep one's eyes closed. Think about something else.

What should I focus on? Something good. David's horse. Stern, so beautiful. Dark and tall, deep-chested and strong.

Once, I daydreamed that a horse like Stern would carry me away from East Prussia, back to Russia. Instead, I finally got my childhood wish, riding the rails back to find Papa.

I rub a rough finger along my cracked and parched lips and notice my filthy, jagged fingernails. I stick them in my mouth to manicure them with my teeth and hear Mama's voice. "Katya, respectable young ladies do not put their fingers in their mouth."

I haven't heard her voice in years. Returning to Russia is like returning to childhood. I pull my fingers out. Remembering Mama is too sad, and so instead, I think of Papa! Papa!

The last time I heard from you, I was still living in Kreuzburg with Aunt Elfriede. That would have been 1934. I was fifteen.

All through this war, not one word from you, Papa. After a while, I stopped writing to you. Instead, sometimes I wrote about you. Just silly little stories about a girl, a windmill and a dog. Stories that you and I — no one else — would understand. Stories where thunderstorms and cuckoos were the only things to worry about. Childish nonsense.

I talked to others who came from Volhynia, from our area around Zhytomyr. They told of horrible things — mass shootings, burned-out villages.

Where are you now, Papa? Maybe you made it to Germany when

the Wehrmacht accompanied other refugees to safety. Maybe you're interned in some gulag in Siberia or, perhaps, in Kazakhstan. They might have forced you to become a soldier like your brother, Uncle Reinhold, in the *Volkssturm*. Maybe you're in a POW camp.

Papa, maybe I'll see you soon. This is why I'm being shipped like a piece of meat back to you. Maybe you will smile at me again.

When my fingers are completely chewed up and my nails have no more scratching power, I shove my battered hands into my pockets and close my eyes, lulled by the train's insistent rhythm.

CHAPTER 32

AND THEN THE long rail trip is over. We're pulled from the boxcar — pulled, because none of us can walk — and we crumple to the ground like empty sacks. Guards prod with their boots and guns, but it doesn't change anything. We're empty — nothing left inside to prop us up.

The sun stabs at my crusted eyes. I dare not open them, for I'll surely be pierced by its beams. I curl up on the ground and wait for death. Please shoot me and let me die. But the mercy shot doesn't come and I'm left alone.

Time passes. Did I sleep? I shiver under the artificial light that's replaced the warm sun — less direct and always moving. I turn my head, gauge my surroundings.

Guards run around . . . shout at each other . . . something about numbers. The numbers don't match.

"Where did they go?" one of them yells.

Another shrugs. "Dead?"

"Or maybe they escaped, huh? Maybe you weren't paying attention, and two hundred prisoners disappeared?" The guard's face reminds me of a split tomato under the light. "What do I tell the *natschalnick*? How will we get the work done?"

Can't they see the condition we're in? We couldn't crawl away if the opportunity came.

They insist we get up, and so we lean on each other — throughout the night — while they count. Morning comes, and we're still leaning, shivering, dying.

Sunlight shimmers through the morning mist, highlighting snow on the not-so-distant mountains. Are these the Urals? Have we finally arrived at our destination? I crouch down to touch the earth, feel the grass and lick dew off my fingers.

Along with the sunshine, the dew wakens my brain. Where's Renate? We're counted again. I listen. There's 241 of us.

Then they count again. Three dead since we arrived, since they started counting. Can't they see that we're all near death?

My nostrils flare. The compelling scent of cabbage floats through the morning air. Maybe I'm dreaming ... dreaming of Siberia ... of Yaya. We stood, like this, for counting. I was eleven years old; Albert, only eight or nine. Somehow, Albert managed to get chocolate from one of the prison guards. There is kindness, even in these people, in these places. I must refuse to think of them as monsters.

When the sun's high in the sky, my spirits low on the ground, I get a surprise. "Soup! Line up for soup, over here!" A guard points.

After waiting yet again in a long queue, we each receive our own battered tin cup — a cup that might once have belonged to a German soldier. Mine is stamped with the Krupp name. Maybe it even belonged to Albert or to David. Maybe to Lili's Hans.

"Dear Albert," I pray in my head. "Dear Albert, remember when we were children, how you would always find the light in the darkest moments? Help me find light now."

Renate's near the end, looking down. After my tin cup fills with greyish-green cabbage soup and a coveted circle of fat floating on top, I go over to her.

"Renate, look . . . real fat!" But her eyes don't see — they're vacant. She's not paying attention to me.

"*Aufwachen!*" I prod with a sense of humour that takes effort . . . an act for my new friend. "Wake up. Dinnertime!" I sing, like a mother to a child.

Renate's grey eyes turn warm. "Katya! Katya!" She repeats my name like it's a link, like she's found something to hold onto.

"Good soup," I tell her. "Just needs a thick slab of bread and a smudge of butter. Maybe a little salad on the side and a piece of broiled meat. That's all."

"Katya!" is all that comes out of her mouth. She grabs hold of my free hand, tighter than I can imagine possible, and says, "Let's stay friends, Katya."

I squeeze tight. "Yes, Renate. We'll help each other. Don't get discouraged."

"*Ja.*"

After we eat, there's more counting. We're divided into sections for the barracks. Each barrack houses thirty. But for us, forty get squished in together. We're skinny, so we can share beds.

Renate and I share a lower bunk. We're lucky. It's hotter up top and these barracks aren't well ventilated. That might be good in the winter . . . if we stay here that long . . . if we last that long. I banish that last thought from my mind. *Katya, you are getting out of here alive. You are not going to die in a filthy barrack like Mama. Nyet!*

I bat back tears of anger. Watching Mama die is a memory I will push away, far away, but like a rat leering through the darkness, its eyes stare at me no matter where I look or what I do.

"Hey, Renate!" I call out, as she arranges her meagre belongings under the bed. "We can whisper like schoolgirls all night long."

"You two better not make noise at night when others are trying to sleep. You think this is all a big party, don't you? You're ignorant, girl." The voice, detached from a visible body, spits out her venom like a snake. "We're going to die here and you chatter like . . . like . . ."

"Shut up!" Renate calls out.

"You shut up!" someone else yells. The tall, muscular woman,

Dagmar, comes out of the shadows and stands face to face with Renate.

The two are close to a physical fight. Renate opens and closes her fist, knuckles white.

"Stop!" I scream. My tone surprises me.

The two women turn their glare from each other to me. I stutter at them. "We . . . we can't beat each other up. We have to stick together against our enemy. Okay?" I move in closer and physically break the electrical charge that sizzles between them. For now, there is peace.

I hum quietly, not wanting to rattle more nerves as the two move off. But my own nerves jangle and there's nothing musical about it.

I unpack my rucksack. A sliver of soap, a pair of mismatched socks stiff with dirt, underwear and a broken comb.

We're called out for another counting session.

CHAPTER 33

WE LINE UP LIKE soldiers in the outdoor meeting area. It's the size of half a soccer field and flooded with electric lights that highlight our sickly bodies.

"Katya Halter!" a guard's voice booms. "*Komm!*"

"*Ja?*" I reluctantly step out of our formation and approach the guard. He batters me with a volley of Russian words. There are too many and they're too fast.

"*Versteh?*" he snarls like a dog.

"*Nitzo.*" I back away, my head shrinking into my shoulders.

His grin reveals a mouth of broken teeth. "Come closer."

My knees tremble as I inch ahead, a quivering mass of fear.

I'm shoved into a smoke-filled, brightly lit office building made out of logs, like our barracks. Three NKVD guards, each wearing faded and stained olive green uniforms with the red star insignia prominently displayed on their caps and collars, tell me things about myself that I already know. That I was born in Volhynia. That my father was a kulak.

That I am being punished for Hitler's crimes. That I'm a no-good German. That I'm a no-good human being.

"*Ja*," I whisper. "I'm no good." How many times have I been told that? Aunt Elfriede told me I was incorrigible. It's true.

"You're good for something." The guard's lips curl. "You'll be the brigade leader — the *starosta*."

I lower my head, feeling shame for this label.

"*Versteh?*"

I shake my head. "*Nitzo starosta.*"

He laughs and speaks in slow Russian. "*Starosta*. You listen to me and then you tell the others. In ten minutes, all women must meet in the common area. We will march together to the open pit mines. Twelve hours you work. Then you return to eat, to sleep. You don't work, you don't eat. *Versteh?* In ten minutes." He holds up ten fingers.

I nod. "Ten minutes," I repeat in Russian, quaking, not sure if there's more. Do I have to bow or salute?

"Go! Tell them," he barks in Russian. "*Dawai!*"

"*Ja.*" Now I understand my new role. I am the messenger. Maybe that's what *starosta* means — although it sounds like the Russian word for star. Fine. I've been acting as translator all along. My Russian's rusty, but I can do it. What choice is there?

Back at the barrack door, Renate waits. "Katya, are you all right? What did they want?"

I tell her what the *natschalnick* told me.

"But we just got here. Are we going to work now? We'll be out there in the dark."

"Renate, you're asking me? I'm just the messenger."

"Yes, you are our *starosta*." She gives me a sympathetic grin. "The Russians' voice." We go into our new barrack home to tell the others.

This is our new life. We wake up before the sun and since it's June, this is very early. We line up in the dark morning for the daily count. We get assigned our duties while they pass out dark squares of bread. Six hundred grams. Then we head out to collect coal in the open-pit mine.

Some women are issued picks to hammer out the chunks of coal embedded in the rocks around us. Others use shovels. We dump the black rocks into wagons or wheelbarrows. Some of us push the wheelbarrows, while others, like me, pull the wagons. It's backbreaking work in the hot sun.

Once I wanted to be a horse. I'd told cousin Wolfgang that horses had the best life. Now I've become a horse. I'm not like a proud and elegant Trakehner, more like an underfed workhorse, a nag. Hitched onto a yoke with another woman, we pull wagonloads of coal up a rocky path. If we don't work fast enough, we get whipped. If we tire and trip over our feet and collapse, we're de-yoked and pulled to the side. But those who don't work, don't eat.

At night, I'm only vaguely aware of Renate, a hump on the bunk beside mine. No doubt she's equally as exhausted and uncaring of her surroundings as I am.

Days turn into weeks. I wake up each morning aching from the previous day's work. Some women, already skin and bones, become walking skeletons, their bodies ready to collapse. For me, the work becomes my escape. As long as I'm working, I'm too tired to think, too tired to feel. My muscles ache, even as they grow hard and lean. I am a horse.

But I am also the chosen one. Anytime the Russian commander wants to change something or demand more work out of us — for it is never less — I am the one called from my sleeping bunk. I become the spokesperson for our taskmasters. This is what it means to be a *starosta*.

The other German women start to blame and, consequently, to hate me for the relentless work, for the poor living conditions, for the lack of food. Like before, I belong to two worlds — too Russian for the Germans, too German for the Russians.

I am incorrigible.

Because of separate work assignments and exhaustion at the end of long days, Renate and I rarely talk to each other. There's only time and energy for supportive glances and quick smiles.

Without a calendar or a watch, I lose track of time. Weeks turn into months. The sun's rays angle lower, set earlier. We trudge back from the pits — often too tired to slap the whining insects that descend on us like clouds. I look forward to the frost that will kill the bloodsucking hordes. Winter, though, will bring new miseries; this I know from childhood.

Renate and I happen to be near each other one evening as we wait for our bowls of watery cabbage soup.

"Katya . . . psst . . . Katya."

I raise a finger slightly to show I've heard her.

"*Wie geht's?*" she whispers.

I shake my head. My whole body feels beaten — not by the hands of men or sticks — by the strain of bending over, of pulling weight beyond my ability. Do horses feel like this?

I should be lining up on all fours, like the animal I've become. A snort-like laugh sputters out of my mouth.

Dagmar, in front, jabs me with a bony elbow. "What's wrong with you? Stop it!" Others in the lineup stare, then apathetically turn away.

I laugh again. Hysterical now.

"Stop it!" Dagmar glares at me.

I'm doubled over now, crouched onto the ground, tears leaking from my eyes. I have achieved my dream — I am a horse!

All of a sudden, big dirty boots approach and stop in front of me. I feel a hard slap across the back of my head. I look up . . . up . . . into the face of a guard smirking down at me. I give him a grin, and he slaps me harder, across the face this time. Something moist drips off my cheek. Tears? But they taste metallic, not salty. I rub blood off my chin.

"*Zatknis!*" he yells at me.

"*Nicht versteh,*" I tell him, still unable to stop grinning.

He slaps my face again, really hard this time, and a couple of my teeth dislodge.

"*Versteh?*"

I *versteh* only too well. I nod, my tongue searching for my lost teeth.

He wants me to shut up. It's no laughing matter. There will be no horse coming to my rescue. No papa. No brother. No words. No daydreams. I understand — totally.

I stay crumpled on the ground. I am defeated. Dirty, cracked boots step over and around me as the other women edge closer to their soup.

Lotte, a quiet girl who rarely talks, finally pulls me up and insists I eat. The soup tastes like blood.

CHAPTER 34

IN THE ANGLED light of autumn, the snow-tipped Ural Mountains embrace our dirty camp with their cold beauty. The first moments of daylight become my time for meditation, my chance to be human and to commune with the divine.

Work is somehow easier since my hysteric collapse in the food queue. Except for these early morning prayers, I no longer think. My body moves and obeys without my brain having to process the command. I've become pure animal.

Our taskmasters show no mercy. They hate all things German. Their murdered, burned, raped, starved wives, parents and children will never return to their scorched homes, and so we will never return to ours. That is the plan.

It's a crazy world of drudgery and miscommunication. I translate the Russian orders, their lectures, their hate — not always correctly. My fellow prisoners don't need to understand it all.

One morning after our breakfast, I'm again pulled out of the work line. "Hey, you!" A guard points at me and motions with his rifle that I follow him. We head straight into the *natschalnick*'s office.

"Here is the *starosta*," he tells his superior.

The *natschalnick* looks me over. His eyes undress me, and I feel heat rise up my neck and discolour my face.

"Too small for a *starosta*," he says, a grin playing on his face. He lights a cigarette, a smelly *makhorka*, to hide his smirk. I notice the package of Belomorkanal on his crowded desk. Just like what Uncle Leo smoked!

"Come closer," the *natschalnick* demands through his exhaled smoke. This man's too young to be my uncle.

I shiver when one of his thick, hairy fingers reaches out and caresses my cheek.

"Soft. Very soft."

The other guard clears his throat.

The *natschalnick* glares at him. "Out! Go away!" he demands.

The door thuds shut behind him, and now I'm alone with the leering eyes of this lusting camp leader. My knees wobble. I'm afraid of collapsing.

"Sit down," he says, his voice turned gentle.

I fall gratefully onto a chair, but my shivers continue.

"I can make things better for you." He tips the ash of his *makhorka* onto a dirty ashtray.

What is this *natschalnick* saying? I keep my eyes down — focus on a bug that scurries for cover near the foot of my chair. So easy to squash — like me.

The *natschalnick* pushes his chair away from the desk and with two long strides, stands right in front of me. The bug gets away from his boot just in time and crawls under the desk.

"Look at me when I talk to you!" He lifts up my chin and stares at me. There's lust in his blue eyes, and I drop my gaze.

He drops his hand from my chin and turns away.

"I need someone to translate documents and interpret during interrogations and — "

"Interrogations? Whose? What for?" The questions jump out of me, in spite of my fear.

"Length of prison sentences will be determined by each prisoner's past." His words are flat, devoid of judgement.

"I can translate for you." If there's any way I can help my co-prisoners, I must.

"Good. You'd be stupid not to. Is there anyone else that you know of? With Russian language skills, I mean."

I shake my head.

"Interrogations begin tonight. You'll be given time off work to sleep. Let me know when you're ready for more. I'll be waiting."

I want to be sure I understand. "More food?"

"If you like." His nicotine-stained finger caresses my cheek once more, and now I do understand, and shake my head as I'm pushed out the door. His touch lingers, like cigarette smoke.

CHAPTER 35

IT'S THE MIDDLE of the night when a hand joggles my shoulder. I stumble with sleep-heavy feet as my tormentor pushes me through the sleeping barracks. Outside, countless pinpricks of light stare down at me. Mama? Do you see me?

I'm pushed inside another building. No stars in here, and I shield my eyes from the room's electric light. A shrunken figure sits, back to me, facing a long table where three NKVD guards sit in a cloud of cigarette smoke. Trial by *troika*.

"Stay where you are," the middle guard tells me. "Translate exactly."

I nod.

"*Identichnost?*"

The prisoner's reply is soft. I can't hear her.

"Louder!" a guard demands.

The head rises. "Lotte Schumann." It's the girl who helped me up the other day when I collapsed. I know nothing about her, but I soon learn enough.

"*Datarozhdeniya?*"

I repeat the questions and then her answer as best I can. "Born July 14, 1924."

"*Mestorozhdeniya?*"

"Born in Insterburg, Germany."

"*Rodnoy Gorod?*"

"Last place of residence was Insterburg."

"*Mat?*"

"Her mother is Hilda, born Baier."

"*Mertvyy ili zhivoy?*"

Lotte's shoulders form a shrug. She doesn't know if her mother is dead or alive.

"*Otets?*"

"Max Schumann." Lotte's father.

"*Mertvyy ili zhivoy?*"

Lotte's head shakes. Her father died near Leningrad. She adds a date. "December, 1941."

"Nazi?"

Her shoulders straighten, and she shakes her head a hard no.

"*Bratyev i sester?*"

Lotte's brothers and sisters include Uwe, Heike, Hermann.

"*Mertvyy ili zhivoy?*"

Again, Lotte shrugs her shoulders. Like me, she doesn't know if her brothers or sisters are dead or alive.

"*Deti?*"

"No children."

"*Rahbota?*"

"I worked as a file clerk," she says. "In the hospital."

"Are *you* a Nazi? Da or Nyet?"

"*Nyet.*"

There are more questions. Questions about her time spent in the Hitler Youth, about the BDM. Questions about languages. Questions about future plans.

The questions get repeated; they crescendo, as if hoping for a different response, to find a reason for suspicion. The lights make the room uncomfortably hot. Sweat runs down the back of the woman's neck and stains her shirt. As the interrogators get louder, she fades. Her answers now are barely audible. I ask her over and over to repeat herself.

Then, after an hour of questioning — there is a clock on the wall — the verdict: five years of forced labour.

I tell the woman, huddled against the light, against the hard faces muffled in smoke. She bursts out in sobs and gets pulled from the room by one of the guards. I'm about to follow her, when a hand grabs me and holds me back.

Nyet. Next prisoner.

I spend another hour going through the whole procedure. And then I do it a third time. Three hours of questioning. Three hours of translating. Finally, I'm dismissed. I get the promised extra sleep and don't wake up until the women return from their long hours of dragging coal.

Renate approaches me in our dark corner. "Katya, what happened to you?"

I tell her.

"You're a lucky one. To sleep instead of to work. It's brutal out there . . . I don't think I'll survive." She collapses on the cot.

"Of course, you will. You must."

"What you just told me . . . about the long sentences . . ." Sobs rack her shoulders.

"Renate, it's just five years. Some might only get three. Only one got eight — "

"I can't hear that, Katya." Renate puts her hands over her ears. "I can't! Stop it!"

For supper that night, I share my bread with Renate while she shares with me a secret. "Katya, my brother joined the SS. It was near the end of the war, and he didn't have much choice, but . . . if they find out . . ."

I chew my half of the dried bread, looking at Renate's sunken face, the dark circles under her fear-filled eyes. "They'll only know if you tell them."

"But if they do find out, then it'll be even worse." Tears slip into her soup.

"Where's your brother now?" I ask. "Is he still alive?"

Renate shrugs. "I haven't heard anything. What happened to your little brother? Wasn't he in kindergarten when we first met at the school in Kreuzburg?"

"Gone. Albert was taken prisoner. I thought I'd find him . . ."

"Your only brother?"

I nod. Memories of my other brother . . . of Emil's pudgy baby toes . . . squirm into the edges of my memory, but I shake them away. No. I'll only let myself remember Albert. He's the one who shares my memories of home and of that awful time out in Siberia.

"I have two sisters," I add. "But . . ."

"Ach! Sisters. I have a gaggle of them myself. Not a friend there. We were always squabbling like chickens for our parents' attention and for a decent dress to wear."

"Hey, Katya," Dagmar interrupts. "Why weren't you out working today? Were you sick?"

"Leave Katya alone," Renate tells her. "None of your business." She turns to me. "It is none of their business. Let them think what they want."

Dagmar glares at me with narrowed eyes. "I'll figure it out." Then she stomps off.

"She'll find out soon enough," I tell Renate. "Everyone must go for interrogation."

Renate grins. "Don't mind me. I just like annoying Dagmar."

Renate stashes some of her bread into the top of her dirty blouse as she chews her lower lip. "When they interrogate me, I think it's best that I have no brother," she decides, as we get up to head back to our barracks.

"Me neither."

"But we have each other," she tells me and puts an arm around my waist.

Lotte stands alone watching us and I pull her close, too. "Right?"

"Thank you, Katya," she sniffles. "I need a friend."

Ever since her interrogation, the first that I witnessed and that somehow remains sharpest in my mind, I've been noticing Lotte. She seems so passive, so vulnerable. But what do I really know about Renate? Has she got secrets that might be dangerous? Listen to me . . . I'm thinking like a suspicious Soviet guard now.

Maybe it's best just to be alone. I drop each of my arms from around Lotte and Renate, drained from showing such emotional support. Friendship, after all, is risky.

Staying up throughout the night becomes routine, but not a routine that gets any easier. Standing under artificial light at three in the morning as I listen to women — women like me — being examined like insects and screamed at until they cry has given me a permanent headache; my throat burns from the guards' constant cigarette smoke, and my ears ring from the sharp yelling at close quarters.

During the day, when I sleep, or try to sleep, I dream that it's me being screamed at, and I try to answer, but nothing comes out of my mouth. In one of my dreams, light shines on my face, and cruel, angry eyes bore holes into the very depths of my being. I wake up sweating and screaming, caught in a beam of the mid-morning sun that highlights the dust of the barracks.

"Don't make so much noise!"

I thought I was alone in these barracks. I lift my groggy head onto my elbow and look around. A few bunks over a hump moves under a blanket. No face.

"Why are you in here?" I call back.

"I'm sick. Let me sleep."

"Sorry," I mumble and turn to the window. The larch trees are changing colour. Blue sky, yellow needles. It's pretty. Will it be cold like Siberia here in the Urals? We'll find out soon enough.

I try to get back to sleep, but it doesn't come, so I just lie there with my eyes half-closed. I luxuriate in the sunbeam, stretch out and indulge in this quiet alone time on my straw mattress, with its scratchy, torn horse blanket.

Suddenly the door squeaks open at the other end of the barracks. It's the *natschalnick*. I close my eyes and feign sleep. But he doesn't come to me. When I open my eyes again, I see that he's over at the sick woman's bed, and he's caressing the lumpy blanket.

"No," the woman whispers, but she's giggling like she likes it, or perhaps that's what she wants him to believe. I'm horrified by her lack of discretion and resolve never to be that desperate.

They're not going to ... but they are.... It's over quickly and then the *natschalnick* gets up and dresses. He gives a quick glance in my direction and, trying to be unnoticed, I don't dare move.

He walks out whistling, while in the background there's the sound of quiet sobbing. Grateful for my Russian language skills, I drift off back to sleep.

CHAPTER 36

THE LARCH TREES lose their golden needles, and the sun hides behind heavy, grey clouds One cold day, a new *natschalnick* shows up at the camp, and as the *starosta*, I'm called into the office to meet him.

I'm terrified. Things have been manageable with the old one. Why did he have to go? Maybe he got too soft — started to see us as human beings. They don't want relationships building between the prisoners and the guards. It's not good for their gulag system, not good for the work quotas.

As I turn the corner to the camp office, a sharp gust of wind blows snow and ice pellets against my face. The hard granules taste like coal and ash. Snowdrifts collect in waves, and by tomorrow, their fresh whiteness will be grey . . . like us. I wrap my quilted jacket closer around me and face the camp office.

"Come in, come in and shut the door. I don't like the cold." There's a cadence to the voice that sounds vaguely familiar. I blink away snow crystals as I search my mind for a clue.

"Close the door," he repeats, flapping his arms around himself as if to keep warm.

His order demands obedience, but before I can respond, the wind closes the door with a reverberating slam.

"Much better." The replacement camp commander smiles. "At least this God-forsaking wind obeys my orders." He sounds friendly, but my throat stays dry with nervousness. "Name?"

"Katya."

"Katya? That's it? No more name?"

Is that humour in his voice? This newly-arrived *natschalnick* speaks in Russian, of course, and so I reply in Russian. "Katya Halter. From East Prussia, in the former Third Reich. Birth year, 1919. Prisoner Number 408." That should be enough information.

"Humph." The *natschalnick* sits down and puts his feet up on his messy desk. "You're the same age as me. What month?"

What does he want, an exact birth date? Is he planning a cake? "March. March seventh."

"Oh." He nods his head as if my birth date matters. "You're a few months older than me. But only a few." He smiles, then looks down as if to hide his expression. "You're from East Prussia, you say?" He keeps his head down, shuffles paper around on his desk, increasing my anxiety. "When did you move to that fascist country?"

"To East Prussia, you mean? In 1931."

"What month?"

"June."

He looks up. "So soon. Really, you wasted no time, did you?"

Are we having a pleasant conversation here? His easy tone unnerves me. What is he trying to get at?

"If you're German, why do you speak Russian, Katya?"

"I was born in Volhynia," I tell him. "My father was a . . ." Should I tell him? Will it get me deeper into trouble?

"Tell me! Who was your father?" The *natschalnick* sits up straight, eyes bright. "Who was he? Was he a kulak, perhaps? Was he the same kulak whose family went up to Yaya in November, 1930? Eh? Are you the same Katya who counted days by scratching the log walls with a red stone? Is that you?" He stares with a frightening intensity.

"Am I the same Katya as that girl in Yaya?" I want to laugh and cry and beat this man up, all at the same time. I know him . . . this is the boy from our barrack.

"Tell me!" he demands, jumping out of his chair, his face harsh and his voice impatient. "Tell me!" he screams into my face.

I back up, feel the door behind me. "We went rabbit hunting," I tell him, my voice trembling with fear and an overflowing thrill. "You always had such crazy ideas. You were . . ." I bite my lips together, before I continue. "You were a role model for me."

The Soviet commander collapses at his desk, and his big hands cover his face, and I know he's crying.

"Sasha . . . Sasha . . . is it really you?" I trip over my clumsy feet, move closer to him, tears flooding my own eyes. I, the German prisoner, put a tentative skinny arm around this Soviet *natschalnick*'s shaking shoulders.

His dark eyes rove wildly, unable to focus on me. "Katya, what have we become? What have I become?"

Under my trembling fingers, his body heaves with despair. I'm speechless, stunned with this moment. I try to soothe, to calm him with pathetic words. "We're all grown up now, Sasha. We couldn't see into our futures . . . our destinies . . ."

"And now we've become the monsters." He laughs, a hard, unhappy laugh. He shoves my arm away. "No, not we. *I've* become a monster. But what are you? What have you done?"

I back away from him. His words remind me of his position, of his power over me. He is a stranger.

"See," he says, shaking his head. "You too! Everyone's afraid of me. And this fear . . . this cowering . . . I hate it. It makes me angry! And when I get angry . . . I . . . I hate myself." Again, he puts his face in his hands and weeps. Loud, body-wracking, childlike sobs.

I look around his office. It's filled with stacks of papers. I recognize my name on top of one, with a number beside it. That must be my file — open — with a photo of me that doesn't look like me, or does it? I glance up and see another photo.

It's framed in pewter and sits on a ledge near a black telephone. It's of this *natschalnick* — Sasha — and on his lap sits a little boy, maybe four or five years of age. The photo has a jagged edge like it's been torn. Is it the boy's mother that's missing?

Sasha looks up and sees me eyeing the torn photo. "My boy. I don't want to talk about him."

"What about your wife?"

"His mother, you mean? Sweet Svetlana." He shakes his head. "Didn't last. She was the daughter of an NKVD guard up in Siberia."

"Oh." This doesn't surprise me. Sasha was always a charmer. "You stayed in Yaya?" That part does surprise me, saddens me. "How long?"

"Not that long. I left a few months after you did. For my birthday, at the end of August. Got to go up to the new gold mine in Kolyma, just in time for winter." Sasha's dark eyes turn darker, and he shakes his head. "Worse . . . worse than this."

"You were looking for your mother," I remember out loud. "Did you find her?"

Sasha's face reddens. "No. I never did find her. Sometimes I think she still might be around. Some old, crippled babushka begging in the streets, hidden behind the wrinkles of life. I've done my share of travelling. This is a big country. Seen a lot of train stations . . . a lot of old women."

Is he including me? Have I become an old woman?

But he looks past me, continuing his tirade. "Our men are all dead . . . except the likes of me." He wipes his eyes with the back of his hand, as if to wipe memories away. "I played their game." He swallows hard, his throat muscles contracting, expanding. "And now I'm stationed here."

I turn back to the photo of the little boy. He's beautiful.

"I survived and here I am, interrogating Nazi scum in the Urals. Being here is supposed to be some sort of punishment. We're all being punished in this country."

His words mean nothing. But his voice . . . his voice shakes the very essence of my being. "Sasha?" I look over at him again. "It's really you. Am I even awake?"

He reaches over and pinches one of my sunken cheeks. "Wide awake! I can't believe it's you . . . Katya! Katya!" His broad smile reveals mottled, grey, old teeth. He grabs my hand, holds it tight. "What about the rest of your family? You had two sisters, whiny little things, I remember. And a not-so-little little brother, what was his name? Al — ?"

"Albert. He adored you, Sasha. Albert's in a prison camp, too. Like me. I have this crazy idea I might find him somewhere in this hornet's nest . . . in one of these camps. But I never imagined I might find you, Sasha! Maybe . . . maybe you can help me." I stutter the last words.

Sasha shakes his head. "Do you have any idea how many German prisoners of war work in these camps? You know how big this country is. You know how things are done here. We don't kill with the precision of your Nazis. We're a bit sloppy with our numbers . . . our bookkeeping."

"But look, Sasha, it's a miracle . . . the two of us together, talking like this. We never expected to ever see each . . ." I dare not tell this once-smug boy how many times I've thought of him and of his brazen willfulness over the years.

"Katya, you've no idea how much you've been on my mind. We were just children, but you were an example to me. When you wrote that letter, I mocked you, but, oh, I was jealous of your hope. And then, when you left on the train . . . the emptiness . . . the despair . . ."

Sasha looks up, and I see the same lonely boy who always put on such a brave façade.

There's a knock at the door. With one swoop of his hand across his face, Sasha regains his leadership posture.

"Come in."

"*Natschalnick?*"

"Yes?" Impatience covers up Sasha's emotional instability.

The guard looks from me to Sasha. "I didn't mean to interrupt, comrade. But there's a fight broken out at Barrack Six. What's your advice?"

Barrack Six? That's my barrack. I hope it's not involving Renate.

Sasha puts on his jacket, grabs a rifle and motions me out. I lead the two men back to my barrack where all hell has broken lose.

CHAPTER 37

THE WOMEN OF Barrack Six form a circle, and in the middle of the circle, Renate and Dagmar snarl at each other like fighting felines. Bleeding from scratch marks, the two women seem oblivious to their audience. Blobs of hair litter the ground.

The jeering, cheering — sometimes laughing — crowd grows silent as Sasha and the other guards approach. Eyebrows rise as they see me. Will I be the next victim?

"Tell the women to back off." Sasha pushes me forward.

I hesitate and my voice falters as I ask them to separate.

"Louder," Sasha demands.

"Move away," I repeat. Dagmar gives me a quick, hostile glance, then aims another punch at the distracted Renate — right into her stomach.

Renate doubles over and collapses. I hurry over to her, while Dagmar, now restrained by two guards, mouths off a stream of obscenities. Renate has no reply.

"What's she saying?" asks Sasha, studying Dagmar's blood-streaked face.

"She just called Renate a bitch, a whore . . . you know . . . all those words."

Sasha sighs and turns to the guards. "Both of them . . . into the isolation cells."

"Shouldn't they get cleaned up first?" I ask, bending over Renate, who's lost a couple of teeth and has bite marks on her exposed shoulder.

"No. First they need to calm down. They'll get some treatment later . . . if they want it."

"But they need water," I insist.

Sasha gives me a long, hard look. He lights a *makhorka* and continues to mull things over. Will he show mercy or will he continue with this tough-man image, the one necessary for his own survival in this gulag world?

"Water, then, to help them cool down." He doesn't give me another glance as he marches away.

That night, instead of interpreting an interrogation, I'm the star of my own session. Sasha is my interrogator — no one else in the room.

"Katya," he says, after a guard shoves me into the brightly lit room, and the door is firmly closed. "Katya, I can't believe it's really you . . . that we're together . . . it's impossible."

"And like this," I add, unnecessarily. We're both speaking Russian. I'm amazed at how easily it flows from my lips.

"Sit."

I sit.

Sasha paces. Up and down and around.

"You're tiring me out," I tell him. "Be still." I'm surprised at how natural I feel with him, surprised at how nothing's changed between us and yet . . . everything's changed. We've changed. Our world has changed.

Sasha plops into the chair behind the interrogation table. Then he jumps up and checks the door lock again. He turns off the bright overhead lights, and now it's only the soft desk light that shines. I relax some more. Craning my neck, I spy a file with my name on it sitting closed on the desk.

He follows my stare. "You don't know how many women just like you I've had to question, to prod, to beat."

"Don't tell me. I don't want to know what you've become. You've had no control over your life, not in this country. None of us control our lives."

Tormented dark eyes stare into my own. "Just like that you will forgive me?"

"Sasha, there's nothing to forgive."

He sighs and slouches further down in his chair. "I could have made different choices. I didn't have to end up a part of the NKVD."

"What? Then you'd have died long ago in a gulag somewhere, buried like my mama in some shallow ditch. Dead because of lice or cold or being worked to death. It's all about survival, Sasha. You taught me that."

"A part of me died when I joined forces with the enemy." He looks faraway . . . past me.

"A part is not all, Sasha. I still recognize you."

His face brightens, and he sits up straighter. "Remember that snowy night we went rabbit hunting and we —"

"Yes, of course. I'll never forget. We danced under the northern lights."

"You and Albert were both . . ." He wipes a stray tear from his face.

"We were giddy with cold. Crazy."

"You think you'd ever dance with me again?" His mouth twitches.

"Sasha! Sasha, we were children then."

There's a long silence. From somewhere far away, I hear singing. Who could be singing in this place? Must be a radio in the guards' quarters.

"Did we sing that night?" I ask, trying to remember.

"You did, not me."

"And then we met that old couple, out there in the snow-covered steppes." I'll never forget their faces.

"We must have imagined them." Sasha grins, erasing the frown lines on his face, exposing his ugly teeth.

"Maybe." I giggle like a girl. "But since we both imagined them, they must have been real. All those wrinkles."

"I think maybe I'm imagining you here right now." He reaches over and takes my hand. "Katya, I need your help."

"You? You need my help?" I laugh so hard that tears flood my eyes and dribble down my cheeks. "Sasha, you need my help?"

He grabs my hand tighter.

CHAPTER 38

"AFTER YOUR TRAIN left me behind, in Yaya, things went from bad to worse, Katya. Spring came and the bugs multiplied. Lice and bedbugs took over the barracks. Typhus became an epidemic. And outside, first the blackflies and then the mosquitoes. They bled us dry."

I shudder, remembering the lice crawling on me. "Like here, Sasha. What do you think it's like for us now?"

Sasha acts like he doesn't hear me. Instead, two of his nicotine-stained fingers climb up my arm, mimicking a louse. I sense more than playfulness behind the gesture and shudder some more.

"I'm sorry." He pulls his hand away.

I close my eyes and try to remember where I am. I'm in a camp office in the Urals, being interrogated by Sasha, the camp's *natschalnick*. Sasha from Yaya. He's no longer a boy, and he's just touched my arm and made me shiver.

When I open my eyes again, Sasha's staring at me, concern in his dark eyes. I'm not imagining this, it's really happening. I must focus, but there's such a confusing stream of emotions running through me that I fail completely.

"Is this a safe place for this kind of conversation?" I ask. The door's shut tight. No windows in this cell of a room.

"You are under my control for the next two or three hours. Nobody questions the questioner. You know that. You've sat in during interrogations, heard the confessions."

"You don't trust those confessions, do you?" I ask.

"My job is not to find the truth. It's just to get a signature, mete out a punishment. War reparations. Germans must pay for the war."

"You mean a death sentence, don't you? We're to be worked to death."

Sasha shrugs. "Your Nazis were no better."

My Nazis? Why not. And *his* Communists. Where does that put us? Are we victims or survivors? Neither option works.

"So tell me more about your time in Yaya," I prod. "When did you finally get to leave?"

"Right." He glances at my arm, maybe at the invisible trail his imaginary louse left behind. From under the desk he pulls a bottle. "Want some? I have a glass, if you need one."

I take the half-filled glass of vodka, but I'm not sure I can drink it.

"Brewed right here in the Urals," he tells me. "The stuff is good. There's a demand for it throughout the area. Sasha's Potato Juice, I call it." He takes a long swig from the bottle. "Go on. Taste it."

I take a sip and swallow. A rivulet of fire slides down my throat all the way to my empty stomach. My eyes water, and I'm choking for air, for water, for relief.

Sasha leans back in his chair and laughs. He takes another swig while I try to recover from a sputtering cough. "I'll turn you into a vodka-drinking woman yet," he promises.

"Please," I gasp. "I need water."

He goes to the door and hollers down the hall, "Water!"

A guard brings a bucket. What must he think? But the man barely looks at me.

"Tell me more about Yaya," I manage to say after rinsing my mouth of the awful potato brew.

"Yes, my hometown. Yaya." And Sasha tells me about how almost everyone in the camp died of typhus that summer. "Those who didn't die wished they did. I spent most of the time digging graves for the bodies."

"My mama . . . she never had . . ."

Sasha doesn't hear me. "And killing mosquitoes, Katya. Those bloodthirsty monsters" — he takes another slug of vodka — "were worse than the bedbugs. Worse than guards with guns."

Doesn't he care? Bedbugs and mosquitoes torment us here, too. "When did you get out?"

"Finally, at the end of that horrible summer . . . I was feeling so lonely and depressed after you left . . ."

Sasha depressed? I find that hard to believe. "How did you go?"

"They threw me on a train . . . yes, maybe like a sack of mail . . . me and a dozen others . . ."

He looks at me, and again I see the mischievous boy who wanted to escape in a mailbag. He'd wanted me to go with him . . . in a sack. Crazy boy with his crazy ideas. And now he's . . .

I blink away the past. "Yaya's empty now? Everyone dead or gone?"

"Oh no, my dear Katya. They'll always find more people for a place like Yaya. When our leader ran out of kulaks, he found others. The Poles. Hungarians. His friends. Family members. Returning soldiers. He's still looking for suitable campers."

"My father might be in a camp," I tell Sasha. "And I told you about my brother . . . Albert."

"Your father? I doubt it." Sasha shakes his head. "Your brother, maybe."

"You doubt what? That my father might be alive? I don't need your doubt, Sasha. I need hope. Even a tiny sliver. That's all I need." I stare at him hard, daring him to defy me.

"I admire your hope, Katya. It got you writing that preposterous letter up in Yaya. It got you out of that place."

"Yes, it did. And you just laughed at me."

"I wasn't laughing when you left."

"So let me hope now."

"Katya, in '37 and '38, they rounded up all the former kulaks and . . ." He makes a motion of a gun to the head. "Trial through *troika*. All ex-kulaks were guilty of Article 58. Treason."

"Show me the grave. Then I'll believe."

Sasha laughs loud and long, slugs back some more vodka, then shakes his head. "You think they have graves for kulaks?" He slams an open hand on the table so hard my glass wobbles. "Katya, this is the Soviet Union. The whole place is one giant pit filled with bodies. Between Hitler and Stalin . . . I've seen many people die." He drinks some more. "Their bodies pecked to pieces by the crows."

"I've seen the crows," I tell him. "I know they're watching."

Sasha nods and slugs back his vodka.

"But not you," I point out. "You're still here." I poke his chest, then shrink back, surprised at my daring.

Sasha pours me some more vodka, then lifts the bottle to his mouth. "This," he says, "is for my wounds. It numbs my pain. Works well." He gulps some more. "Drink up, Katya."

"Vodka won't stop the crows," I point up.

"Tell me what will?" he asks.

"Depends on the wounds," I reply and take a cautious sip. "What are your wounds, Sasha?"

He shakes his head, grinning. "Private."

CHAPTER 39

WE ALL HAVE private wounds. I remember David and me together at Rauschen — a shameful, private wound. "Where did you fight, Sasha? Maybe you fought against Albert. The last time I saw him was before Christmas when he got furlough for his birthday." It seems so far in the past . . . a lifetime ago that we sat around the table using fine china and sipping real coffee.

"How old is he now?"

"Twenty-four."

He shakes his head. "Younger than me. Just a boy. Maybe we did shoot at each other, your little brother and me. I was everywhere. Stalin doesn't like weak soldiers. There weren't enough guns for everyone. I'd wait for the inevitable dead, so I could grab a weapon." He grinds out his cigarette. "You know what happened to those captured by your Germans?"

"They were killed, I assume?" Somewhere in this cell, I can hear water dripping.

"By whom?" Sasha asks.

"By the Germans. We killed Soviets, of course." What's he trying to say?

"Partly right. Those that didn't die of starvation in your camps, those who survived and returned home were then punished by Comrade Stalin."

"But why?"

"For surviving . . . and for letting themselves be captured by the enemy." Sasha slugs back more vodka. "You Germans were master killers. You had your death camps, your firing squads, your mobile gas vans and your ovens. Here, in this country, we kill by chaos and neglect. Or we shame soldiers to death. Paranoia. Your Hitler had a plan . . . a blueprint for destruction." Sasha spits on the floor. "It's all the same in the end." He lifts the bottle to his mouth.

"Is there nothing to talk about besides death and killing?" I beg. "I want to remember linden blossoms and storks . . . my dog . . . dear old Zenta."

Sasha's face crinkles into a smile. "Here's something to remember. Something good. Something I've got that helps me carry on and doesn't give me a headache."

He stands up and digs out of his pocket a foil-covered square. "Ever since I've been a guard, I've carried chocolate. Remember Sepp?"

I smile and nod. Sepp was a guard in Yaya. He gave Albert some chocolate and showed kindness to us children more than once.

"And remember the drunk?" Sasha asks. "What was his name . . . you know . . . the one who sat and guarded the trail when you wanted to mail your letter?"

"Igor." I can still picture him, face scrunched up as I wrote my name in the snow.

"Yes, maybe I'm becoming Igor, but I want to be like Sepp." Sasha breaks off a piece of chocolate. "Have some."

I take a piece and lean back in my creaky chair.

Sasha slugs back more vodka. "It's not easy. Being human is not easy. Not here. Not now."

Eyes closed, I let the sweet dark square melt in my mouth as I remember how more than ten years ago a guard named Sepp gave my little brother a piece of kindness. That chocolate is still melting, still spreading its goodness around.

When I open my eyes again, I say, "Sasha, finding you in all this mayhem, tasting this chocolate, has given me more hope than you can imagine."

"You and your hope!" Again, he lifts the bottle to his mouth, but when he puts it down, he's smiling.

Cobwebbed corners of the interrogation cell glimmer silver. Rust-coloured stains on the floor — old blood — resemble tarnished copper. Today it might have been my turn to be interrogated and to spill blood — smashed nose, knocked-out teeth. Instead, I'm being asked to spill my soul. To Sasha. Sasha!

"When did you know it was me, Sasha? I look different. Did you know I was here? How long have you been a gulag commander? What happened to your son?"

"Stop!" Sasha grins. "So many questions. Instead of the vodka, it's the chocolate that has loosened your tongue!"

The silence is loud. The clock ticks, water drips, my heart beats. So many rhythms, so many movements, so many lives.

"Tell me!" I demand. "Where does your boy live?"

Sasha turns to the photograph. "I don't know where he is." Tears slide down his cheek. "The little man's turning five this November." His mouth twitches. "Like your brother, he's vanished." He wipes his tears away with the back of his hairy hand. "I've no hope to see him again."

"He wouldn't be in the gulag, would he? But why . . . what has he done? He's just a child." Surely the Soviets aren't still imprisoning their young.

"No. He's not in a camp. His mother didn't like how he interfered with her lifestyle, so she sent him to live with her family. But the little rascal was too much for them." Sasha shrugs his shoulders and lifts the bottle. "They put him in a state orphanage. Problem solved."

"I was so afraid of going into an orphanage after my mother died."

"I know. I was there." Sasha reaches over and for a moment puts his hand over mine. I pull away. "My Svetlana took off with another man while I was off fighting the Great Patriotic War. I couldn't come home to look after Misha, and she didn't have time for him. Wrote and said she didn't want to be reminded of me."

"Misha? You named him Misha?" Now I reach over and touch Sasha's hand. Misha was the name of the chocolate-giving guard's son. "And so now you've no idea where your little boy is?"

"The trail's gone dead. It led me here, to the Urals. I'd heard that there was a Misha in an orphanage near Shadrinsk. Same age. But when I went to meet this boy, it was obviously not him. Dark features. My boy was light. Blue eyes . . . not unlike yours."

I can only peek at Sasha's eyes — eyes flooded with longing — before uneasiness forces me to stare at the stained floor.

"Sasha, I'm sorry about your son." I look up. "May I go back to the barracks now? This is too much for me to absorb. I'm . . . I'm . . ." I struggle to find the right words.

"Of course." He stands up. "It's too much for me, too, Katya." His eyes are bright with tears and red-rimmed from vodka.

"The others will wonder why I'm not bruised and bleeding." I want to lighten the mood.

Sasha moves around the table and kisses me hard along my neck and then my face. I push him away, but he's stronger than me.

My clothes, my hair . . . all is disheveled.

"There," he says. "Now perhaps, you have something to show the others."

"Sasha!" Tears stream down my face as I leave the room, not seeing anything or anyone around me.

Back on my bunk in the barracks, I sob myself to sleep. But in the morning, I awaken to a sense that something good has happened, and I lie there swatting at bugs, but smiling.

CHAPTER 40

THAT MORNING, while lining up for our morning bread, I stretch my neck for a glimpse of Renate. She should be out of isolation by now and joining us for breakfast.

"Renate's been sent away," another woman quietly tells me. "Dagmar must have done serious damage."

"Away? To where?"

"Some hospital." She shrugs. "Russian hospital in a bigger place."

She'll get better care than here. "How's Dagmar?" I whisper back.

"Ask her yourself." She nods to the woman behind me.

I turn to face a scratched and bruised Dagmar.

"Renate's your friend." Dagmar growls. "Tell her to stay away from me. I didn't want to hurt her. She's crazy, if you ask me. Went berserk on me."

"You mean she started it?" I find this hard to believe. Renate's so quiet.

"I mean she's annoying. If you're supposedly our *starosta*, then act like it. Control the crazies."

"Renate wouldn't hurt a fly."

"Don't hold up the line," someone mutters and pushes us forward.

I'm ready to move on, but Dagmar pulls me back by the shoulder and hisses into my ear. "I'm the real *starosta* around here. Renate had it coming."

I pull away. "What do you mean?"

"Don't worry so much about poor innocent Renate." Dagmar spits onto the ground between my feet. "I caught her with a guard . . ."

Renate with one of the guards? I find that hard to believe.

Dagmar's grip on my shoulder tightens. "You worry about Katya. You're the interpreter . . . half-Russian . . . the one with connections . . . think you're special." She spits again, this time right onto one of my scuffed and splitting shoes — a pair that I salvaged from a dead woman. "I don't like special."

I don't want to be special — I want to be ordinary.

"But I'm watching you, so be careful . . . or you'll end up like Renate." Her eyes focus on my neck, and I reach a hand up to cover it, feeling self-conscious. Did Sasha leave bruises? Dagmar smirks and raises her eyebrows before she finally releases my shoulder and pushes me forward.

How safe am I with these women, especially now that Sasha has reappeared in my life? Or maybe I imagined last night. I give my head a good shake, but I can't forget the chocolate, the vodka and Sasha's angry lips.

We slurp down our morning *kasha*, a watery gruel made of buckwheat, accept our dark chunks of sawdust bread and march to the coal pit.

Having Sasha as the *natschalnick* doesn't change my days or my diet. He's cancelled further interrogations for everyone except me. So it's back to the old routine. Doesn't matter if it's raining, hailing or snowing. We haul coal like stupid oxen, then drag ourselves back to the camp barracks. My soup's no warmer and my bread's no thicker than anyone else's.

But Sasha has changed my nights. Again and again I'm called out for late-night meetings. Not really interrogations . . . no, these are more like one-sided arguments. They always end with Sasha drunk and desperate for something I can't give him.

Lack of sleep is killing me. "Sasha," I tell him. "I don't want your kisses, I want to sleep."

"You can sleep with me. I have a big empty bed . . . room for you."

"No, Sasha. No. But maybe more food?" Doesn't he see how badly we're being treated? "For all of us, not just me."

He shakes his head. "Impossible. The whole country cries for food. You German prisoners eat what Russian workers eat . . . and you don't even have to look for it, or cook it."

Sasha gives me more chocolate. "I'm trying to find a way out for you, an early release, Katya. But I have to be careful . . . it's dangerous for me to side with the enemy."

"I understand." And it's true. He's a prisoner of this system, too.

Sometimes I actually like being in the coal pits — to get away from the emotional demands of Sasha. The strain of physical labour means I have little energy for mulling things over. While I work, almost asleep, trudging like an animal through the rocks, dragging the coal-loaded cart behind me, my mind focuses solely on the next step.

But on those nights when something wakes me — rats, bedbugs or the screams of a nightmare, mine or another woman's — from a too-short sleep, I rewind my thoughts about Sasha and his desperate demands.

Those nights, it's easy to believe I've imagined Sasha . . . imagined his face attached to an NKVD uniform. A bittersweet dream of the past, mixed with chocolate. Some nights I cry, but most nights my pain is hard and dry. This is no place for tears.

Days and nights run into each other. It's all one long trudge. How long have we been in these Ural coal pits?

There's not much snow — and it gets ugly from the coal and all our trampling. The cold gets colder. Like the other women, I keep my bare, chaffed hands under my armpits whenever possible. Dark mornings marching out to the pits are indistinguishable from the trudge back at night.

Stopping to catch my breath one evening, I glance up at the stars, cold and remote, glittering in profusion.

"Hey, star watcher!" a guard calls out to me. "Keep moving."

I'd no idea I'd been watching long enough to attract attention. The others have moved ahead and I hurry my steps to catch up.

The last woman in the long, straggly line is Dagmar. "What did you see up there?"

"My mother. A baby brother. Maybe an old friend." I'm not ready to see the others. Papa, Aunt Helena, Albert, my sisters . . . no, I don't see them up there . . . not yet.

Dagmar hisses at me with her normal venom. "You have to stop that kind of talk. Hear me?"

I nod. "I know. I didn't . . . I wasn't . . ."

"Listen, girl. We're all suffering, okay? You're not any worse off than any of us. You don't see me daydreaming into the stars."

"No." *Why is she so angry?*

"Right then. Focus on this. I'm telling you for your own good. You start daydreaming, it's the first sign that you're going . . ." She makes a circle at the side of her head, not saying Renate's name but implying it just the same.

"Cuckoo!" I say for her. And it takes all my willpower not to repeat it over and over. I say it just to myself, with each step I take. "Cuckoo, cuckoo, cuc . . . koo . . ."

"You are going to end up just like Renate." Dagmar squishes her eyes and warns me, "Careful, girl. I hate everything about cuckoos." She moves on, and I wonder if what she says is true. Am I going nuts?

Sasha calls me into his office over and over again. He's intense. Too intense . . . and always drunk. Wants only to embrace me. When he cries, I can't comfort him . . . I feel only repulsion.

I don't know what to do. I don't want to be near him. What if someone finds out about our strange relationship? It can't be good — for him or for me. I'm not sure how much longer I can go on like this. I thought he would help me, but he's almost as powerless as I am.

CHAPTER 41

I'M CALLED OUT for an interrogation, and this time it's not Sasha waiting in the small, low-ceilinged cell of a room that reeks of sweat and blood.

"Katya Halter?" asks the strange NKVD officer — someone I've not seen before.

I nod.

"Sit down." He motions with his head.

I swallow nervously and sit down while doing a quick glance around. No Sasha lurking in the shadows. No one in the corners.

"How long have you known Sasha Oleniski?"

I clasp my hands together on my lap. Try to stop their shaking. How much do they know? Should I tell them the truth? Of course, I should. They already suspect something. Will I be making things worse for him? Maybe I'll make things worse for myself.

I shrug, try to act nonchalant. "We met once as children. In another camp."

"Are you lovers?"

Is that their main concern? My hands separate, turn into fists, and I feel the heat rise in my face. "No!" I shout too loudly. "Of course not." Sasha has it all wrong.

"It is forbidden for our officers to have affairs with you fascist women. Are you German?"

I consider this question. Normally I would answer yes, yes, yes. But now, it might not be the best answer. "I was born near Zhytomyr, outside of Kiev," I tell him. "You decide what I am."

"You're registered as a Nazi prisoner of war," the officer says, waving a file in my face.

"I lived in Germany during the war, yes. But I've never been a Nazi. And . . ." I add, fumbling to defend myself, "I was born and raised here, in this country." Does that help me? "What am I?" It's an honest question.

The guard drops the file, picks up a *makhorka* and blows smoke into my face. My eyes water, my throat burns.

"You speak Russian well," he says.

I'm not sure how to reply. Do I say thank you?

"Comrade Oleniski has been transferred to another camp. We all travel around. It keeps us on our toes, stops us from forming relationships that could tie us down. You understand?"

"Yes, yes, of course."

"He left a letter for you."

"He did?" I gulp down my surprise.

"Yes. We had to read it. But you can have it now. I've had to remove some parts, but its intent will no doubt cheer you up. We don't want to cause" — he sucks on his cigarette and continues — "we don't want to cause unnecessary hardship." Then he exhales, grinds out his butt, hands me the letter and shows me the door.

Clouds hide the moon. It's dawn before I can read Sasha's words.

My Dearest Katya,

You taught me this, to write a letter. You taught me to not give up. You showed me hope. I'm being transferred to Siberia, to a town in the far north.

A heavy black pen crosses out some words, but I can guess. Some random place in the middle of nowhere. That's where they send people they don't trust.

Here's some hope for you. If I see your father, I'll tell him I chatted with you. If I see your little brother, I'll give him chocolate. Join me and we'll go rabbit hunting again, we'll dance under the northern lights.

Katya, I need you in my life. Don't give up. Maybe you could write me like you wrote to your father. I still have connections. I could help you if you let me. You are my destiny.

Always yours,

A hopeful Sasha

I can't write back to Sasha — this life allows no letter writing — and maybe that's for the best. Like Papa, Albert and David, Sasha's simply another man of my life who disappears. It's just us women, that's how it's always been.

Later, when I struggle to re-read Sasha's letter, the light has faded, and it's hard to decipher. Still, I ache with loneliness. I wipe my cheeks. Tears can freeze, leave salty stains, and then everyone will know the secret of our hearts. Sasha's right, some wounds are private.

I look around. It's not good to be unaware. Dagmar stares at me — she misses nothing — and comes closer.

"You got mail?" she asks. "I didn't know we were allowed to receive letters from home."

"Home?" I laugh. What would that be? Federofka? Kreuzburg? Wehlau? Stablach? "I don't have a home."

"Let me see the letter. Where's it from? Who's it from?"

"It's none of your business," I tell her and stash the letter between my flat breasts.

"Of course, it's my business. The Russians might call you our *starosta*, but they're not in charge here in the barracks. Everything in here is my business." She pounces for the letter.

Her aggression stuns me, but only for a moment. Our fight becomes a regular dog fight — scratching, biting and hair pulling. I will not let this woman take Sasha's letter from me.

Dagmar bares her teeth and lunges again and again for Sasha's letter. I bite her hand just as she's about to grab it. She howls and comes at me like a bull, her head lowered, bashing into my stomach. I double over in agony.

I sense, rather than see, an audience gathering around us like flies. Renate, my only friend, still gone. There's no one to support me. These women only jeer, cheer or stare with detached interest.

It doesn't take long for NKVD guards to arrive, and Dagmar and I are disentangled. We're both covered in scratches. I pant like a dog and swallow blood.

"Animals!" one of the guards says, laughing. "A dogfight! I should have sold tickets, made some bets. Okay. Showtime over." He dismisses the spectators.

Meanwhile, I'm hunched over, regaining my breath while my heart pounds, and tremors ripple through my broken body.

"And you two." His voice becomes a snarl. "You think you're going to sit in an isolation cell and recover? Huh? No." He shakes a finger at us. "You will have half-rations, and we'll find you a special project. You can work your wounds away."

He calls out to another guard. "Igor! Take these girls out to the pits for the night. They can load one of the wagons." To me, he says before I'm dragged off, "Whatever did Sasha see in you?" He spits into my swelling, bruised eye.

CHAPTER 42

DAGMAR AND I are accompanied by two guards, the shorter one, called Yuri, in front, and giant Igor behind us. The stars shine bright in the sky, not that I spend a lot of time looking at them. I need to watch where I'm going. The snowy trail's rutted and icy. It's as dangerous to trip over as tree roots.

My left eye swells so that I can barely see out of it, but I manage to manoeuvre the dark trail with Dagmar and Igor close behind.

It's a thirty-minute walk in daylight. Tonight, it takes us twice as long. When we arrive at the pits, an old German army truck sits empty in the starlight.

"Fill it up," Igor snarls. "When it's full, we'll head back."

The guards turn away and flip a coin, no doubt to see who gets to nap first. The winner, Igor, takes a few slugs of vodka — Sasha's vodka, maybe — and makes himself comfortable in the cab of the truck which, after a few false starts, grudgingly rumbles awake.

With no shovel and only tattered gloves on our grubby hands, we pick up handfuls of black ore and throw it into the back of the truck. Plops of ore on metal ring loudly into the night. Dagmar and I have said not a word to each other and Sasha's letter is still safe with me.

Yuri, meanwhile, makes a fire and then sips from his own bottle. It doesn't take long and he, too, nods off.

Dagmar hollers loudly. "I hate this place!"

Yuri jumps up, rifle pointed. "Shut up and work!"

"Why did you scream like that?" I whisper.

"Just testing." She kicks at the ore. "Want to see how alert our escorts are."

"Let's get this over with," I tell her. "I need to sleep."

Dagmar turns to me, arms full of coal. "At least tell me who wrote the letter. Why did you get mail and none of us have received anything? What's happening back home?"

"The letter's not from Germany," I tell her. "It's from here, in Russia."

"Oh." Dagmar's eyes seem to glow in the dark. "Why didn't you tell me? A Russian letter?"

She dumps the coal, and as it scatters she starts to laugh — a loud, crow-like sound that fills the frozen landscape. This time neither guard hears us. "We were fighting about a Russian letter. That's insanity!"

"I guess we're in an insane world," I agree.

Dagmar and I work in silence for a bit, side by side, our hands now as black as the coal we carry. Work keeps us warm, but exhaustion slows me down. My feet are like numb blocks of ice. The scratches on my face and neck freeze, and my salty tears no longer sting.

Strangely, having Sasha's letter close to my skin keeps me warm, even if its message is goodbye.

"So if it's a Russian letter," Dagmar says into the cold silence, "who's it from?"

Does she know about Sasha, about our nightly visits?

"Is it from your father? Didn't you say your father could be in one of these camps?"

Sasha said all the kulaks were shot. I dare not hope anymore for Papa's life . . . or for his letter.

"Or what about your mother? She still out here somewhere?"

"No." That I know, for sure. I kick at the ore, loosen it with my feet. "She's dead. She died in a place like this, further north. I was a child."

"So you've been through this hell before." Dagmar's voice softens and reflects kindness.

Fresh tears form. I blink them away and gather more ore.

"Who's this letter from, Katya? I need to know." The menace is gone from her voice. "It's about hope. Understand?"

Of course, now I understand. We desperately need hope. "It's from a fellow prisoner, from my time back in Siberia," I tell her.

"Still a prisoner, after so many years?" Dagmar shakes her head but seems satisfied with my answer. "What kind of country is this . . . this frozen, dirty hell?" Dagmar lets out a long wolf-like howl. Like a caged animal.

Yuri stirs, glances our way with unseeing eyes, then nods off again. We approach his dying fire and warm our feet and our hands.

After a bit, we traipse back to our work.

"Maybe we'll soon get letters from Germany," I tell Dagmar, wanting to cheer her up, not believing my own words.

"Yes," she nods in agreement. "Doesn't the Red Cross have rules about that kind of thing?"

"Rules?" I laugh, in spite of my resolve to cheer her up. "This is the Soviet Union, Dagmar. They make their own rules. And then break them whenever it suits them. Maybe nobody even knows we're here. Maybe they think we're already dead."

"Well, there's a Russian who wrote you a letter. Someone knows you're here."

I look at the still mostly empty back of the truck. "Let's get this filled." I'm too tired to hope right now.

CHAPTER 43

"I CAN'T CARRY any more ... not one more piece." I'm leaning against the back of the truck, piled with coal, just enough that our taskmasters will be satisfied. I glance over at Dagmar. "Maybe we should sleep now, like them?"

A loud snore filters out from the crack of the truck cab window, while the other guard, Yuri, sits slumped over by the dead fire.

"Sleep out here? No way!" Dagmar shakes her head. "I'd rather have bugs as sleeping partners than spend the rest of the night out here like a lump of coal."

"You wake them, then," I tell her. It won't be easy, considering all the vodka they've consumed. But Dagmar's right, it's cold out here.

"We should just take the truck and drive away ... far away!" Dagmar suggests.

"Where would we go?" I kick a frozen tire. "Do you even know how to drive?"

"Can't be that hard if these drunks can do it."

We both laugh. We're giddy with lack of sleep, exhaustion, cold and desperation. And we laugh some more . . . like we're drunk, or may-be . . . like we're friends. How did that happen? Just a couple hours of sleep, just a bit of warmth, and we'll be happy. How our standards have dropped.

Now that we're not moving around, cold seeps in under our clothes, pricks at our skin, attacks our bones, chills our blood.

"Dagmar, you've got the louder voice. Maybe you try waking them up, and I'll get this fire going again. With all this coal, we have no excuse to freeze out here."

Between the two of us, we manage to prod and shout the guards awake. They're groggy and grumpy. The fire's not doing well either. We need to pour some petrol over the coals.

"All gone!" With a stupid look on his unshaven, drunken face, Yuri turns an oil can upside down.

Not only is the can empty, it turns out the truck's gas tank is empty, too. These fools kept the truck running while we worked, and now it's out of fuel and the motor's frozen solid. Soon we'll all be frozen solid!

Igor lights himself a *makhorka*, wasting a match that could be cre-ating heat. He blows smoke our way. "Stupid women!" He sputters a chain of abusive words, the gist of which blame us for our predica-ment.

We should have just let the guards sleep — we should have slept next to them in the cab. That's how desperate I am for sleep. Instead, the four of us trudge back to camp on foot. What choice do we have? The truck, loaded with coal, stays behind.

We make it in time for breakfast. At least the tea's hot, even if it's weak. How I stay awake the rest of that day, I don't know. My body's a machine. It just keeps going — walking, working, freezing. The bread, broken into crumbs in my pocket, tastes like dirt. I no longer have energy to talk, to notice much, and I'm left alone.

Later that day, Dagmar falls to the side during our return trudge back to the barracks when our shift ends. I don't check on her. My body — no longer connected to my thoughts — moves me forward. Behind me, someone takes pity on Dagmar, and two women struggle to drag her back to the barracks.

The winter continues its frozen hold, but the cloudy skies spill little snow. There's nothing to brighten up the filth of our day-to-day existence. Everything in this place is grey and dirty, ugly. Our hands, coloured black from the coal. Our nails, cracked and claw-like. Our faces, smudged grey like rock. Our thoughts, smoke-filled and suffocating. We look like the crows that laugh at us from the gnarled trees.

Every few weeks, we get new guards. They continue to expect me to make sure everyone is up and accounted for. I am their *starosta*, even if Dagmar claims the real power. As the Russian's accountant, I keep track of the numbers, of the daily roll call. That's how I know about the dead.

Some women die in their sleep. It's my job to go to their cot and shake the sleeping awake. If they don't respond, I slap them, and if they still don't open their eyes, I take their cold, limp hand and check for a pulse. Sometimes, tears that I thought were frozen dribble down my cheeks.

When I'm sure there's no more life in the bones huddled on the cot, I cover the face of the dead woman and head out for the *Appell*. I report the number of dead. *Dva or tree*. Sometimes only one. I show the number with my fingers. Heads turn, then quickly look away. A slow dribble of death. Other women are delegated to carry the bodies out.

The ground's too frozen for proper burials, so they just pile up near the latrine, and we, the living, line up twenty metres beyond for our breakfast.

Morning after dreary morning, throughout this unending first winter, I hold the hands of the dead. I resent this responsibility. I'm no nurse, and I'm no leader.

One afternoon, the sun's shining and water drips from the roofs. Spring weather comes and goes, indecisive. But the ice does melt and somehow I, too, get a semblance of life back. Somehow, I've survived this first winter in the Urals.

Surely, with the change of seasons, there will be a spring for me, too.

CHAPTER 44

THE FROZEN GROUND, worn smooth and glassy by our constant
back and forth, transitions into a muddy quagmire. Ankle deep in
mud, we squelch through the mess in bare feet. Soon, with the mud
and the coal dust, we become black stick figures — or maybe crows
without wings. Only our eyes show who we once were.

I make a daily effort to scrub off the dirt, but my tattered washrag
no longer cleans. What I really need is a long soak in a tub of hot water.

"Katya!" whispers a figure one day after wash-up. "Katya! It's me,
Renate."

"Renate? Is that you?" I peer at the pale stick figure in front of me.

"Yes!" She giggles and reaches out to hug me.

I hug her back. "I never thought I'd see you again," I tell her. "Where
have you been? You look so . . . white . . . so clean."

"Sick." She lowers her eyes and stares down at her muddy feet.

"What? We're all sick. Typhus?"

She shakes her head.

"Tell me, Renate. Why were you gone?"

"You won't tell anyone?"

"Tell anyone what?"

She glances around before she whispers. "Remember, I was sent to isolation?"

"Right, you and Dagmar. You were fighting."

"So somehow, someone left a long nail behind in my dank jail cell."

"And?"

"Unfortunately, it was a rusty nail . . . but it was the answer to my problem."

"What problem?"

Renate takes a deep breath, looks around before she whispers, "I was with child, Katya."

"You?" I'm speechless.

"I tried to abort the baby in that pit of hell." Renate's pale face turns paler. "It almost killed me along with the child . . ."

"Renate!" I'm stunned. I had no idea. "Who?"

"One of the guards. I decided you had the right idea. You and Sasha. Don't think I didn't know what was going on with you two. I figured, Katya's clever, that's the way to do it."

"Do what?" This time it's me who looks around to see if anyone's listening, but we're alone.

"Survive, *Dummkopf.* You were sleeping with the enemy in order to survive, so I got myself my own — "

"Renate!" I'm weak in the knees and lower myself to the ground, where I lean against the stone well.

"Yes, well. Things didn't turn out." Renate dabs her eyes. "Got a couple of months off work, though." She giggles and reaches a hand down to me. "You promise you won't tell?"

"Of course," I agree. She doesn't ask about Sasha, and I don't tell her, yet I can't stop my own curious question. "Which guard?"

"He's gone," she tells me.

"They send all the guards away," I tell her.

"Gleb was exiled to some remote place."

"Gleb?" Which one was he? The faces of the NKVD guards blur together. "Was he good to you?"

Renate sighs and slides down beside me. "Sometimes . . . if he wasn't too drunk."

"Do you know where they sent him?" Maybe he was sent to the same place as Sasha.

Renate shrugs. "No idea." She waves an arm. "Far away. It's all the same to me."

"Is that why you and Dagmar fought?"

"Yes. Mostly. We'll never be friends. How is she?"

"The same. She rules our barrack."

Renate looks down. "I must avoid her."

"It shouldn't be too hard. No one has energy to fight." I don't mention that Dagmar and I are now friends. "Have you received any mail from your guard?"

"No." Renate looks at me in surprise. "I don't expect to."

"Do you miss him? Did you love him?"

"So many questions, my friend." She shakes her head. "I'm sure he's forgotten all about me, Katya. New camp, new woman. Come, let's get our soup before it's cold." She stands up and pulls me up behind her.

Renate is stronger than she looks. Her winter break did her good.

The other prisoners take little notice of Renate's return. Sickness, after all, is routine. But now, with the spring melt, there's a change in routine. Instead of shipping coal, we spend the next few days cutting down trees. It's frustrating work with dull axes. We cut spindly aspen, birch and larch — it's all that grows in this rocky land. At least the trees are skinny. They match our wood-chopping muscles.

Then we drag the tree bones along the muddy trail and create a wooden road — a bridge of sorts. It's backbreaking work, and the guards grow impatient because it takes us a whole week to create our two-kilometre sidewalk over the spring mud.

I'm grateful to get away from the coal dust. Mud is cleaner than coal.

CHAPTER 45

I MISSED MY birthday again this year. No matter. What's a number, anyway? I've turned seventy-seven, I'm sure, and not twenty-seven. Sometimes I want to scream, but who'd hear me? We've become deaf to each other's cries. Our growing insanity is worse than the hunger, than the work, than the unkindness of the guards. I will stay sane. I will not be buried in coal dust.

Sasha's letter helps me more than I care to admit. Every night when I go to sleep I'm conscious of its presence. I don't need to reread it because each word is seared into my brain.

With the longer days comes the heat. It's worse than the cold. It's oppressive and inescapable. Hot outside and hot inside — in our air-less, stuffy barracks where the stench of human sweat and sickness threaten to suffocate me. Through the cracks near my bunk I watch stars, or feel rain, or catch a slight breeze. It's worse than on the crowded train, because barracks don't move — I'm not going anywhere.

Outside, plodding to the coal pits, I breathe mosquitoes. Their whines . . . incessant . . . demanding . . . I call them Little Annies — in honour of my cousin. Like her, they know how to poke and get under my skin. At night, they bore into my ears, trying to suck at my brain with sharp, hungry needles.

More women die in the heat. We're all close to death and it stresses our guards — not because they care — because they have work quotas to fulfill. We need better food.

One day, they give us seeds. "Plant yourselves something to eat." A guard gestures with his rifle.

"What kind of seeds are they?" I ask.

The guard shrugs. "Plants."

We use our hands to bury these mystery seeds because the shovels are out at the pits. After all, shovels at the barracks could be used as weapons. The sickest women are allowed to stay behind and tend our garden. We're all sick, but we haven't got the strength to protest or argue about who's sicker. It's Dagmar who decides.

Every day, when I return from the pits, I hurry over to the green life emerging from our patch of tilled ground. The seeds are mysteries, like birthday gifts, and I'm impatient to see what they have inside them.

As the little sprouts break out of the stony soil, they're met with the dirty air of the coal pits, and the lettuce and kohlrabi grow spindly. We have better luck with the beets, onions and carrots. These root vegetables stay protected from the deadly air, even though the rocky soil gives us the oddest shaped carrots.

Except for the growing seeds, the summer of 1946 stagnates. Each day stretches out hot and dry, monotonous — like the work, like the daily *Appell*, like the faces. Sleep is the only reprieve. More and more, death seems to me a better choice than living.

I envy the dead — the wretched, blackened, mosquito-bitten bodies — that we bury in shallow graves quickly before the crows get them.

One day, Dagmar gives me permission to stay back at the camp. I can no longer walk on my infected foot. It started as an ingrown toenail and now, with all the filth, it festers and my toe balloons in size.

"Thanks, Dagmar," I mutter.

"Take care of yourself," she mutters back. "You're our *starosta*, remember?" She smiles. "I need you to stay strong, Katya."

After giving myself a footbath and some tearful, crude surgery, I lie in the shade of a scrawny tree. I'm not sure what kind it is ... deformed by the pollution of this Ural mine ... like us. On its branches sit a murder of crows. Big, black and devilish ... they're like living pieces of coal with flapping wings and beady eyes.

One of the birds stares at me, and when the others fly away, it stays behind, ogling me sideways with a taunting eye. Its raucous caw sounds like a laugh. When it's finally done studying me, the crow shrugs its wings and takes off. As it glides overhead, I feel the swoosh of its flight, and I clench my hands so tight, my jagged nails cut into my blackened palms.

Hobbling around until I find a fist-sized hunk of coal, I return to my position near the tree. "Come back, you devil crow. Come back and laugh at me. I dare you!"

The tree stays empty while the sun crawls across the sky. Shadows shift. I'm grateful for a slice of shade and nod off.

How much time passes before a harsh laugh wakes me? Looking up, two dark pools of bird intelligence stare down at me. I stare back while my hand reclaims its weapon. The crow hops from branch to branch, coming closer, more daring, more curious. I let it satisfy its curiosity.

Finally, it stops hopping — still keeping a safe distance between us. We exist together, each sensing the other, each aware of our differences — and of our similarities. My hand tightens around the stone. Resolve growing inside me.

Another crow lands on a branch and then another right behind it. I take advantage of the distraction, of my crow's diverted attention. With all my pathetic strength and a focused aim, I hurl my stone.

Thwack! A sputtering of wings and feathers. Did I get it? Birds flutter away in confused panic, but one crow falls to the ground and I'm certain that it's my crow. It flaps a wing, then lies still. Elation surges through me.

Is it aware of my victory? After our time together, I want this crow to know it is me. I hobble closer, and my shadow falls on glassy eyes that stare with unblinking intensity back at me. Is that recognition in those black pools of despair? The eyes close.

I've won — the bird is dead. I stick one of its feathers into the scrawny bun at the back of my head.

Not only is the victory mine, but I've caught myself some dinner. Today, I will feast on crow meat. Sasha, my rabbit-hunting companion of childhood, you would be proud.

The other crows settle back onto the tree and watch as I pluck the feathers off their dead companion. I gather scattered coal and strike flint to make a fire. There's no time to waste. I don't want to share my feast with the others. This victory is all mine.

A crow without its feathers is not a big bird. I cook my skinny fowl behind the latrine, near the fresh graves. Nobody comes here.

The aroma of roasted crow mingles with the smells of death and decay and human waste. No one pays me and my crow meat any attention. I chew the dark meat slowly — I have to because it's dry and tough, and my teeth are weak and wobbly. The crow's breast tastes like ash or maybe like death. But as I chew, the meat mixes with my saliva, and I swallow it because it gives me life.

When the others come back from the pits and their long trek in the muck, Dagmar stops in front of me, eyes wide and blinking. "Feeling better?"

I nod.

"You've got a feather stuck in your hair." She reaches over to pull it out. "You've been fighting with the birds, Katya?"

"Don't!" I push her hand away.

"Fine." She cocks her head sideways. "I hope you're not growing cuckoo feathers, Katya."

"Crow," I correct her and glare with defiance. "I'm growing crow feathers."

"Looks good on you," she mutters. "Better than cuckoo, Katya. Much better."

That night, I pull out a saved crow bone and gnaw on it like a dog. The next day, when I hunt for my crow stone, it's impossible to distinguish from all the other stones scattered about.

I return to work, keeping the feather tucked in my hair. I decide to share my crow victory with Renate, but she shows no interest in my story. Her eyes, flat like her un-pregnant stomach, see nothing — even beady crow eyes show more spirit. Since her return to our camp, she's not been herself.

But I've changed too. I keep my crow feather stuck in my hair and no one takes it from me. When I catch my reflection in a cracked barrack window, beady eyes stare back at me.

I am the crow.

CHAPTER 46

WITH NO CONTACT from the outside world, it ceases to exist. It's just us, the coal and the heat.

And the bugs. Lord, save us from the bugs. The lice are everywhere — our hair, our clothes, our private parts — everywhere.

"Come here!" Dagmar calls out to no one in particular, late one afternoon before our evening meal. "Look at this!" She points at a rag on the floor beside her bunk.

I'm the only one who draws closer. "What?" Can't she pick up her own sweater?

"Watch. Watch the sweater."

I stare at the lump of wool. "It's ... mov ... moving."

"It's crawling, Katya. The sweater has legs."

We watch as countless tiny legs carry it forward. The lice show the power of numbers, of what a collective can be. Lice are our role models. The individual is nothing. The bugs cooperate with each other, each louse doing its share, carrying its weight.

"Such good little good communists," I mutter.

Dagmar shakes her head and kicks the sweater away. "Disgusting."

The lice have multiplied by the millions. I'm terrified — not so much of the tiny creatures — of the disease they carry and pass on from bite to bite. Typhus, the disease that killed Mama. I check constantly for signs. No, I can't end up like her in some lonely grave in this country of death.

But one morning in late summer, I wake up with a dull headache. When I stand, the barracks spin, my muscles ache more than usual. I force myself to the pump, pour cold water over my skin. My head pounds in protest, and I want to crawl back to my bed.

"Katya! Look at you."

Dagmar points at my neck and backs away. And suddenly I'm itchy all over and I understand. It's the rash. The purple rash — typhus. Eating the crow has not saved me, after all.

Renate now notices, too. "Katya, we have to tell them. We'll all be infected . . ." Her voice turns high-pitched. "We're all going to die!"

"Stop it, Renate. I'll let them know. Don't worry, I will."

Someone gets a guard, but when he saunters over, his face turns white. "Go!" He pokes a rifle butt into my back. "To the *natschalnick*. Now!"

The *natschalnick* makes me wait outside his office. When he comes out he points to a truck. Two other women — their necks and faces blotchy and purple — are shoved into the back of the old British-make army lorry along with me. We drive off down a rutted dirt road. Where are they taking us?

I don't know the women by name, only by sight. One of them knows me. "So, Katya, they bit you too. Being a *starosta* couldn't save you."

I ignore the spite in her voice and reach for my feather. It's gone, I've lost my crow feather — just when I need it most. "Where are they taking us?" I ask.

"To a hospital."

"Really?"

"Yes, they want to cure us," she says. "So that we can do more work."

I look over at the other woman. She's unconscious and seems near death.

"They better hurry," I reply. "What's her name?"

"She's Sabine and I'm Frieda."

"Which hospital?" I ask.

"A Russian hospital," says Frieda. "With Russian medicine."

"Does it work?"

"What? The medicine?" Frieda laughs. "I heard the guards talking. They say that entire camps are being wiped out."

"Why do they care about us?" I ask. "I mean, they're killing us anyway."

Frieda laughs. "We can't die until we've got the work done, girl. Are you stupid? Sabine might have saved herself, but she kept it a secret. And now look at her. Soon that'll be us."

Sabine's flushed with fever, eyes closed. Her mouth moves but her garbled words make no sense.

Singing erupts from the front cab. Our captors must be in good moods. No doubt they have some help from the always-present vodka. Even though it hurts my neck, I lift my face to the wind and to the fluffy clouds in the blue summer sky. Sunlight stabs at my eyes, and I cover them with my hands. My aching muscles and bones protest as we manoeuvre over the bumps, and I shiver with fever and with fear.

Sabine, in her delirious state, cries out, "I'm coming. Wait for me. I'm coming."

Frieda shakes her head. "My head hurts . . . I can't listen to her."

A few minutes later, Sabine stops crying. She stops breathing . . . and Frieda and I ride on in silence.

We rumble into a town crowded with rusted army vehicles, paint-hungry buildings and tired-looking people. I sit up, wanting to be alert in spite of my fatigue. The truck engine goes silent in front of a stone church. A church? Why are we here?

Two Russian nurses, dressed in white, stand in the doorway. Ah, not a church — this is the Soviet Union, after all. There are no churches. I relax and slip into timelessness.

Mama holds Emil, only he's smiling like he's a doll — it is a doll — and I want to pull it from her arms. I scream in anger, only to wake up drenched in sweat, lying on real sheets on a lumpy mattress. Where am I?

Bright lights hurt my eyes, and I shut them again, more comfortable with the dark.

Only now, I'm at the windmill with Zenta, and his happy dog tail keeps whacking my face. I wake up pushing the tail away, laughing, only it's a nurse's hand, sponging my face with a cold washcloth.

"Who are you?"

"I'm Tanya."

"Where am I?" Stained glass windows behind her glow like jewels. But I lose consciousness before I hear the angel's answer.

I'm with David — we're walking on the beach and the wind blows as the waves roar. The sound is so loud I need to cover my ears, and when I open my eyes, there's an electric fan blowing cool air over my sweating body.

I hear voices, but when I try to sit up and figure out who's talking, I collapse back down onto my pillow.

I squish bugs while a boy with dirty hair laughs at me. It's Sasha. I wake up, blink my eyes in the night and wait for the tickle of the bugs' legs, for the bite of their blood-sucking mouths. But I don't find any bugs. Not a single one. And no Sasha.

What have they done with my parasites, my pets? I scratch my head. Just thinking about lice makes me itchy . . . and now I realize I don't have any hair. Panic wells up in me, and I flail my arms and gasp for air. A figure in white hurries over.

"What's wrong?" she asks. Now I know she's a nurse, not an angel. Angels don't speak Russian.

With my hands still fingering my bald head, I cry, "Where's my hair?"

The nurse laughs. "It'll grow back. Is that your only worry? No more lice." She shudders for effect. "Now you all look the same. It's a good thing each of you has a number, or we'd never know who is who."

202 / Gabriele Goldstone

It's then I notice the others in the room. Along each side of the wall, five or six beds, all with hairless heads. Man or woman, we all look the same — like babies — or maybe like old men. Across from me is number four east. Does that make me number four west?

"I need a mirror! I need to look at myself."

"When you're strong enough to walk, you'll be able to look."

Again, I feel twelve years old. The shame of Yaya creeps over me. Why am I so vain? Still weak, I fall back into an exhausted sleep. In my dreams, I'm at school and everyone's laughing and pointing at me and my shorn head. I wake up in a sweat. I'm still here, in a Russian church-turned-infirmary somewhere in the Ural Mountains. I'm like an old dying woman on the outside, but inside — inside — I'm still twelve, stuck in the horrors of a childhood that won't let go.

"Grow up, Katya," I tell myself. Around me various shapes huddle under blankets. More people like me. One of the huddled shapes gets up and moves towards me.

"Katya?" The bald figure stands beside me.

"Who are you?"

"It's me, Frieda. I'm going back to the camp today. I'm better now."

"Good." I close my eyes, shut her out. The light's too bright for my sensitive eyes.

"You'll get better, too." One of Frieda's skinny arms reaches over, and she touches my hand. "See you soon."

I don't want to return to the camp. No, not back there. I want to go home ... but where is that? Federofka? No, it's a collective now. Kreuzburg? With the aunt who hated me. Never. Back to Richter's, in Wehlau? But David's gone. Dear David. Stablach? The munitions factory will be shut down. The war's over. Should I go to the big city ... to Königsberg? There were so many bombs. So much destroyed. It might take years to fix everything, but I could help. Maybe that's where I'll find my sisters. Maybe Albert, too.

For now, I'm in Russia ... in the Soviet Union. This is my chance. That's why I'm here ... to find Papa. If he's still alive, I must get to him. Sasha doesn't know everything. He might be wrong. And what about the others? Aunt Helena, Gerda, Marissa . . . here I lie, just thinking of myself. I need to think of the others. Natasha. Natasha helped me. She gave me bread, strawberries . . . I finger my empty earlobes. I need to find her some hoops.

Sasha said he'd help me. I need to find Sasha.

"*Medsestra!* Nurse! Nurse!" Why did she walk away?

CHAPTER 47

A SYRINGE JABS my upper arm. When I wake up, I'm refreshed, energized, ready to . . . ready to what? A nurse approaches. For a brief moment, she steps into the light coming through the coloured church windows and she's a rainbow. It's Nurse Tanya.

"Patient Four West, you're awake." She's now out of the light, although light still shines from her eyes. "I think maybe you're feeling better?"

"Yes, Tanya. Much better."

"You've returned to the living." Her smile turns sad. "Many will not live."

"It's because I ate the crow," I tell her, remembering the bird's insolent stare and my victory over it. "I didn't need the feather, after all."

"What?" She puts a hand to my forehead. "Your fever is gone."

I push her hand away. "Never mind. I am better."

"I'm relieved and happy for you, but you're still weak. You must enjoy this last day in bed."

We both know how valuable a bed is — a total luxury. Rest. When one's truly sick, one can't appreciate the comfort, the ability to stretch toes to the edges, to be focused only on one's body and not let the outer world intrude. It's good advice Tanya gives me. If I feign sleep I might be left alone for a little longer.

"It's been almost three weeks since you've arrived. The fever's done, so tomorrow at noon, you'll have to go back to the camp. We just don't have enough beds for everyone."

"Frieda's gone?" I scan the beds.

"Yes, like you, she's one of the lucky ones. Not everyone survives typhus." Tanya shakes her head. "And all the medicine can't help those who give up. You wanted to live ... that's why you're still here."

I don't mention the crow this time. Instead, I reach for her with a pale, shockingly clean hand, as she turns to go. "Thank you ... for everything."

Tanya whispers. "Not all Germans are bad. We must look out for each other." She squeezes my hand and moves on, through the rainbow.

I lie on the cot, staring up at the stained-glass church windows and listen to the whimpers of the sick. While I wiggle my toes gratefully under the blanket, I don't want to stay here.

Tanya comes back later with a white scarf. "For your head," she says. Her German is broken, but she tries.

"For my vanity," I acknowledge. "*Spasibo*."

"When did you learn Russian?" she asks.

"At home. Growing up in Volhynia we spoke German, Ukrainian and some Russian, too."

"You are from my country? Maybe I've heard of Volhynia. Is it in Ukraine?"

"My father was a kulak," I tell her. "Yes, in Ukraine ... west of Kiev."

"Where's your father now?" she asks, as she pretends to take my pulse.

I shrug. "Maybe in a camp somewhere."

She shakes her head. "If you don't know, then he's dead." She turns her hand into a pretend gun and points at her head. "All the kulaks are dead now."

I swallow hard and nod. It's what Sasha said. Maybe it's true.

The next morning, I'm greeted by one of the camp guards. He stands by my bed, rifle draped over his shoulder.

"Katya all better." He nods approvingly, a grin on his face, like he's responsible. "Now back to work."

Tanya, beside him, nods. "This patient must take it slow. Light duties." She gives me a slight wink so that the guard doesn't notice. Or maybe she just has something wrong with her eye.

"We go back together," the guard continues. "You and me." His tone seems friendly, conversational. It's like I'm not some prisoner and he's my guard . . . in spite of the gleam of his rifle under the electric light.

"I'll help her get ready," Tanya tells him. "Don't worry, I won't let her escape." This time her wink is obvious.

"No hurry," the guard replies. "We've got much time, Katya." He shifts his rifle to his other shoulder, and begins humming before he saunters towards the door to light a *makhorka*.

"Katya?" Tanya smiles. "You see that? He likes you."

"What?" Terror rises in me and I can't swallow it down.

"Use him to your advantage. This life will kill you, if you don't play smart. I've seen it. Don't be a martyr. Enjoy what you can get."

"Where are my clothes?" I ask, not wanting to hear her talk.

"I've been saving something for you." She comes back with a dress I've never seen before. The tiny blue and yellow flowers are faded, but it's in much better condition than mine was.

"Whose is this?"

"Doesn't matter. It's clean, mended. You need a new dress."

She pulls it over my shoulders, straightens it over my flat breasts. I've lost weight since this sickness and I'm like a skinny child, lost in this flowing field of cotton flowers. Tanya studies my outfit, head tilted sideways. "You need a belt. I'll be back."

Tired, I fall back onto the edge of the bed to rest and ponder the situation. With a start, I remember Sasha's letter. Where is it?

When the nurse returns with a ruby red sash, I push her away. "Where are my other clothes?"

"Burned," she tells me. "They were so lousy, torn and filthy. Your old dress had no life left in it. No flowers." She shakes her head. "You look pretty now."

"I had a letter tucked inside that faded dress . . ." Tears flow down my face. "A letter that meant a lot to me."

"I'm sorry, my girl. It's all gone. Here, let me tie this around your waist. What a waist. Tiny like a child."

I wipe my tears, mumbling the lines of Sasha's letter to myself. You taught me to not give up. You taught me hope.

"My Katya, listen to me. Let this guard love you. He's a good man — just in a bad place. It'll make it easier."

"Never mind. I can look after myself." I take a deep breath and walk to the door.

Outside, the guard drinks from a bottle. When I stand in front of him, his eyes leer, but he smiles. "*Frau, komm,*" he insists, stashing the bottle into a jacket pocket and opening the cab door of the truck.

Tanya's wrong. No Russian is a good man when he has a bottle in his hand.

I'm frustrated, afraid and too weak to pull myself up into the truck cab, so the guard pushes me in from behind. His hands on my back are strong, and I gulp down the helplessness fluttering inside me.

CHAPTER 48

"ICH SERGEI." He turns his eyes from the road over to me and smiles again, a bigger smile that exposes rotting teeth. Maybe his attempt at German is to impress me, but the smile does the opposite.

All our teeth are rotting. I've got teeth missing on both sides of my mouth, but I never have much food to chew, so it doesn't matter. Our watery soup doesn't require teeth.

"*Spazieren fahren,*" Sergei says, only one hand on the steering wheel. With his other hand, he picks up the bottle lying between us and takes another swig. This guard says he wants to go for a leisurely drive. He knows more German than the average Russian. As if to prove this, he adds, "*Lange weg,*" and winks as he hands me the bottle. "*Trink.*"

I push it away.

The long way takes us down a bumpy dirt road and into a tiny village. Here he stops and gets the almost empty bottle refilled at a ramshackle shack — flaking paint, tin roof — a vodka distillery. There's an exchange of rubles and a couple dozen more bottles are put into the back of the truck. "For my friends," Sergei tells me. "Lots of friends." He grins again. "Thirsty friends."

I sit in the cab and watch as he talks to an old, creased man. Nearby, a wrinkle-faced woman sits on a bench in front of a fence, which is as broken as her teeth. Her face scrunches up as she looks me over, making me feel exposed and even more vulnerable.

If this guard tries to rape me, I'll have no strength to fight him. I bite my lips and look around. Should I try to make a run for it?

Behind me, there's the rutted road that led into this village. Maybe a dozen homes, like this one, line the street. No doubt everyone who lives here is watching me and this guard. There'd be no place to go . . . not as a German prisoner.

Then, as if to help me in my indecision, the old woman gets up from the bench and, leaning on a stick, hobbles closer. She rattles off a stream of Russian words, speaking so fast that I don't understand.

I shake my head.

"Ah, Nazi?" she now asks.

I shake my head. "*Nein, nitzo.* Not Nazi. *Ich* . . ."

But the old woman doesn't let me finish. She spits into my left eye — squishes saliva around with her mouth muscles — and then spits again into my right.

My faltering Russian language skills leave me tongue-tied. I've no way to redeem myself before this judge and can only wipe my eyes with the end of the ruby sash.

Sergei doesn't see what's happening. He's too busy passing a bottle back and forth with the old man. But when a couple of scrawny chicken strut by, Sergei makes a leap for one of them. He wrings the neck in a split instant. And now the old man curses, the old woman wails, the truck motor rumbles to a start and we're off, the truck door slamming shut like an afterthought. The chicken lies dead at my feet, and Sergei, drunk and reckless, manoeuvres the wheel like a madman.

"*Abendteuer!*" he shouts and honks the horn like he's in a parade.

Adventure? I clutch the seat, impressed — in spite of my fear — with his German.

"How did you learn German so well?" I ask, my words bumping up and down with the rest of me as we make our getaway on the rutted road.

"I worked with Germans before the war. Mennonites. On a collective near the Volga. Good people." He takes another big gulp of the homemade brew. "Gitler no good." He shakes his fist at me for emphasis. Then he pounds it on the steering wheel, and the truck veers violently. "Stalin no good."

He looks around, fear on his face. But it's only me who's heard him, and the fear dissolves into laughter, and Sergei laughs and laughs and drinks.

I smile.

"Hey, *trink, Mädel, trink*!" He forces the bottle to my lips.

The rutted road now comes to an intersection. Ahead lies our camp, near the city of Chelyabinsk, its smoke stacks billowing in the distance. Forty kilometres, the sign says. Sergei winks again and turns off the road.

"*Nein. Nitzo.*" I grip the edge of the seat. "Where are we going?"

"To the river. We will roast our chicken by the river. Picnic!" He makes a smacking noise with his lips. "*Essen. Gut.*" He reaches over and pats one of my trembling thighs.

CHAPTER 49

THERE'S NO ROAD leading towards this river where Sergei wants his picnic, and we careen cross-country over an uncultivated field. Our collection of bottles in the back of the truck clatter in loud protest, while the open bottle between us spurts out its clear contents.

"Give me the bottle," Sergei insists. "Don't waste good vodka."

"Slow down!" I beg, my head bouncing against the cab ceiling as I pass him the bottle.

He drinks, laughs and exaggerates the up and down motion like a hyper child.

My chest slams against the dash, and when he swerves wildly to avoid a big boulder, I fall against him. Sergei clamps his right arm, still holding the bottle, around my shoulder and squeezes.

"Hold tight. We are having fun!" he shouts out. "*Abendteurer!*" He pulls me closer and puts the bottle to my mouth as if I'm a baby. "Drink! Drink, my woman, drink!"

I've no choice, because I want this man to focus on his driving. Am

I doomed to die in a truck accident out in an empty field? The vodka — spicy hot — burns all the way down to my queasy stomach. I close my eyes only to tear them open again. I have to watch. Rocks jut up, and dips lie in ambush as we twist and turn around the hazards. I'm nauseous with terror, vodka and dizziness.

We come upon the river so suddenly that I'm sure we'll drive right into it. It's wide and fast, brown and unfriendly.

Sergei jerks on the handbrakes, and I careen against the window.

"Time to eat." He grins and grabs the neck of the dead chicken. With his other hand, he clutches tight the almost empty vodka bottle and jumps out of the truck. I sit there, rubbing my forehead, grateful to still be alive. My racing heart slows down as I take deep breathes.

Sergei finishes off the bottle and drops it, before he pulls me through the open door. "*Frau, komm!*"

I crumple to the ground, but Sergei helps me back up. He gives me one of his rotten tooth smiles and carefully brushes dirt off my dress. "You still look pretty."

I shudder and my heart speeds up again.

"Now we need a fire." Sergei heads towards a dying birch, yellow before its time and leaning precariously over the river.

For a moment, I remember another birch in another forest with another man, dear David, in East Prussia before the war.

"Perfect for us, Katya," says my Russian guard. "Find more wood!"

I wander around gathering sticks and broken branches. It's been a wet year, and there's not much fuel lying around. I walk along the riverbank but come up with little kindling.

"*Stoy!*" he calls to me and motions with his hand. "Come back."

He's afraid I'll run away. The thought has crossed my mind, except where would I go? Could I maybe pretend to be Russian and look for Papa and Albert . . . or even Sasha? I adjust my babushka, make sure it's secure. Maybe I could find Aunt Helena or even Gerda, our dear maid who was like a second mother to me. My thoughts run wild. So many people in my life who've disappeared. And they're all here . . . somewhere in this country.

This country. I look up at the Ural Mountains. The Soviet Union looms huge around me, and everyone here is homeless. Nobody trusts anybody.

I keep plodding along the riverbank, further and further away from Sergei. His voice grows fainter. He's still calling but making no effort to come after me. I start to run, excited with the thrill of freedom, feeling like a rushing river in a hurry to reach some bigger sea. Five . . . ten . . . more time passes. I slow down. The thrill's now muted. Exhaustion takes over, like a dark cloud covering the sun.

I'm panting like a dog and need to sit. Ahead, a willow bends over the river, and I sink down against it, soaking up the late August sun . . . close my eyes . . .

When I awaken — waving some buzzing insect from my face — the sun's close to the horizon, and a cool breeze flutters my head scarf.

I blink at the fading light, unsure of my surroundings. My body aches, my head throbs as I re-orientate myself and consider my options. Ahead, the forest of larch and birch trees is tinged with the first whispers of gold against the snow-tipped Urals. If I follow the river north, what will I find? Unfriendly Russians? Another camp? More guards?

Behind me waits Sergei, with his rotten-teeth smile and his potato vodka.

Maybe he's returned to camp and reported me as escaped? They'll send dogs after me. My only chance would be to cross the river. It flows fast, like it's in a hurry to leave me behind. And this old willow offers no magic bridge to the other side.

Besides, what will happen to Sergei? Will they blame him for my disappearance? They'll punish him. He wasn't mean to me. Would he hurt me? He hasn't even tried to kiss me. He was more like a boy wanting some fun. Wasn't that what he said . . . adventure? And what about that chicken?

I get up, brush grass and dirt off my new dress, straighten my scarf and follow the riverbank south, back towards Sergei. Maybe I'll just check on him. He was so drunk, he might have fallen in the river and drowned.

Walking along the river, absorbing the beauty of the summer

214 / Gabriele Goldstone

evening, I again glimpse flashes of David and me in the amber forests, a golden time. A bubble of nostalgia drops over me and I indulge in its warmth — sucking on it like a piece of chocolate. This could be a beautiful place if I wasn't a prisoner. But right now, in this moment, I feel free.

Like any bubble, the moment doesn't last. Up ahead there's smoke. Sniffing like a dog, I follow the scent to Sergei's fire. There he sits, oblivious to me, poking sticks into the fire, flames flickering light on his rugged face, like sunlight on the mountains.

I drop down and crawl closer, drawn in by the aroma of roast chicken. Saliva drips from the corners of my mouth like teardrops. I lick it back, then wipe it with my dirty hands. Still it flows.

A huge, rough, hair-covered hand reaches towards the clump of willows where I'm crouched. Thick fingers wiggle blindly.

I wait. He waits. Finally, the aroma of roast chicken wins. Trembling, I take his offered hand, and he pulls me closer. I slip down beside him, compelled by my hunger.

"Smells good, *ja*?"

"*Ja*," I tell him, focused on the roasting meat, anticipating its texture, wanting only to savour it in my mouth.

"I saved some for you." He tears off a chunk of breast meat. "Eat."

"*Bolshoi spasibo*." I truly am grateful.

"It's hot. Careful. I'll hold it for you."

Fat dribbles down my chin as I bite into the crispy skin. I eat slowly, chewing each morsel, letting my tongue play with the texture of the white meat before swallowing.

"I thought you were hungry. Eat, woman, eat."

I grin at him, and now I eat like a hungry dog. When I'm done, I wipe my mouth with the back of my hand.

Sergei says, "I wanted to lick that fat off your lips. You're too fast."

Of course, it's inevitable. Was this meal worth it?

"*Frau, komm!*" he says and pulls me against him.

I don't have any fight left in me. If this is going to happen, I won't resist. Sergei puts one arm around me and rocks me gently. "Life can be good, my woman. We have to find the moments. *Ja?*"

Sergei hums — a deep, soothing bass that vibrates from his throat. I relax. We watch the fire die, warm in each other's arms, and we sleep.

Nothing more.

At the crack of dawn, Sergei wakes me with a squeeze. We scramble into the truck and manoeuvre across the field, back to the main road, back to the camp.

"You will have to join the workers today," he tells me. "Hospital says you're better."

"*Spasibo*, Sergei."

"*Danke, Frau.*" He bows his head slightly, then looks my dress up and down, like it's see-through. "Sasha told me to look after you. You should thank him."

"Sasha?" I gasp. "Where is he?"

Sergei shakes his head as the *natschalnick* comes towards us. "*Frau, geh.*" Sergei nods towards the trail, in the direction of the pit. "*Arbeiten.*" His tone, cold and unwelcoming, reminds me of what I am. Our moment is over.

CHAPTER 50

AS I SCRAMBLE to join the women lined up to drag themselves to the open pit mine, I'm surprised at my energy. But by the end of the day, my strength has been sapped, and I collapse on my straw mattress in utter exhaustion. How can I possibly survive another season of twelve-hour days, coal shipping, cabbage soup and sawdust bread? My reprieve in the hospital has made this life so much starker, so much more hopeless.

Only the lice get enough food. An army of the parasites reclaims me as theirs.

Two weeks later, another prisoner is sick. She's to be sent to the hospital. This caring for the ill is new. Are they afraid of losing all their workers?

Sergei is again the driver and insists that I come along as interpreter, even though he's quite capable of doing his own translating. I jump at this chance for another moment with him. The girl, Maria, now unconscious, lies on blankets in the back.

"I should stay with her," I tell Sergei.

"No. You stay up front with me."

I make Maria comfortable. Her forehead is cold, her pulse faint. "She might die, Sergei."

"With or without you." He grabs my hand and pulls me into the truck's cab.

Again, the bottle passes between us. "No," I tell him.

"Yes. Medicine for your soul."

I remember our night by the fire, his strong arms, the vibrations of his hum, and I drink this liquid fire. It tastes bad but feels good. Sergei smiles and pats my thigh. I let him.

We drop the girl off at the hospital. The nurse, Tanya, smiles at me. "Dear Katya, you look pretty. Sergei, you think so?"

I blush while Sergei laughs. "Too skinny."

It's true. I've no hair, my breasts are flat, and even my periods have stopped flowing. I'm barely a woman.

"You have to live life while you can." Tanya winks, like we're sharing a secret. "This one here," she shakes her head at Maria, "she won't make it."

Sergei spits on the ground. "You talk too much, nurse. Make her better. That's your job." Then he grabs my hand and whistles as he pulls me back to the truck.

Tanya waves before turning to Maria.

Sergei puts the bottle between my thighs as we drive. He hums. I breathe deep and take another sip of the vodka.

Like good friends, we continue on to our spot by the river. He takes his time and the ride is almost gentle. We talk little. I don't drink much more of the vodka because my head is starting to spin.

This time I don't try to run away. Together we build a fire, and when the flames die down, he pulls a dead rabbit out of the back of the truck.

"I like variety. You too?"

I nod. "When did you shoot that?"

"Early in the morning. Special for you."

In spite of the roasting meat and the vodka, I sense Sergei's melancholy. It draws me closer, like a fire.

"What's wrong?" I ask him, stirring the embers with a willow stick.

He takes another slug. "Lonely. So many women and none for me."

"No wife?" I ask Sergei.

He shakes his head, looks over at me with dark eyes of hope.

"No, Sergei. You must find a Russian woman."

He sighs and drinks some more. "You speak like a Russian."

"No. Why not befriend one of the nurses at the hospital?"

"Maybe." Sergei pats one of my legs stretched out in front of me and folds one of his own on top. "I like you better."

I don't move. I like the feel of his leg on mine. Is this the vodka?

"You're a good woman, Katya. Sasha needs you."

"Sasha!" I stiffen. Why is he in this conversation? "I'll not see him again. Someday I'll go back to Germany, and he'll stay here guarding the gulags."

Sergei passes me the bottle. "Drink! To Sasha."

And I do. And I remember another fire . . . in Siberia . . . when Sasha and Albert and I danced in the snow while the night sky burned with colour. I tell Sergei.

"Ah, so that's your connection to my friend. I was wondering."

"We were just children. I don't know this man called Sasha . . . I know only the boy . . . a long time ago."

"*Ja. Ja.* Now I understand."

"We hunted for rabbits."

"And did you share rabbit with Sasha?"

"No luck," I tell Sergei. "We had only our hands, you know."

Our legs stay touching. Sergei edges closer. I'm enveloped in the sweat of his skin, the dirt of his clothes, the wood smoke, roasting rabbit and my own sweat and dirt. We sit like that, prisoner and guard, vodka spinning in our heads, leaves raining down around us, the river moving by, captured in a life I feel powerless to escape. I becomes we.

Entwined legs, roaming fingers, kissed tears, vodka thoughts. I let Sergei enter and for a moment it hurts and I cry — but it doesn't feel wrong. It feels sad and melancholy and good. We barely talk. His slow rhythmic movements belong to the river, to the wind, to the smell of falling leaves.

And then we eat the roasted meat, the rabbit that Sasha and I could never catch. With each sip of vodka, we toast the memory of friends we've lost. Then we drive back to the camp. And then we separate.

The very next day, Sergei leaves in the back of one of those army trucks.

"*Auf wiedersehen*, Katya," he calls.

I run up to the truck, not caring what anyone thinks. "Thank you, Sergei. And if you see Sasha, tell him . . ." But the noisy truck rumbles on, and my words get lost in the dirty diesel exhaust.

Tell Sasha that we ate the rabbit — the rabbit that Sasha and I chased as children — and that we toasted his memory.

CHAPTER 51

"KATYA!" Renate calls out.

I join the queue forming for the daily trudge to the coal pit, trying to quell the confused feelings for Sergei surging inside me. Hugging myself, I notice how chilly the morning feels. Summer's over.

"Come closer." Renate grabs my hand. "Others are wondering about you."

"So am I," I tell her, smiling. "I'm wondering about me, too."

"You and that guard," she whispers, as we continue on side by side, keeping up with the others. "There are rumours."

I shrug. "This place is full of rumours. Tell me one that gives me hope — like when are we getting out of this place?"

"No rumours there. Just winter coming with more bad soup and —"

"Stop, Renate. If you keep talking about such depressing things, I'm going to fall back and walk by myself."

We walk on in silence. I cling to Sergei's body in my thoughts, but he has Sasha's yearning eyes and David's lingering smile. No one can take these memories from me, and I will not regret those moments.

Another winter in these Urals approaches with steadfast insistence. Reality blows cold off the mountains, and the only rhythm in my life is the shuffling of feet as we drag ourselves to the black pits.

It's bitterly cold this November. The winter wind stalks us, showing off gales of power with a swoosh not unlike bird wings and then backs off again. The crows bide their time . . . watching for those who fall behind. I will not die. No, I ate the crow, and I will not die here. But as the days shorten, my resolve grows weak like the sun.

How many of us have died since we arrived in the summer of '45? Better to count how many are left. Of maybe the original four hundred women, only half of us still live in spite of the replacements, women trucked in from other camps.

Yes, there are more camps like this. Maybe worse than this, if you want to believe the stories. I believe — that's why I don't listen.

I pull up my collar against the bitter wind. My thin blue and yellow dress and quilted jacket are useless for warmth. My bones jut out in awkward places. Did I always have such a hollow neck and sharp elbows? I catch a reflection of myself off a passing truck window and can't believe how much my eyes have grown. Why didn't they shrink along with the rest of me?

My hair's coming back — curly now. Sofie would be jealous. I like how it feels — soft and thick — and imagine Sergei touching it. But Sergei's gone. My scalp-massage morphs into a vigorous scratch. The lice like it, too.

One cold morning, Renate and I finish loading up a wheelbarrow with coal and take a short break to catch our breath. Guards are focused on lighting up their *makhorkas*, difficult with the wind blowing.

A coal fire glows near a passed-out guard, and Renate and I take advantage of his inattention to warm our hands. It's best to keep moving, to work or to at least to stomp one's feet. When you're too exhausted to move, you freeze instead.

Renate's like a scarecrow — grey skin and bones, dressed in rags — looking like she might blow over in the wind. She's in worse shape than me. I've grown more confident around the guards, although none are as human as Sergei or Sasha. Still, it's possible now to see things through their eyes. We've not had any sadistic guards, just men doing their jobs — not much more than prisoners themselves.

I push Renate close to the fire and stay nearby, keeping an eye out for trouble. When she suddenly screams, I turn around with a hammering heart. Renate's fallen into the fire! A few quick steps and I pull her out. The guard, three metres away, looks up with unseeing red eyes that close again.

Renate's quilted jacket, stuffed with cotton, burns with bright flames. I fight with the jacket, struggle to suffocate the fire, but the jacket sticks to her skin. She's a living candlewick. I drag Renate over to deeper snow, push her down, and she rolls in the snow, round and round. The smell of burned flesh mixes with the smouldering cotton. Finally, the flames sizzle out, leaving a black mess of charred clothes and melted snow.

The commotion finally attracts guards, and a couple hurry over, tripping around their drunken co-worker. Did I say these guards are human? There are exceptions.

Renate lies in the snow — wet and blackened. They ignore her and scream at me to go back to the pit.

"*Nyet!*" I yell back.

A rifle, its bayonet gleaming, points at me. "We'll look after her. Go!" When I turn back to help Renate, the butt of the rifle swats me across the face. I fall, finger my swelling face, then get up to join the work brigade. The other guard yells at a whimpering Renate to go back to the barracks. "Find dry clothes," he orders.

The day takes forever to end. When I'm finally back at the barracks, I immediately search for Renate.

"Where is she?" I ask Dagmar.

She shrugs. "Probably kissing some guard."

No one's seen her. I trudge back down the trail, looking for my friend. They wouldn't have left her out here, would they?

It's dark, and I trip over a log. As I pick myself up off the ground, in

the light of the half-moon I see that it's not a log. . . . It's Renate. . . .
She's become a long, narrow ice cube, forgotten near a burned-out fire.

A hand sticks out, a foot, some of her hair. "Renate?"

I can't drag her back on my own. I'll be in trouble for leaving the
barracks, but I'm beyond caring. I run towards the guards' office, and
one of the men comes out.

"What's all the noise? What's going on?" He pulls out a flashlight,
shines it in my face.

I cover my eyes from the bright light. "You've got to help. Someone's frozen."

He follows me, complaining all the way. We find Renate, and together we drag the human icicle back to the barracks.

There's still a pulse. I sit nearby all night as Renate's body thaws.
Her fingers, toes, nose, ears are bubbled and discoloured. She blinks
with unseeing eyes.

"Renate?" I whisper. "It's all good. You're warm now." I tell one of
the guards, "We need to take her to the hospital."

He shakes his head. "Too late," he mutters and walks away.

I keep her wrapped in blankets, wash her burns, make her drink tea.

Weeks later, Renate hobbles from barrack to barrack or along the
path to the pit on stumps that used to be feet, but she sees no one and
never speaks again. A ghost.

One evening, when I come back from a long, back-killing day,
Renate's gone. Where do they take the crazies — the *dokhodyaga*? I
hope they shoot them.

CHAPTER 52

WE DON'T TALK about Renate. We don't talk much at all. The winter days are short, the nights long. Did we miss another Christmas? It's hard to tell. Besides, what is Christmas here? Merely a day on a calendar ... and we don't even have a calendar. Regular time doesn't belong in this world.

During one evening *Appell*, a guard passes out newspaper-thin brown postcards. I translate the guard's words.

"Where should we send our cards?" Dagmar shouts.

"International Red Cross offices. Berlin, Frankfurt an der Oder, Hamburg, Munich." The guard shrugs. "You pick."

"What do we write?" someone else asks.

"Twenty-five words," the guard says. "All positive. No hint of your location."

I translate. Women stare at each other with blank faces.

"Find your missing family," the Russian guard adds, in a kinder tone. "Tell them you're still alive."

The women all talk at once while I pass out broken pencils. One for every six prisoners. It's a struggle to get them back.

A woman called Margarete is the first to receive a reply. The letter, from her parents, says that they've made it to the British zone. Where's that? What does that mean? Did her parents move to England? We know nothing about the outside world.

A piece of paper covered in numbers — possibly torn from some magazine — falls out of Margarete's letter. It's a calendar! We crowd around Margarete, craning for a look at this one-page record of time. She dares not hang it on the wall, in case a guard tears it down.

Where are we on this timeline? Somewhere in December, the month where the numbers end.

"What does it matter?" Margarete shrugs. "January, 1947, will be just like January, 1946."

Others murmur agreement, and Dagmar snarls, "We don't need to be told what day it is. Useless. I hate it!"

I try to cheer her up, cheer us all up. "We can keep track . . . we can plan a Christmas celebration this year." I sense questioning pairs of eyes staring at me in the gloom.

"How shall we celebrate, Katya?" Dagmar's in a caustic mood. "Put up a Christmas tree? Go down to the *Christkindl Markt* and trade in our rations for *Lebkuchen* and chocolate?"

"Shush, Dagmar. You're so pessimistic," says Lotte, who's usually absolutely quiet. "We need to salvage what we can. Anyone with candle stubs? Christmas is mostly a mood. We'll create one."

"Good idea," says an old woman we call *Oma Irmchen*. "I'll make stars out of scrap wood and straw . . . like when I was a child."

"Oh," says Dagmar. "Next thing, we'll be pulling names for gifts."

"Another good idea." Lotte claps. "We're a creative bunch. We'll come up with something."

Dagmar shoots back. "Right, and when are we going to knit our little treasures? Under the moonlight?"

Their squabbling reveals more energy than these barracks have seen in a while. It's contagious, and I like it. "We have to agree on a day."

Oma Irmchen points out the obvious. "Christmas Eve is always on the twenty-fourth."

"*Ja*," I nod, as a murmur rises among the others. "But what day is it today? That's what we need to figure out."

We study Margarete's calendar by moonlight. It's impossible to know. The date of mailing is circled and noted, but that was back in October. How long did this letter take to arrive? We're still stuck in timelessness, and we're not sure quite how to get out.

The next evening at supper, Dagmar pounds the table and demands better food. A guard rushes over and pulls her out of the dining hall.

"What's wrong with Dagmar?" Lotte asks.

I shrug. "She's crazy sometimes."

Later, when we're back in the barracks preparing for sleep, Dagmar gets shoved through the door.

"You okay?" I ask, looking up from my cot. I can't see her face too well in the dim light.

"I'm fine." She looks rather proud of herself. "They didn't touch me — just yelled. Nice and warm in that office."

I'm suspicious. "What have you been up to, Dagmar?"

"Electric light. Not just warm, I could see everything. Clearly. Even their calendar on the wall. Christmas is in five days. I saw the crossed-out dates. Today's the eighteenth. Tomorrow will be the nineteenth."

Dagmar's courage astounds me.

I don't bother pointing out that the Russians use a different calendar. Maybe it doesn't matter. Maybe it's just better to agree on a date. Whether it's German or Russian, who cares?

And so, in spite of our work, our bedbug-infested barracks and our meagre rations, we prepare. We save bits of food and we create pathetic little gifts. I'm stitching together a birch bark journal from the grove of birches we pass through on our way to the pit. Unravelling a bit of Renate's old sweater, I use the yarn for the stitching and my sharpened crow bone for a needle.

Of course, I can't provide a pencil with the journal, but a thin splinter of coal works fine. I wrap more yarn around the top half so that fingers won't stain, laughing at myself as I do it because, of course, our fingers are already black.

Every day, I collect a few more strips of bark, hide them in my jacket. It'll be a small journal, small enough to hide.

Not everyone anticipates Christmas. Several just laugh or frown at our preparations — led by Dagmar, who's not as tough she pretends. As long as they don't give us away, I don't care. It's their loss.

The twenty-fourth dawns. We're as excited as children, but first we have a long day of work ahead of us.

CHAPTER 53

MY FINISHED GIFT stays tucked beneath my jacket. I've learned to keep important things on me at all times. Those who hide bread in the barracks, for late night snacking, are only hungrier when their precious bread is gone.

The birch bark tickles my skin as I work and reminds me of its presence, filling me with anticipation.

We trudge wagonloads of coal up the uneven slope, fulfilling our daily norm. The work has become so automatic we barely pay attention to what we're doing. The guards, like dogs, bark out commands. "*Dawai!*" is their favourite one. But to hurry is impossible.

"*Zatknis!*" they yell if we talk to each other.

Zatknis! I wish *they'd* shut up. We're just machines to them. We aren't women anymore. What breasts we had hang on our skinny, bony bodies like empty sacks. Crab lice invade our private areas, our crotches itchy, inflamed and encrusted with scabs. Constant bowel irritations leave us cranky and filthy. We could use diapers except how could we wash them?

No, we're not machines, not women . . . we're animals. Sasha or Sergei would not want to touch me. Not anymore. Albert wouldn't recognize me. That stranger I kissed on the train one Christmas, back in another life . . . he wouldn't come near me.

The birch bark journal digs into me, and I adjust its position. Once I wanted to be a writer. Once I found power in words. I blink back tears. Now I eat crows for power.

I open my mouth and taste a snowflake. Like a useless word, it melts on my tongue. But then out of my throat comes a sound. Softly, I hear myself humming the melody of "Leise rieselt der Schnee." Softly falling snowflakes feel Christmassy, even here in Russia.

The short day darkens, and my mood lightens as we drag ourselves back to the barracks. We wash coal dust from our faces and hands. I scrub extra hard, but the sliver of soap we share is not enough. Then I join the lineup for our watery cabbage soup, hoping that today I'll get some floating fat. I eat as much for the warmth as for my stomach, shovelling the soup into my mouth like coal into a furnace. Ten shovelfuls. Ten swallows.

We eat in silence. Eating soup is like praying. Only the dull clunking of wood spoons on wood tables signals the end of this holy time.

Back at our barracks, however, we get into Christmas mode like eager children. We spread previously picked pine boughs out on the wobbly table in the centre. We bring out the candle stubs that have been salvaged from the guards' trash. Someone ties red yarn in bows around the bunk posts nearby. Pine cones dangle from the yarn.

Most importantly, we drop scraps of food into a rusty can. Dried blueberries and cranberries mix in with pine nuts and walnuts.

"Walnuts!" I cry out. "Where did the walnuts come from?"

Lotte timidly explains. "I was called into the commandant's office because my work norm is dropping."

"And?" I ask. Lotte is the last person I'd expect to do something as risky as steal, especially from a guard.

"Well, he was doing his regular yelling, and then he had a coughing fit and it wouldn't end, and so I offered to hit him on the back and it worked, and he spit up a nut, and then he threw his bag of nuts at me.

They spilled all over the floor. 'Pick them up!' he screamed. 'Get them out of my sight. If you women don't kill me, these nuts will!'"

Lotte offers a rare smile. "And so I did. I crawled around and collected them, thanking him over and over while he was still teary-eyed from his hacking."

We all laugh. These nuts are a special treat except, of course, we have no nutcracker.

Dagmar's up and at the door. "I'll be right back. Don't start Christmas without me. I know where to get a nutcracker." I knew she had the Christmas spirit.

We sit around giving each other hugs, something we never do. Lotte, more talkative than ever, tells of how her mother would heat chestnuts in the fire to keep beds warm at night.

"My mama did the same!" I tell her. I take a deep breath, inhaling a memory of roasted chestnuts.

Someone else talks about the coal that St. Nicolaus never left her as a child.

"I'd like to shove coal into the guards' shoes!" Lotte's completely animated tonight.

We all agree and continue sharing stories until Dagmar returns — with a guard right behind her.

"What?" he shouts. "What is going on here?"

Dagmar won't look at me. Won't look at any of us. I'm sure it's not her fault. We're silent . . . like children caught in the act of opening gifts before parents give permission.

"Making yourselves comfortable, I see." The guard laughs. "I was told to watch out for this kind of behaviour. The Soviet Union has no use for religious fanatics." He rubs his hands together. "Coincidentally, I just got a call that one of the factories in Chelyabinsk needs more coal . . . immediately. I'm sending the whole lot of you out to the pits to fuel them up. You can leave now. A Christmas present from Comrade Stalin to all you sorry-looking fascists." He laughs. "And you won't have to walk. The truck's waiting for you."

"But it's night! We're tired," I protest.

"Half-an-hour drive. Four hours of work. If you hurry and work hard, you'll have time for a nap before breakfast."

We grab our outerwear while he rips down our evergreen boughs and spits out the flickering candles.

Christmas, 1946. Better to forget.

CHAPTER 54

ON SOME RANDOM day, the wind changes direction and the snow melts, dampness replacing ice. This fickle promise of spring does little to cheer any of us.

Then, one morning during *Appell* — the routine, ridiculous, tedious and meticulous daily counting session, when the dead and the dying are reprimanded, and the living are rewarded with more work and less food — something besides the weather does change.

I'm called to the front of our shrinking group. "Katya! Translate!" A paper gets thrust into my hand. It's stamped March 18, 1947. It's from Moscow; the writer, some Kremlin bureaucrat.

I read. "Regarding the German female prisoners of war in Camp #376, Ural."

Ah, someone with power knows we exist. This might be promising. I lift my chin and face my audience.

"With the utmost of charity, we will begin repatriation. Prisoners will be selected, beginning in May. You will be notified on short notice and given transport to the border."

My pulse quickens. A guard grabs back the letter. I stare at the others. Who will go? What determines who goes and who stays? I join my co-prisoners, and we all walk a bit faster out to the coal pits. When I glance at faces, I see light in eyes that quickly look away. None of us wants to see their desperate hope reflected in another.

April drags on and on. May might never come this year.

I think of Mama. I will not die nameless and without a grave, like you. Again, I remind myself, I killed the crow. I ate it. I will live.

May. Finally. We know it's May because of the celebrations. International Workers' Day. We stand at attention as a parade of Soviet officials march past us. Ruddy-faced *kolkhoz* workers drive by in the open backs of re-purposed German army trucks, spades and rakes at their shoulders like weapons. Music blares. Speeches are made — something about how communism has raised the standards of living for proletariats. Later, after the visiting officials leave, the guards celebrate with vodka.

The warm air stirs new life in bright green leaves, in blades of grass, in dandelions, while we continue to fade. Even on blue-sky days, women die. In spite of the hope of release, the despair of a winter now past insists on its toll. Even strong, brazen Dagmar verges on giving up.

"Dagmar," I tell her. "You've got this far, you can't fade now."

She's lying on a cot, staring at the bunk above her, her face covered in bedbug bites.

"I can't, Katya. I just can't live like this . . ." She turns to face the wall.

I do my daily trudge to the coal pit and back. My feet could walk this route even if I were dead. That evening, when I return to the barracks, there's a different energy in the air. A document has been posted over at the dining hall — a list of names. Fifteen women are to leave the next morning.

My name is not on the list.

But Dagmar's is. I hurry back to the barracks and manoeuvre around the agitated women. Some are weeping, some are comforting the weepers, everyone is emotional. Where's Dagmar? She's no longer lying prostrate on her bed.

I find her out by the water pump, cleaning herself up for the journey home, but she can't wipe the grin off her face no matter how hard she scrubs. She bears no resemblance to the dying woman I saw on the cot this morning, and I slink away, unable to bear her joy.

She calls out to me. "Katya! Your turn will come, I'm sure!"

I kick at some stones along the ground, fight back the tears and nod. That night, I barely sleep. No one does. Women whisper together. Some cry. Even the bedbugs sense the excitement and skitter with more enthusiasm than usual.

Almost half the women in our barrack are going home. The rest of us must stay behind. The fifteen who will be leaving are the weakest, the sickest. I'm happy for them. Maybe eating the crow gave me too much life. Maybe it will kill me in the end.

Coal-grey skies mark the morning of departure for the chosen ones. Low clouds, caught between the mountains, mirror our own captivity on the ground. Where's the train?

The lucky ones wait, the guards wait, we all wait. The skies, tired of waiting, spit down on us. Finally, when it appears that no train will arrive, the workers who are to remain, like me, get sent to the pits. It's late afternoon and still raining. A distant rumble, sounding like thunder, must be the late train. But instead of greeting it, I'm forced to veer off into the pits and soon hear only the shouting of our taskmasters.

When I return in the growing dusk, after a restless, wet shift, I wash up and join the queue for soup. We're all quiet, tired and sad. Emptiness fills me — but not like soup, more like stones. Of course, I'm happy for them . . . for Dagmar, especially . . . but I'm jealous, too.

I slurp soup and, with wobbly teeth, nibble what passes as bread. Depression weighs me down like a load of coal. The clatter of wooden spoons acts as percussion to our silent meal.

As we drag ourselves back to the barracks, Lotte comes close and locks arms with mine. I pat her arm and speak words I don't believe. "Our turn will come. For now, think of all the room we'll have to stretch out in. We can each have our own . . ."

She pulls away, shakes her head and reaches for the barrack door. As it creaks open, sobbing greets our ears. In the semi-darkness, with only the electric light from outside shining through one dusty window, lie the women — the women who didn't get away after all.

"You're still here?" I squeak in disbelief.

Dagmar, sitting cross-legged on a lower bunk near the door, replies. "Psychological torture or bureaucratic bungling, take your pick. I hate this place. I hate, hate, hate it!" Her eyes gleam madness. She pulls at her straggly hair, and I think of a witch.

"But maybe tomorrow?" I suggest, my voice soft, attempting to calm her hysteria. "A train delay doesn't mean you're not leaving."

"Maybe tomorrow. Or next week, or next month. Or maybe it's all a trick." She leans towards me with a menacing leer. "Maybe we'll die waiting." Then she collapses, shrivels up, and I turn away, unable to provide the comfort she needs.

Instead, a cold, crass thought won't leave me. If Dagmar dies, there'll be more room on the train for others. Why, maybe I could take her place. But I keep my selfish thought to myself and fall asleep to a cacophony of sobbing. When morning dawns, we all face another grey day. Clouds still hover, still caught between the mountains — like us.

No one dies waiting for the transport that finally takes them out ten days later. Dagmar jumps with renewed energy into a freight car. The doors slide shut, and they're gone. Of course, we've got mixed feelings about their departure. We don't say much. It's all been said.

I work beside Lotte. She's easy to ignore . . . small, shrinking and quiet.

The day after the others have left, the two of us work without saying a word. There's nothing to say that's worth the energy of speaking out loud. We bark out our names during *Appell* like the well-trained dogs we've become. At dinner, we sip our soup and clatter our spoons, but even though there are fewer of us, the soup's no thicker and the chunks of bread no bigger.

Then, we head to our bunks. Too tired to pray, too sad to sleep. We listen to the sounds of the empty beds that fill our barracks.

But only a few weeks later, another ten names appear on a new list nailed to the door of the dining hall. Lotte and I read each other's disappointment, and yet there's something else in her eyes. A tiny light that I haven't seen before.

"Lotte, we will have our turn, too!"

She turns away. That hope is too fragile to speak out loud. Have I jinxed it?

Two more weeks pass before this group of ten leaves. They travel in a regular coach with seats — like human beings.

Days are longer, our shadows shorter. The flies, the lice, the bedbugs, the mosquitoes — all multiply, ravenous for our blood. With fewer of us for the parasites to feast on, we each get a bigger share of the vermin.

A few days after summer solstice, the *natschalnick* calls to me at *Appell*. "Translate, Katya. Tell them, when the next train arrives it's for you." He smiles and I see relief in his blue eyes. "*Idi domoy!*" he shouts.

"Go home!" I repeat, translating words we've all been waiting to hear.

"*Vse!*" he adds.

"Everyone!" I repeat, no longer caring that my smile reveals my rotting teeth. I shout it again. "Go home! All of us!"

The *natschalnick* turns and heads back into his office.

Lotte and I exchange glances — this time we don't look away from each other's hope.

"Lotte," I say. "You're crying."

She points at me and smiles. A real smile revealing her own missing teeth. We hug. We hug everyone. We weep. We smile some more.

A week goes by, but again there's some mix-up somewhere. We stay put. Now, however, we no longer go out to the coal pits. We just sit and wait. I'd almost rather be working. Waiting and hoping and not hoping; it's much harder when there's nothing to do but slap mosquitoes.

CHAPTER 55

ON A STEAMY afternoon in July, when nothing's moving except the black flies, the ground beneath me shakes long before there's any sign of a train. Anxiety twists my insides into knots as the locomotive, black smoke rolling from its stack like a thundercloud, rumbles into Camp #376. A string of passenger cars tag behind the locomotive. Passenger cars? For human beings? Tears blur my vision and with impatience, I wipe them away. I need to see.

After the train squeals to a hissy stop, a Red Army commandant, head held high, jumps off. He adjusts his belt and scans our camp. Here we are, a huddle of weeping women, trembling like children at the sight of Nikolaus. I spot Sergei close behind the commandant and turn away, unable to make eye contact. His smile freezes, his head drops and he shadows his commandant into the office. Doors thud shut.

I imagine the office. Papers shuffled, *makhorkas* smoked, numbers argued. The officer comes back out, Sergei again behind him. Our local guard barks at us, and we shuffle into a lineup. The *natschalnick* clears his throat and shouts, "It has been decreed by our just leader, Comrade Stalin, that each one of you will go back to Germany."

Silence.

He clears his throat again. "Today."

My heart races, my knees buckle and I collapse to the ground. I can't . . . I won't . . . I don't believe this. Beside me, a bug crawls in the dirt. This bug will stay, and I will go? I look up, catch Sergei's eye this time as tears flow down my cheeks into the dirt.

Hours later, paperwork complete, we board the train. Some of us must be carried. This train car has seats — it's a regular passenger car — for us. Lotte grabs my hand and squeezes it. I squeeze back, but suspicion makes my hand weak. This might be a trap.

The guards seem like parents seeing their children off, and I almost feel sorry for them. Once I'm sitting on the train, I look out the window at the camp. There's Sergei. He waves at me, and I wave back. He trails a finger down each cheek, mimicking tears.

Unlike me, the train clicks and clacks out of Camp #376 without hesitation. I'm crippled by hesitation, by fear and doubt — and by Sergei and our shared moments by the fire. I want to sit by myself but can't shrug off Lotte, who clings to me like a child. She, too, can't fathom the change.

"Sit, Lotte. Just sit and look out the window."

She nods, and I sit down across from her, but she doesn't look out the window at all. She just looks at me, waiting for my direction. I sigh and stare out at the shrinking camp, the waving guards, and the ugly barracks.

As the train picks up speed, the coal pits come into view. My body, crippled — but not broken — from more than two years of pulling carts of coal, is still here. I'm taking it with me. I glance down at my hands. They've been scrubbed, but coal dust will no doubt stain them forever. But they also were the hands that killed my crow, and I clench my fists with a sense of victory.

Leaning my head back, I take a deep breath, and a surge of giddiness, of freedom, of adventure, pulses through me.

And then I realize that I don't even know where we're going. What did they say? Frankfurt an der Oder? Where is that? On the Oder River, obviously. Where's the Oder River?

I have no money, no home. But I have my freedom. First thing I must do is find my family . . . my sisters, maybe Albert. I'll find some work, and we'll build ourselves a new home and maybe I'll find an old desk and —

"Having a bath will be a good thing," says Lotte. She stretches out her tanned, thin, sinewy arms and studies her battered hands. "Maybe I'll buy some Nivea. That would be good."

Her words startle me back to the present. "What did you say?"

"We're finally going to become human again. Everything is going to get better, Katya. Just you wait and see." She grins and licks her lips, either with anticipation or from the strain of speaking.

I turn from her, smiling out the window but not seeing the Soviet landscape that stole two and a half years of my life. "Reading a book will be a good thing. Reading a newspaper. Having a home."

"You think we'll find it?"

"Home? If not, we'll build it again," I tell her.

We ride on, each with our own plans for the future. It's been eight long years since war invaded my life. Can I even find my life again? My self?

"Never touching coal again will be a good thing," I say out loud.

"Or seeing crows," Lotte adds, closing her eyes and shutting everything out.

"You hate crows, too?"

She nods and mumbles. "Crows are — "

I squeeze her hand. "Don't say it, Lotte. There will always be crows, but we won't have to eat them."

Still, I keep my eyes wide open, watching for any sign of crows. But as the train picks up speed and rumbles out of the Urals, away from the coal pits, the trees become blurry forests — and crows become mere birds again.

AUTHOR'S NOTE

My mother inspired this book. Born in eastern Volhynia, an hour west of Kyiv, in 1919, she died peacefully in Canada, in 2011. She and my father (ex-Luftwaffe pilot and also a former POW in USSR) married in 1952 and immigrated to Canada in 1953. When I was growing up in Winnipeg, she let slip bits and pieces of her previous life, and I built the narrative of *Crow Stone* around her jumbled memories. Here are some facts behind the fiction of this story.

- About two hundred thousand German female civilians were dragged into Soviet labour camps during the final months of World War II.

- While walking through a park in Königsberg, my mother saw red blood on white snow; heard horses moaning as they lay dying.

- There was no time to bury the dead during the East Prussian winter exodus. She told me about the porcelain-like faces of unburied babies on snowy roadsides.

- Rape was inevitable.

- Soviet soldiers used her to find her sisters.

- Young children were often separated from their families. My aunt was nineteen when she became the foster mom to such a child. She looked after a little girl until 1952.

- There was a relative who wouldn't share a potato while preparing for the last-minute flight from the Soviets.

- Her younger brother did come home for his birthday in 1944, and later sent a POW postcard dated January 17, 1945. It was the last anyone heard from him.

- Poles beat on the freight car as she travelled east.

- Her naked buttocks were pinched to determine her health and labour capabilities.

• She saw lice moving sweaters.

• Her Russian language skills helped her survive. She became a *starosta*.

• She helped sober up a drunk Soviet officer.

• A woman in her camp caught fire; Mom rolled her about in snow, but still the woman turned into an ice cube and later went insane.

• Mom killed and ate a crow while in the Urals. I learned about this near the end of her life. We were sitting in a nursing home, staring out at a tree. where a crow perched on a limb. She said it was waiting for her — like before.

GLOSSARY OF FOREIGN WORDS

G = German, R = Russian

Abendbrot (G). Evening bread; a cold supper.

Abendteuer (G). Adventure

Achtung (G). Caution

Adeen, dva, tree (R). One, two, three

Amis (G). Slang for Americans, commonly used during the war and later under occupation

Appell (G). Roll call

Arbeit macht frei (G). "Work sets you free"

Arbeiten (G). work (verb)

Aufpassen (G). Watch out

Aufstehen (G). Stand or get up

Aufwachen (G). Wake up

BDM (G). Bund Deutscher Mädel (League of German Girls)

Belomorkanal (R). Soviet brand of cigarettes

Bleib (G). Stay

Bolshoi spasibo (R). Much thanks

Chefin (G). Supervisor

Danke (G). Thank you

Dawai (R). Hurry or come on

Die große Liebe **(G).** *The Great Love* (movie)

Dokhodyaga (R). Crazy person

Essen (G). Eat

Finger weg (G). Fingers off or away

Frau, geh (G). Woman, go

Frau, komm (G). Woman, come

Fräulein (G). Unmarried woman

Frohe Weihnachten (G). Merry Christmas

Gauleiter (G). Nazi official governing a designated area.

Gdyeh (R). Where

Gut (G). Good

Hitler Jugend (G). Hitler Youth

"Ich weiß es wird einmal ein Wunder gescheh'n" (G). "I know someday there'll be a miracle"; song sung by Zarah Leander in 1942 movie *Die große* Liebe

Ich weiss nicht (G). I don't know

Idi domoy (R). Go home

Ivan (G). Nickname the Germans gave the Soviets or Russians

Junge (G). Boy

Kaput (G). Broken

Kasha (R). Buckwheat groats

Kolkhoz (R). Collective farm

Komm, Mädchen (G). Come, girl.

Krupp (G). German steel company

Kulak (R). Soviet term for a rich peasant

Lange weg (G). Long way

Lebensborn (G). Literally, fount of life; birthing centres for Aryan, mostly unwed, mothers

"Leise rieselt der Schnee" (G). "Quietly falls the snow"; title of well-known Christmas song

Liebling (G). Darling or love

LKW (G). Last Kraft Wagon (truck)

Mädel (G). Girl

Makhorka (R). Tobacco/cigarette

Medsestra (R). Nurse

Mensch (G). Man

Mensch ärger Dich nicht (G). A board game also known as Parcheesi.

Mertvyy ili zhivoy (R). Dead or alive

Mischling (G). Nazi term to describe people of mixed Jewish heritage

Natschalnick (R). Boss

Nein (G). No

Nicht versteh (G). Don't understand

Nitzo (R). No

Nyet (R). No

Oblast (R). Province or territory

Oma (G). Grandma

Osmotr (R). Inspection

Ostarbeiter (G). Nazi term for forced labourers from east-occupied regions

Ot sebya (R). Push

Pomogite (R). Help

Schweine Ohren (G). Pigs' ears, a German pastry

Sehnsucht (G). Yearning

Sieg Heil (G). Hail victory, a Nazi greeting.

Soviets (R). Also called Russians or Ivans by the Germans

Spasibo (R). Thank you

Spazieren fahren (G). Take a drive

Starosta (R). Person in charge

Stoy (R). Stop

Tot (G). Dead

Troika (R). Group of three

Ukhodi (R). Go away

Urah (R). Hurrah

Ushanka (R). Fur cap with ear flaps

Versetzen (G). Translate

Versteh (G). Understand

Vne! Trapeedca (R). Out and hurry

Volkssturm (G). Literally, People's Storm; a male militia formed by Nazis in final months of war

Vse (R). Everyone

Vykhodit (R). Come out

Warum? (G). Why?

Wehrmacht (G). Nazi military

Weihnachtsmann (G). German version of Santa Claus

Wie geht's? (G). How's it going?

Wie lange? (G). How long?

Wo? (G). Where?

Zakaz (R). Order, attention

Zatknis (R). Shut up

LIST OF PLACES

Berchtesgaden: Hitler's Bavarian retreat

Chelyabinsk: major industrial city and Oblast just east of the Ural Mountains

East Prussia: most easterly province of Germany until 1945. Now divided among Lithuania, Russian Federation and Poland

Federofka (Federowka): village 35 km northwest of Zhytomyr, Ukraine. Now Kalinovka

Königsberg: city and port on the Baltic. Renamed Kaliningrad in 1946

Kreuzburg: town 20 km south of Königsberg (Kaliningrad). Now Slavskoye

Kurgan: city and Oblast in the Ural region 146 km southeast of Shadrinsk

Metgethen: western suburb of Königsberg. Now Imeni Alexandra Kosmodemyanskogo

Nemmersdorf: village on eastern edge of East Prussia. Known as the scene of a horrific Soviet massacre of civilians in October, 1944. Now Mayakovskoye, Kaliningrad Oblast

Pillau: town on the Vistula Spit. Now Baltiysk, Kaliningrad Oblast

Rauschen: former East Prussian spa town on the Baltic. Now Svetlogorsk, Kaliningrad Oblast

Shadrinsk (Chadrinsk): industrial city in the Kurgan Oblast of the Urals, 146 km northwest of Kurgan

Stablach: military base 8 km northwest of Preussisch Eylau (now Bagrationovsk)

Urals: mountain range running north to south that divides European Russia from Asia. Mining area

Vistula Lagoon: brackish water frozen in winter. Crossed by German refugees en route to Pillau between January and March, 1945

Volhynia: area in northwest Ukraine bordered by Belarus on the north and Carpathian Mountains on the south. Colonized by German settlers in the second half of the 1800s. Later, divided between Poland and Soviet Union

Yaya: town in Kemerovo Oblast, Siberia, along the Trans-Siberian Railway. Transit labour camp in 1931

Zhytomyr (Ukrainian spelling): city in northwest Ukraine; known as Shit-omir in Germany

SUPPLEMENTAL READING

NON-FICTION

Alexievich, Svetlana. *Secondhand Time: The Last of the Soviets*. New York: Random House, 2017. First published 2013.

Applebaum, Anne. *Iron Curtain: The Crushing of Eastern Europe, 1944–1956*. Toronto: McClelland and Stewart, 2012.

Bacque, James. *Crimes and Mercies: The Fate of German Civilians under Allied Occupation, 1944–50*. Vancouver: Talon Books, 2007.

Bergau, Martin. *Der Junge von der Bernsteinküste*. Heidelberg: Heidelberger Verlagsansalt, 1994.

Clough, Patricia. *In lange Reihe über das Haff: Die Flucht der Trakehner aus Ostpreussen*. Munich: Deutscher Taschenbuch Verlag, 2006. First published 2004.

Dallin, David J., and Boris I. Nicolaevsky. *Forced Labour in the Soviet Union*. New Haven, CT: Yale University Press, 1948.

de Zayas, Alfred. *A Terrible Revenge: The Ethnic Cleansing of the East European Germans*. New York: Palgrave MacMillan, 2006. First published 1994.

Douglas, R.M. *Orderly and Humane: The Expulsion of the Germans after the Second World War*. New Haven, CT: Yale University Press, 2012.

Duffy, Christopher. *Red Storm on the Reich: The Soviet March on Germany, 1945*. New York: Da Capo Press, 1993. First published 1991.

Egremont, Max. *Forgotten Land: Journeys among the Ghosts of East Prussia*. New York: Farrar, Straus and Giroux, 2012. First published 2011.

Hitler, Adolf. *Mein Kampf*. Munich: Eher Verlag, 1925. Translated by Ralph Manheim. Boston: Houghton Mifflin Company, 1971.

Karner, Stefan. *Im Archipel Gupvi: Kriegsgefangenschaft und Internierung in der Sowjetunion 1941–1956*. R. Oldenbourg Verlag Wien, 1995.

Klier, Freya. *Verschleppt ans Ende der Welt: Schicksale deutscher Frauen in sowjetischen Arbeitslagern*. Munich: Ullstein Verlag, 2000. First published 1996.

Koschorrek, Günter K. *Blood Red Snow: The Memoirs of a German Soldier on the Eastern Front*. Minneapolis, MN: Zenith Press, 2005. First published 1998.

Kossert, Andreas. *Damals in Ostpreußen: Der Untergang einer deutschen Provinz*. Munich: Pantheon Verlag, 2008.

Kossert, Andreas. *Ostpreußen Geschichte einer historischen Landschaft*. Munich: C.H. Beck Verlag, 2014.

Lorenz, Hilke. *Weil der Krieg Unsere Seelen frisst*. Berlin: List Taschenbuch, 2014. First published 2012.

Mitzka, Herbert. *Meine Brüder hast du ferne von mir Getan*. Einhausen: Hübner Druckerei und Verlag, 1983.

Nesaule, Agate. *A Woman in Amber: Healing the Trauma of War and Exile*. New York: Soho Press, 1995.

Pausewang, Gudrun. *Ich war dabei*. Düssseldorf: Patmos Verlag, 2004.

Peter, Erwin, and Alexander E. Epifanow. *Stalin's Kriegsgefangene*. Graz: Leopold Stocker Verlag, 1997.

Pieklakiewicz, Janusz. *Pferd und Reiter im II. Weltkrieg*. Munich: Südwest Publishing, 1981. First published 1976.

Polian, Pavel. *Against Their Will: The History and Geography of Forced Migrations in the USSR*. Budapest: Central European University Press, 2003. First published 2001.

Reski, Petra. *Ein Land So Weit*. Berlin: List Taschenbuch, 2002.

Roeder, Giselle. *We Don't Talk about That*. Victoria, BC: Friesen Press, 2014.

Urban, Luise. *East of the Oder: A German Childhood under the Nazis and Soviets*. Stroud, Gloucestershire, UK: The History Press, 2013.

von Arburg, Adrian, Jurij Kostjaschow, Ulla Lachauer, Hans-Dieter Rutsch, Beate Schlanstein, and Christian Schulz. *Als die Deutschen weg waren: Was nach der Vertreibung geschah: Ostpreussen, Schlesien, Sudetenland*. Reinbek bei Hamburg: Rowohlt Taschenbuch Verlag, 2007.

von Lehndorff, Hans Graf. *Menschen, Pferde, weites Land*. Munich: Deutscher Taschenbuch Verlag, 1983. First published 1980.

von Lehndorff, Hans Graf. *Ostpreußisches Tagebuch*. Munich: Deutscher Taschenbuch Verlag, 2013. First published 1975.

FICTION

Kempowski, Walter. *Mark und Bein*. Munich: Penguin Verlag, 2019. First published 1992.

Kerr, Philip. *The Winter Horses*. New York: Knopf Books for Young People, 2014.

Pausewang, Gudrun. *Traitor*. Translated by Rachel Ward. Minneapolis, MN: Carolrhoda Books, 2006. First published as *Die Verräterin* (Ravensburg: Ravensbürger Taschenbuch, 1995).

Sarles, Marina Gottlieb. *The Last Daughter of Prussia*. Stockton, NJ: Wild River Books, 2013.

Sepetys, Ruta. *Salt to the Sea*. New York: Philomel Books, 2016.

Solzhenitsyn, Aleksandr. *Prussian Nights: A Poem*. Translated by Robert Conquest. London: Collins and Harvill Press, 1977.

Wheelaghan, Marianne. *The Blue Suitcase*. Edinburgh, Scotland: Pilrig Press, 2010.

ACKNOWLEDGEMENTS

I'm immensely grateful to the late Ron Hatch and to his wife, Veronica, for accepting *Crow Stone* for publication. It's a story I've carried for many years before setting it down on paper, and then more years of letting it sit before finally sending it out. Having *Crow Stone* published as an actual book has taken a huge weight off my shoulders.

I'm also very grateful that Wendy Atkinson, along with Kevin Welsh, honoured the contract I signed with Ronsdale before Ron's passing. I'm aware that book publishing is a challenging business and appreciate their dedication to the Ronsdale authors.

I'm so pleased with the book's cover and want to thank Julie Cochrane, its creator, for incorporating my mom's 1947 POW release paper into that cover.

Thank you to Robyn So, my editor, whose astute eye helped me shape my vision without damaging my fragile writer self.

Thank you to my friends and family who put up with my historical ramblings and know when to leave me alone. Thank you also to Christina, Deb, Jodi, Larry, MaryLou, Mel, Mindy and Pat, my writing critique group, who have encouraged and tough-loved me through my drafts. Nobody said it would be easy. Thank you for being there.

And thank you to my late mom for setting the example to keep going and to keep hoping. Yes, *Crow Stone* is a dark story, but as she once said, those two-and-a-half years went by quickly and helped her appreciate the good times. May any of our dark days pass quickly, too. As someone so aptly said, *If you're going through hell, keep going.* One day at a time.

ABOUT THE AUTHOR

Gabriele Goldstone's well-received novels have been nominated for numerous awards. She writes the books she wishes she could have read while growing up in Winnipeg, Manitoba as the self-conscious firstborn of postwar immigrants. gabrielegoldstone.com